'If I receive any letters from a lawyer, I'll make sur

up with nothing! Don't forget, I'm British, and British Law protects me, not you!'

I was frightened and confused. I was British too. I obtained my British passport over fifteen years ago, but I was still frightened by what he said.

I did not know anything about British law. In my country, Thailand, foreigners have few rights, I thought it must be the same in Britain.

His words floated around my head. Yes, my husband knew how to frighten me. That is how I ended up with nothing, absolutely nothing, and homeless.

It is not easy to adapt overnight from living in a nice house in Glasgow, with two lovely daughters, to living in a high-rise tenement in the worst part of Glasgow. At the time, I did not think I could take my daughters there, it was so dangerous. I had no experience of that side of life.

I was too ill and exhausted to go to work because I had been up all night, terrified. I walked towards the Women's Aid office and knocked on the door. Kirsty opened it.

'Nuch, I told you, I would get back to you next week. I don't have a place for you at the moment.'

'It's okay, I understand. I just want someone to talk to.' I was crying and shaking.

'Ok, talk to me.' Kirsty gave me a cuddle.

'I was so scared staying in that block of flats, full of people drinking or on drugs. The screaming, shouting and banging was endless. Do they never sleep? I couldn't eat, I couldn't sleep. I miss my children. I felt there was no reason to live anymore.'

Kirsty nodded.

'Last night, in desperation, I tried to jump out of my window on the fourteenth-floor. I couldn't find the key to open the window, that's the only reason I'm still here. Could you give this letter to my daughters, in case I feel like that again, and succeed next time?' I was crying, I handed her the letter.

Dear Nicola and Teresa

It's really important to me that you know, whatever happens to me, it's nothing to do with you two.

I just could not adapt to where I am now from where I used to live. I no longer want to live in fear and just want it to end.

My family in Thailand don't know what I'm going through. I don't want them to worry about me. Can you tell your grandparents and your aunties that I love them very much and don't want them to be upset. I have just found my way to stop the pain.

Lots of love as always,
Mum xxxooxxx

'Okay, sit here, don't go anywhere, I'm going to make a phone call.' Kirsty walked into her office and picked up the phone. She talked for ten minutes.

'Okay Nuch, I've a refuge flat for you. You'll be safe there. But it won't be ready today, it'll be tomorrow. I want you to go back to the flat for one more night and stay safe. Can you do that for me, just one more night?' She held my hands.

'Yes, I can.' I nodded, still crying.

'You promise.'

'Yes, I promise.'

'You come back here tomorrow morning, at nine, with your belongings. I'll take you to the refuge flat in Cambuslang and you'll be safe there.'

I felt better walking out of Kirsty's office. This was my third day living in this horrible place.

I went back to the flat, I pressed the lift for the fourteenth floor. When the door opened, there were three men in it. They looked rough and smelled of alcohol, I was frightened to go in.

'It's okay, I'll take the next one.'

One of them shouted, 'What's wrong with this one!?'

I was so scared. I started to walk upstairs to the fourteenth floor. I remembered Laura's advice. 'Don't speak to anyone in the lift and avoid eye contact. Always keep your door locked, don't open it to anybody.'

Ten minutes later, I heard a loud argument outside my door. I looked through the keyhole, I could see men fighting outside. I ran into the lounge to hide, in case they smashed my door in. I was so scared I was shaking.

TWO

I was born on 25th July 1966 in Lampang Province, the third largest city in northern Thailand. My Dad is called Somchai, he had short black hair back then, greyer now, slim, five feet five inches. He has dark brown eyes, and tanned skin.

My mum is Sri, she had short black wavy hair, greyer now, slim, five feet, with dark brown eyes, and tanned skin from working in the sun.

My parents are from the north of Thailand, their natural skin tone is lighter than people from other parts of Thailand, but because they worked outside regularly, their skin became quite dark.

In Thailand, people do not like to have dark skin because it means to others that you work outside in the fields, and you are poor. The pharmacies sell skin cream to lighten the skin, we call it white lotion, the opposite concept to the tanning lotion sold in the West.

Our house was in the Mae Mo district, which has a cool climate with lots of trees, rivers, lakes and mountains.

Mum and Dad built it from wood which they cut, in the days when you were still allowed to cut the trees.

The house was built on sections of teak tree trunks, raising it up from the ground about 2.5 meters high, creating an open space underneath.

The roof was made from corrugated metal sheets, high and steep, to protect against the rain, and to keep the inside cool. There was no internal ceiling.

The outer walls were made from layers of teak planks, a hard wood, not affected by rain or strong sunlight.

The windows were formed from spaces between the planks, there was no glass. We had mosquito nets over the beds.

The toilet and shower were outside. It was a squat toilet, there was no seat, we straddled two-foot pads and faced the door. To flush it, we used a plastic bowl to scoop water out of a large bucket.

The shower consisted of a plastic bowl which we used to pour water over ourselves, there was a drain in the bathroom floor.

The space underneath the house was much cooler than upstairs, it was sheltered from the strong afternoon sun.

This design was safer because it was harder for snakes and scorpions to get inside the living accommodation, and it protected the living accommodation from flooding in the wet season.

The downstairs area had a wooden floor which was about two feet off the ground. We used this as a daytime living room, playroom, workshop or even dining room. We had our meals on the floor mat. When it was cooler, usually in the evenings, we stayed upstairs.

I liked the cool breeze in the open space downstairs. I spent most of my time there during weekends, doing homework, playing with my big sisters, or having an afternoon nap.

Mum cooked on the balcony upstairs, it was too hot to cook inside the house.

She preferred a charcoal burner, *Tao*. She made her own charcoal from trees on our land which she burned in a large kiln in the garden. This process took one day, one night.

She had to check the kiln every two hours, day and night, if the fire went out, the charcoal was ruined.

She sold any spare charcoal, it made a good price, because it had such a good reputation.

She was very resourceful, in terms of providing for the family. She would gather ants' eggs from nests, high in the mango trees in our garden. These were a local delicacy, and expensive.

She had an ingenious collection method, a long bamboo pole with a bucket attached. She would poke the nests with the bamboo pole, and the ants and their eggs would drop into her bucket.

This produced a collection of eggs and some terribly angry ants. These ants have a nasty bite, and so, to separate the eggs from the ants, she would add charcoal ash.

Mum explained that there was something in it which the ants did not like, and for some reason, after adding the ash, the ants would not bite when she separated them from the eggs.

She worked all day until bedtime, she never stopped. She is in her late seventies now, but she still works hard.

Dad was thirty-one and Mum was twenty-six when I was born. I was her fourth daughter, number six, if you include the two miscarriages.

She miscarried twice with all the hard work. I suppose, you could say, it nearly killed her to help Dad build the house and do her own work. She was tough.

At that time, the coal mine for the power station was not long started, there were few workers then, and no houses round about.

I remember Mum telling me that when they first built the house, there was no electricity, they used oil lamps for light, and charcoal for cooking.

There was no piped water, Mum and Dad carried all the water from the river, ten minutes' walk from the house.

They had to fill the water tanks in the house every day, for the toilet, washing dishes and cooking. Mum washed our clothes in the river, then slammed them on rocks to scrub them clean.

At first, they used a rainwater tank from the roof for drinking water. By the time I was born, there was tap water and electricity. Mum and Dad still drink the rainwater, but I prefer bottled water.

Later, when we had a water supply, I helped her with the washing by putting powder in the sink, scrubbing my clothes clean by hand, then rinsing them in the sink.

By this time, our house was no longer isolated, there were more houses round about, this became Ban Viang Sawan Village, in Mae Moh District.

I often wondered what it had been like for Mum to give birth when the facilities were still extremely basic. 'Mum, what was it like to give birth when you had all of us, back in those days?'

'I gave birth to all your big sisters in the house. There was no telephone in those days, your Dad had to run around to find the village doctor. When he arrived at the house, he would tie my hands up to the beam running across the ceiling. I was in a sitting position, my legs bent at the knee. I pushed hard and when the baby appeared, the doctor would get hold of her and pull to help me.'

'Sounds painful.'

'Yes, there was no painkillers, you were the only one that I gave birth to in hospital.'

'Why?'

'I was in severe pain, I kept pushing for hours, but there was no sign of you coming out. The doctor told your Dad to take me to hospital, otherwise we both might die.'

'How did you get to hospital and how far was it?'

'We had no car, your Dad asked a neighbour for a lift.'

'How far was it to the hospital?'

'There was no hospital in the district, we had to go to Lampang City Centre, about ten kilometres away.'

'Were you scared?'

'No, I was excited. I thought you were going to be a boy because I was in so much pain and kept pushing for hours! I was not in as much pain with your three sisters, compared to you. It took me less than an hour to push them out! The two miscarriages were girls, so I was quite sure the sixth one would be a boy'.

'How did you know the two miscarriages were girls?'

'I was six months pregnant; I saw they were girls.' Mum replied, she looked sad.

'Were you disappointed I was a girl?

'We hoped for a boy because your Dad had lots of land to work. But, we were happy with a healthy baby.'

After listening to Mum, I never wanted to have her experience of giving birth. It sounded so painful; I was not sure I could cope.

One day, I looked at a photo of my sisters and I on the wall. Jang, my third sister, and I, sat next to each other on the dining chairs.

Sang, my second sister, stood next to Jang. Prang, my eldest sister, stood next to me.

'Mum, is this the only photo of us when we were babies?' I asked.

'Yes, it was taken at a local photo shop. I didn't have any money to buy a camera and it was too expensive to have photos taken, we couldn't afford it.' Mum replied

'How old were we?'

'You were one, Jang was two, Sang was four and Prang was five.'

'So, you don't have any photos of Sang and Prang when they were babies?'

'No.'

'That's sad. How much was it to have a photo taken?'

'I don't remember exactly; it was about forty baht (one-pound sterling).'

'That's terrible Mum. It was only forty baht.'

'It may not seem much now, but that was your Dad's daily wage at the time. It was a rip off!'

'Why didn't you go to a different shop?'

'There was only one in the village.' I could see Mum was sad because she had no photos of Prang and Sang as babies.

Dad started work in The Mae Moh Lignite mine over sixty years ago, it became the biggest power plant in Thailand. When he started, he earned seven baht per day, less than a penny.

To supplement his income, after work each day, he went to the river or lake near our house, with his nets to fish for food for us. He caught fish, snails, and river prawns.

This allowed him to keep his wages for our education, or to pay for the doctor or hospital, if any of us were ill. The public must pay for all medical treatment in Thailand.

Dad usually caught *Pla Nin*, black tilapia fish and *Pla Duk*, catfish. Occasionally, he caught *Pla Lai*, eel. Mum made soup or grilled them for us.

My favourite dish was fish roe soup because there were no bones. Dad always ate the fish heads because he did not mind the bones. He kept the rest of the fish for us.

I ate fish head sometimes because I love fish eyes, but not often because Mum was afraid that I might swallow a bone.

Mum loved eel curry, but she said it was not good for children, I am not sure if that was true or because she wanted to keep it for herself!

I remember one evening, when Mum was busy, she asked me to kill some catfish which Dad caught in the river. He kept them alive in a bucket, so they were fresh.

She said to me, 'Just smash their heads until they're dead. Then cut the stomach open and pull all the guts out. Leave the roe if there is one.'

I could not do it, I was too squeamish, so I put them back in the river! Mum was mad at me, we had only boiled eggs, vegetables with chilli dipping sauce and rice for dinner.

There were no state benefits of any kind in Thailand, we had to pay for everything. Mum grew fruit, vegetables, and herbs around the house.

I remember mangoes, jack fruits, bananas, pumpkins, limes, tomatoes, basils, chillies, onions, and garlic. Sometimes, she picked mushrooms and bamboo shoots in the forest.

She would sell some and keep the rest for us. She would also sell fruit and vegetables from our garden. She sold them on a table on the main street, ten minutes' walk from our house.

Mum worked really hard to make extra money to help Dad, and of course, this was to help us all.

Later on, she taught herself dressmaking. She did not take any courses, she learned by taking old clothes apart and looking at the patterns to see how they had been sewn together.

After a lot of practice, she was confident she could start doing it well enough to earn some extra money. She started altering and making clothes for people in the village. She also made us some clothes from the left-over fabrics.

The only reason she stopped dressmaking was because she trusted people to pay at the end of the month when they had money, but unfortunately, they often did not pay in full. Dad did not like her having to keep asking people for the money they owed her.

We had five dogs altogether. One was called Toon, she had four puppies, Mum wanted to give three away.

'Mum, look at them, they're so cute, please can we keep them?' I begged Mum.

'It's hard enough to feed the four of you, never mind four more puppies.' She replied.

'They won't eat much, they're just puppies.' I was desperate to have a puppy.

'They won't stay this size forever; they'll get bigger every day.'

'Please, they won't cost you much more, they'll just eat whatever is left over from our meals'

'Okay, I give up, but you need to ask your Dad.'

Asking Dad could be awkward. Luckily, it was the end of the month. He always came home drunk after he was paid.

'Here's my wage envelope.' Dad handed the white envelope to Mum.

'It's already open, again! I told you not to open it.' Mum raised her voice.

'Well, my workmates wanted to have a few drinks.'

'Your friends don't have a big family. You have four kids to take care of, and you might have another four dogs soon.' Mum counted the money.

'One hundred and fifty Baht has disappeared.' Mum was angry.

'I bought a bottle of whisky; they don't sell half bottles.'

'You can sleep outside tonight; I don't want you in my bedroom.' She was mad at him.

Dad slept outside that night; he was always in trouble when he opened his wage packet. The only good thing was, when Dad was drunk, he would give us anything that we asked for.

'Dad, Toon's had four puppies, can we keep them all?' I asked politely.

'Four?'

'Yes, we want to have our own pup each.'

'That's okay. Here, I've twenty baht left in my pocket; you can buy milk for them tomorrow.'

'Thank you, Dad. You're truly kind.' I put the money away before he changed his mind.

Prang picked the bitch puppy with brown fur, just like Toon. Prang called her Brownie. Sang picked the male pup with a black and white coat, she called him Spot. Jang picked the black male pup, she called him Black. I picked the white bitch puppy; I called her White.

'What colour is their dad?' I asked my sisters curiously.

'I'm not sure.' Jang replied.

'Well, my Brownie has brown fur from her mum.' Prang said.

'Perhaps their dad was black and white.' Sang said.

'How does that explain the ones who are all white or all black?' I was still curious.

'They're not human, perhaps they had more than one dad.' Mum said when she overheard our conversation. 'That's why we call women who sleep with more than one man, at the same time, a bitch!'

We each looked after our own puppy. We kept our dogs outside or in the living space downstairs, occasionally they would go upstairs.

It is normal to keep dogs outside in Thailand, our weather is hot all year round. We fed them with boiled rice, mixed with mince, or our leftovers.

Mum shared the work around the house between the four of us, sweeping, and mopping the floor, washing dishes. We washed our own clothes.

Mum washed most of my clothes because I was the youngest. My big sisters were jealous of me because I was the favourite, I had an easier life.

I was scared of spiders, often Prang and Sang would swing a dead spider in front of me to force me to do their housework. Jang had a fear of spiders too, otherwise she would have ganged up with Prang and Sang.

We did not have any toys to play with. Dad did not have money to waste on toys, so he made models of animals from mud for us to play with. He also taught us how to make them ourselves.

I was not keen on making mud models because they made my hands dirty. I loved them when Dad made them for me, he was good at them, using stones for the eyes.

I could make basic animals, such as a dog or a pig. My favourite one was an elephant. It was too complicated for me to make, with giant ears, long tusks and a huge trunk. Dad carved the tusks out of wood. If he had lots of time to spend, he made them well, but often, he was too busy.

We used to play this game where we tried to jump over a string of joined up rubber bands. We made long strings out of the brown rubber bands used for tying hair or tying up bags. We could make them in a few minutes.

Maybe, a hundred bands for one length to jump over.

Two of us held the string between us, while others would try and jump over it. Sometimes, our friends would come to play at our house, at weekends there could be six of us. Whoever jumped the highest won, usually it was my eldest sister Prang because she was the tallest.

I loved making paper dolls out of sheets of card. I drew boys and girls onto the card and then cut them out. This was one of my favourite pastimes, I would spend hours doing it.

If I wanted to change the clothes, I would use a different coloured sheet of paper and cut out a shirt or a skirt. I would stick it over whatever the dolls were wearing, giving them new clothes.

Another of our favourite games was hopscotch. I loved playing this with my friends and sisters.

We played an unusual version; it was hopscotch with coconuts for shoes! Mum would cut a coconut shell in half, make a hole in it, and thread a little string through the hole.

We put our feet on top of the coconut, like shoes, with the string between our toes. We held the string at arm's length and ran as fast as we could towards the finish line. If you fell over that was you out of the race, you were disqualified.

Jang was good at it. It was funny to watch, especially when somebody fell over.

We loved playing with little plastic spinning tops, they were cheap to buy and great fun. Whoever spun it the longest won.

We made our own playing cards out of cardboard, we cut them to size and wrote numbers and letters on them. We had to play in secret because Dad said it was gambling. One night he came into the bedroom and caught us playing cards, he was irate.

We still played, but we were careful because he said he would slap us if he caught us. We did not play very often after that; we were too scared of him.

THREE

In 1971, when I was five, Mum put me in a local kindergarten five days a week, seven hours a day. We learned the Thai Alphabet, the sound of each letter, and how to write them. We had forty-eight consonant characters, twenty-six single and combined vowel characters, and five tone characters.

Because I am left-handed Mum told the teacher to slap my hand if I wrote with my left hand. This was because in Thailand we have a saying that you are not going to be clever if you are left-handed.

'What would you like to be when you grow up?' Mum asked.

'I want to be a nurse when I grow up, if I'm clever enough, I want to be a doctor.' I replied.

'You're going to be clever in school because you write with your right hand.'

At playtime, the teacher did not slap my hand, so I used my left hand for colouring pencils or painting with a brush.

So, here I am, writing with my right hand, but drawing and painting with my left hand!

We studied our lessons 09:00 – 12:00, lunch break 12:00 – 12:30, then an hour and half for a nap 12:30 – 14:00.

It sounds strange now, but we would all lie down and sleep on the floor on straw mats. Then we had an hour of music, singing and learning about music, and playtime until our parents collected us.

My favourite lesson was learning the sound of Thai letters.

I remember, one day Mum could not find my lunch box. She took me to kindergarten without it and said she would bring my lunch to school before lunch time. She turned up at school a couple of hours later with a cooking pot!

'I'm sorry, I couldn't find her lunch box.' She told the teacher.

I was speechless!

'No worries.' My teacher replied smiling.

One of my friends said, 'You eat from a cooking pot!' Everyone was laughing.

'You better find my lunch box, everybody laughed at me.' I said to Mum angrily when I returned home.

'Snap out of it, some people have no food for lunch.'

I did not speak to her all night, but she was right. I was lucky to have food.

Dad bought his first bicycle in 1973, I was seven and had started local elementary school. Bicycles, in those days, were for transport only. Nobody cycled for fun.

Dad took us on his bicycle to school every day. It was about two kilometres from our house and was the only school in the village.

He extended the back seat of his bike with bamboo so he could put four of us on it, one on the front and three on the back. I was squeezed in, at the back, between my two big sisters.

'Mum, I would rather walk.' I said at the time. I did not dare complain to Dad.

'Some people can't afford a bike.' She replied.

'I'm embarrassed, people laugh at five of us on one bike!'

Mum told me, 'Just get on with it. I know you don't want to upset your Dad, if I could afford another bike, I would take two of you.'

Luckily, a few months later, our neighbour felt sorry for us. He offered to take one of my sisters to school with his daughter who was in the same class.

16

Prang started elementary school at age seven. This was for seven years, then six years in secondary school.

By the time I started elementary school, it was only six years, then three years of lower secondary, and then three years of higher secondary.

There were forty students in my class, we remained in the same classroom for all our subjects, but with a different teacher for each subject.

At elementary school, we studied nine core subjects. Thai language, mathematics, science, history, health and physical education, technology, arts, music and English. My favourite was mathematics.

The classes started in mid-May and ended in March, five days per week, eight hours a day, eight in the morning until four in the afternoon, with a thirty-minute lunch break.

We had to arrive in school before eight, because our National Anthem, *Pheng Chat* is played every morning at eight am.

All students were expected to attend and sing the national anthem. Two students would raise the Thai Flag up the school's flagpole, followed by a Buddhist chant. This is still the same, I can never see it changing.

The Thai National Anthem is also played on TV and radio stations, over government building speaker systems, and in most other public places, at 08:00 and 18:00 every day.

During the *Pheng Chat,* wherever you are, whatever you are doing, you must stop, and stand to attention, to show respect. At the cinema, it is played before the film starts, you must stand to attention, the National anthem is especially important to us.

The Thai Flag has five horizontal stripes, red, white, blue, white and red, the central blue stripe is twice as wide as the others.

Red is said to symbolize the blood of life, white, the purity of the Buddhist faith, and blue the monarchy.

If you were late at school, for the *Pheng Chat,* you were punished in front of everybody. The teacher would hit you three times on your bottom, with a stick.

I was late one morning, running as fast as I could. I was ten metres away from my class's line when the National Anthem started. I hesitated wondering if I should stop to respect the song, or keep running to the line, and hope no one noticed I was late.

I decided to stop to respect the song, I thought it was the right decision.

'Why are you late?' Mr Paiboon, the head teacher asked.

'I forgot my homework book, I had to go back for it.' I replied.

'It's unlike you to forget your homework book, you're the cleverest in the class.'

'I took it out of my schoolbag this morning to recheck my answers, I forgot to put it back.'

'I believe you, you have the highest marks in your class, you never forget your homework, but I can't let you off for being late, or I will have to let off other students too.'

'I understand. But if I had not gone back for my homework, I would've got punished in class anyway. Plus, I wouldn't know if I had all the answers correct.'

It made no difference, Mr Paiboon brushed aside my explanation, and hit me three times with his stick in front of the assembly. I felt so embarrassed, and ashamed.

There were exams for each class twice a year, mid-term exams in September (mid school holiday was in October), and final exams in March.

If our mark was less than fifty percent, we had to repeat the year. This meant another school fee for our parents.

At the time, this was about two thousand, five hundred baht (seventy pounds sterling) per term, which was about a quarter of my Dad's monthly wage.

The girls' uniform was, white blouse-untucked, with the school logo on the first line on the right breast, the second line was our school ID number.

Mum made our uniforms. Our name was on the left breast, embroidered in red. There was a blue bow, tied at the neck, heavy blue skirt, covering the knee, with six pleats in the front and six in the back, and black leather shoes with white socks.

She could not afford to have our names embroidered by a shop, she did the best she could, and wrote our names on our blouses, and then embroidered over her writing. Unfortunately, Mum's writing was poor, because she left school after primary four, and so the names did not look good!

Our hair had to be short, the rules allowed a bob no longer than one inch below the ears. Fringes had to be above your eyebrows. Mum also cut our hair, to save money, unfortunately this was not her best skill, and one side would often be longer than the other!

The boys wore a white shirt tucked in, with a left breast pocket with their name above. School, initials and logo on the first line on the right breast, the second line was our school ID number. They wore khaki shorts with a brown leather belt, brown socks and brown trainers. Their hair had to be cropped-short.

Pupils did not do anything naughty going to, or coming from school, because their name and school were so visible on their uniform.

At PE, boys and girls wore the same uniform, yellow t-shirts with the school logo, black leggings for girls, black shorts for boys. We all wore white trainers and socks.

We studied hard in Thailand, every subject came in a schoolbook, there was a separate homework book for each subject, our school bags were heavy.

This was different from Scotland, my children often had sheets of paper instead of books, their school bags were light, in comparison.

My class finished at 16:00, but you could only go home if the teacher was satisfied with your performance.

We learnt the multiplication times tables, up to twelve, calculators were not allowed in class.

Every day at 16:00, the teacher would ask you to stand up at your desk to recite a table.

In order to get it right, I did my tables every day up to number twelve, before I went to bed. We repeated them in such a way, they sounded like a song. If you did not get it right in class you had to keep standing, and the teacher would move on to someone else, returning to you at the end.

If you did not get it right on your third attempt, then you would be hit with the stick, three times on your bottom or on your hand, in front of the class.

I am fifty-four now, but I still remember those times tables. I have lived in the UK longer than Thailand, and nowadays I think in English and translate to Thai, but when it comes to mathematics, I still think and calculate in Thai.

I was clever in school, our teacher would often ask me to do everything first, and I was allowed to leave class before the others.

After the multiplication tables routine, we had to go to our English teacher, and spell five English words which we had learned that day.

Most students got it right because we were allowed to pick the five big words.

FOUR

Mum taught Prang how to cycle. Prang taught Sang, and Jang, they all learned quickly.

Prang did her best to teach me, unfortunately, as soon as she let go, I fell off and broke my left elbow.

It was a really bad injury, it forced the bones forming my elbow apart, it was really painful, and my elbow became very swollen.

Dad took me to the public hospital in the city centre. There was always a big queue there, because, while it was not free, it was subsidised by the State, and cheaper than the private hospital.

Dad saw the long queue and spoke to the receptionist. 'My daughter needs to see a doctor now.'

'Sorry, you have to wait in the queue.' She replied

'She's just a young girl, she's in a lot of pain.'

'I'm really sorry, everybody's in pain here, many are ill. You have to join the queue.'

Dad was angry, and worried about me, I was crying with pain. My arm was swollen up, it was huge. Dad cut my sleeve to relieve the pressure on the elbow.

He took me to the private hospital, which is not subsidised at all, it was much more expensive, it has little or no queueing.

I was lucky Dad had a good job and had saved up enough money for treatment there. Otherwise, I would have had to wait in agony all day at the public hospital.

A doctor saw me and took me straight to X-ray. Dad and I could see, on the X-ray, that the two elbow bones had split apart. The doctor explained that this would have to be corrected by straightening the joint under general anaesthetic.

After the operation, I woke up with a plaster covering my left elbow.

I had to keep it on for two months. This was really difficult because I was left-handed.

My elbow healed well, but afterwards I was double jointed in the elbow. I never rode a bike again until I was forty-seven!

Sometimes, there were evening movies in the school football field for villagers. Mum would dry peanuts from our garden in the sun, deep fry them, add salt and make up packets to sell at the movies. It was a good little business.

One night she sold them all. 'Prang, will you cycle to the house and get more nuts, we've run out, people like them so much!' Dad asked Prang.

'Where the hell is she? She has been gone twenty minutes; we've run out of nuts. I'll kill her.' Dad moaned to Mum.

'Why don't you go and check on her.'

Prang was eleven, she had picked up a ten-kilogram sack of nuts from the house. It was too heavy for her to cycle back with, so she put the sack on the bike and pushed it along. She was rushing so much to get back, she lost her balance, the bike wobbled, and the nuts fell off. The sack split, spilling the nuts out onto the road.

Dad found her, and when he saw the nuts everywhere, he lost his temper and slapped her hard on the shoulder.

Prang was crying when she came back, she told Mum about Dad. 'Don't you hit your children, they're not animals.' Mum shouted at him.

I seemed to be the only one in the family that Dad hardly put his hand on, because I was the youngest and cleverest. He had lots of hope for me.

Every school summer holiday, Dad took me to another province, Uttaradit, to visit his family. It was about two hundred kilometres from where we lived.

I was lucky, he could only afford to take one of us on the train, I went to see them every year, for as long as I can remember.

I had three uncles and two aunties; Dad was the oldest of his siblings. I had ten cousins all together. I loved meeting up with them and looked forward to it every year.

I wondered about Mum's family. I often asked, but, at first, she would never tell me anything. Around the time I was twelve, I started to get answers.

'Mum, where are my grandparents?' I looked at Mum, I had never met any of her family. I knew nothing about her parents.

'I'm ashamed. I can't tell you; I ran away with your Dad when I was sixteen. I still feel like a bad daughter.' Mum looked at me, she was sad, she had never talked about it before.

I kept questioning her, I was not going to give up easily. 'Mum, I'm twelve years old now. I want to know about my grandparents, all my uncles, aunties and cousins.'

Mum nodded.

'You're a Mum yourself, how will Granny sleep every night not knowing what happened to you. She's not seen or heard from you for twenty years; she'll be worried about you.'

'Your grandparents had twelve children, they were very poor, and couldn't afford to bring them all up. Money was very tight.'

'Why did they have twelve kids in the first place?' I asked.

'They had no money for contraception.' Mum continued, 'I wanted to get away from the poverty and have my own family. I ran away with your Dad when I was sixteen, he was twenty-one.'

'Was Dad serving in the military then?'

'No, he was lucky. Military service in Thailand is decided by possible candidates going to the army office and picking out a slip of paper from a box. You can't see what's in the box. Depending on what colour you pick, you can be drafted to the army. Red meant you went to the army. Black was the lucky one, you didn't go if your ticket was black. Your Dad was lucky; he chose a black one.'

'Why didn't you tell granny that you wanted to move in with Dad?'

'Because he didn't have any dowry money to give to your grandparents for taking me away, he didn't have a house. He had nothing to offer, he worked hard, but at that time, he had nothing.'

I nodded.

'We had nothing to start our life together, we slept under trees until we could build our home. Then he started work labouring in the coal mine, the pay was enough to start our life together. So, we ran off.'

'What made you decide to tell me now?' I asked.

'I was thinking I should look for my family when we've enough money to buy a truck, and we can afford to take a few days off work'.

'Can we not just take the bus or train?'

'No, I don't know exactly where they live, or even if they're still alive. I know the name of the district, that's all. It's about four hundred kilometres from here. I don't know if they still live there or if they have moved away. It's a long journey, we'll need a truck to drive around looking for them.'

A year later Dad bought a pick-up truck. Mum was thrilled, she decided it was time to look for her family.

'When your Dad is off next, we're going to Kamphaeng Phet to look for your grandparents, and my brothers and sisters'. Mum told me.

I was so excited, I hoped I would be able to get to know them all.

There was not enough room for all of us in the truck. Mum only took me; she asked our neighbour to look after my big sisters.

It took us five hours to get there. Mum asked around the district, eventually, we managed to find my grandparent's home.

'Mum, Dad'. Mum shouted outside the house.

A skinny old woman with white hair came out. 'Who are you?'.

'Sri, your daughter'. Mum replied.

'I thought you were dead'. She was crying.

They hugged each other, crying loudly.

'I'm so sorry I ran away, I thought Dad would kill me if I came back.'

Mum kept saying sorry for running away. In the end, with hindsight, my grandparents understood her reasons.

Granny's house was very basic because they were poor. It was one open space, no bedrooms, only a roof woven from grass. The floors and walls were made with bamboo tied together with rope. The poles and beams were cut from hard wood.

They cooked, ate and slept in that one open space. They had old, thin mattresses to sleep on, with mosquito nets above.

I met some of my uncles and my aunties who lived nearby, but some of the family had moved away.

Mum's youngest sister was a year older than my eldest sister, some of my cousins were a similar age to us. I cannot remember all their names now.

Sadly, my grandad passed away a few months after I met him, I did not have a chance to know him well.

FIVE

In 1979, I was thirteen, when I returned from visiting my grandparents. I started my first year in Mae Moh Vitaya lower secondary school. It was in another village about five kilometres away. Dad took me there every day, on his motorbike.

Jang was already there in her second year, Sang was in her third year.

Prang was in a private high school in Lampang city centre because she failed the entrance exam for the secondary school in the village. Fortunately, there were more options in the city centre. My sisters took the school bus.

You must pass entrance exams to get into our public schools, colleges or universities, but no exams were needed for private schools. In Thailand, if you are in a private school, people assume you are not clever enough for public school. The fees are much higher, unlike the West, where private's schools are for rich families.

There were a few new subjects in elementary school, such as knitting, crochet, cooking, baking, gardening, and dressmaking.

Our school uniform was the same, but with the new initials and school logo. I could have my hair longer, but it had to be tied back, any fringe had to be above the eyebrow. No make-up was allowed.

I was so excited on my first day in high school. I felt everybody knew me already. My name was on top of the school board because I passed the entrance exams with the highest mark. Since starting elementary school, I always had the highest marks, except for PE.

I failed PE every year. We had a different type of sport each term, basketball, handball, table tennis, badminton, volleyball and gymnastics.

I did not like any sports; I was not good at them. Sometimes, I made myself sick, so I did not have to go.

Mum had to bribe the PE teacher every year for me to pass my re-sit. I had to pass every subject in order to move on to the next year. There was only one unit in PE, so it did not affect my total mark.

Every day, my classmates would wait for me to arrive, so they could copy my homework. If I arrived late, I would get a hard time from my classmates. We would put our homework books on the teacher's table, before the class started.

The teacher would use my correct answers to check on the rest of students in the class. Sometimes, my book was stolen from the teacher's table by other students!

I decided I deserved a reward for my hard work. 'Mum, can I have a watch for a present?'

'Okay, as long as it's not more than two hundred and fifty baht (five pounds sterling).' Mum replied.

'I would love a digital watch.'

Mum agreed, she gave me it a few days later. It was my first digital watch, not many people had one then. I was so happy with it.

My big sisters were jealous because I got presents twice a year for my good schoolwork. They were not good at school, Sang and Jang just managed to pass every year.

Prang failed most of her exams. Mum and Dad had to pay extra for her to re-sit exams, most years.

Sometimes, she had to repeat the class if she failed her re-sit. Mum and Dad were not pleased. After poor exam results, Dad often slapped the back of her head.

A couple months after I started secondary school, Na, my classmate handed me a note. 'Hey, someone asked me to give you this note,'.

'From whom?' I asked.

'Why don't you just read it.' She replied.

I opened the note.

'Hello, my name is Chat. I'm in the second year, 2/1. I just want to say that I really like you, and wonder if we could meet up some weekend?'

I recognised the name; he was top of the school board. I assumed he liked me because my name was on top too.

I liked him, he was slim, dark and the same height as me. Usually, I preferred a taller boy because I felt that they could protect me, but I did not care much about Chat's height because he was clever in school. I knew he would get a good job.

We swapped notes once or twice a week, there was no internet, or mobile phones.

A few months later, we swapped our ID school photos. I kissed his photo and put it under my pillow before I went to bed every night. I was in love!

Every time I walked past his class, I would look for him, he did the same every time he walked pass my class.

Sometimes, we met at lunch break, but not too often. We did not want to get into trouble from the teachers, if they found out, we would be expelled. I knew that if my Dad found out, he might seriously assault or even kill me. He had a terrible temper.

After he finished third year, Chat moved to a higher secondary school in the city centre and we lost touch. We had not swapped addresses; letters were too risky in case my Dad opened one.

In 1982, when I was sixteen, I finished my third year in the lower secondary school. There was no higher secondary school near our village. I enrolled myself into Lampang Vocational College for a three-year course in accounting as the main subject, with secretarial as a second subject.

Our college uniform for girls was a white blouse, with the logo badge on the right chest, with the number of collar dots indicating your year.

We wore blue knee length skirts with or without pleats, plain black leather shoes without socks or ties, natural hair colour, no dye. Short hairstyles were allowed, fringes had to be above the eyebrow, any hair longer than shoulder length had to be tied back. No nail polish, no make-up, no perfume.

The boys wore a white shirt, tucked in, our college logo badge on the right chest, pocket on the left. Dot(s) on their shirt collar, black trousers, black belt, black socks and black leather shoes, short hair above the ears.

I woke up at 05:00 to catch the 06:00 free bus for the power plant staff. It was twenty minutes' walk to the pickup point, it dropped me off outside my college. I usually had an hour spare every morning before the class started.

My three sisters and I were now at four different schools or colleges, in the city centre.

My college gate was locked at 08:00 when the Thai National Anthem started. You had to arrive before the gate was locked. You could not enter after that, unless you had a letter from your parents or doctor explaining why, otherwise it counted as one absence.

In each subject, you were allowed ten absences per year, if you had more than ten, you were not allowed to sit the exam on that subject.

If you were off sick, you had to hand in a letter from your parents or doctor, but it still counted as an absence.

The gate opened at lunch time, 12:00 – 13:00, if you did not want to have lunch in the canteen, you could eat outside college. Most of us had lunch in the canteen because it was cheap, and we only had thirty minutes' break. The gate would reopen again at 15:30.

We changed classroom for every subject, sometimes to a different floor or building, there were five floors in each building, no lifts.

We did not have any spare time between classes, we had ten minutes to go to the toilet or move to the next floor or building. If you were late, that was also counted as an absence.

I picked accounting because I was good at maths. I picked secretarial because there were new subjects, such as shorthand, recording and typing.

I found accounting hard, it was no longer just about maths. Shorthand was new to me, I loved learning new skills. Sadly, I have forgotten all the shorthand.

I loved typing, I trained to touch type. In fact, we did not have a choice, if the teacher caught us looking at our keypad during exams, we failed straight away. If we did not look at the keypad, we could pass, if we did not make too many mistakes.

All our assessments, no matter the subject, were typed on a typewriter, if we made a mistake on a page, we had to retype the whole page again.

Computers were not allowed for typing assessment, no changes were allowed. At that time, there were no computers in our college.

SIX

I was not close to Dad, none of us were. He always looked so serious; I hardly saw him smile. There was not much conversation between him and us, it was more questions and answers.

I overheard Mum say to him. 'You never joke and play with the children. They're all scared to come to you with anything, all those stupid rules, not allowing them out after 18:00. In bed with lights off by 22:00. No hanging out with friends or cinema, at weekends.'

'It's not stupid, ok!' Dad shouted. 'I want them to do homework and study after school. If they're out, they can't study. If they're not good at studying, they won't get a job and they'll be poor all the rest of their lives. I want them to save up, instead of spending their money on the cinema. There are boys at the cinema, not just girls. I don't want them to meet any boys before they graduate'.

I remember one evening when Prang was seventeen, she came back home after 18:00 on a Saturday. Dad was waiting for her at the front door, he was angry.

'Where were you!?' He shouted.

'I missed the bus.' Prang replied, shaking and crying.

'Were you with a boy?'

Prang was too scared to say anything. Dad started slapping and kicking her. She wet herself.

'Don't you kick her'. Mum shouted.

'If you want to punish her, hit her with a stick not with your hands and feet!'.

'They're my children, I'll do whatever I want. Don't you dare tell me what to do, I'll kick you too'.

Dad often beat Mum if she stuck up for us, but sometimes he would just beat her for no particular reason, or because they had a minor argument. He also had regular affairs.

Mum put up with it when we were younger, because if he left, she would have nothing. There was no intervention by the police for domestic violence, no laws protecting women, and no child maintenance.

Once we grew up, she did not have to worry about him leaving any more, she started to fight back. Their disagreements became quite violent, and he would often end up in hospital if he lost the fight!

I remember Mum found out about an affair when she was dressmaking, they had an argument, Dad attacked her, and she stabbed him in the head with her dressmaking scissors. He needed hospital treatment after that one. She was tough and took no nonsense from him.

Prang walked out of the house when she turned eighteen. She could not stand Dad's rules anymore.

'Mum, I've rented a one-bedroom apartment in town. I've taken a job in a restaurant at night, so I can still go to school during the day.'

'I'm worried about you; how will you study if you're tired after working at night?'

'I'll survive.' Prang replied.

I did not blame her for walking out. I was worried and would miss her, there was no internet or mobile telephones then.

Dad went crazy when he found out Prang had left.

He warned us. 'Money earned at night is dirty. She's a whore working at night, don't you speak to her or keep in touch with her.' He never spoke to her for five years.

We did not share his extreme views, we secretly kept in touch with her.

Jang had a boyfriend when she was eighteen, she was in her second year in commercial college.

She showed me his picture. He was slim, dark tall handsome with curly hair. 'If Dad finds out, he'll kill you.'

'Don't tell Mum just in case she tells Dad.'

'Okay, I won't, but be careful, he might find out from someone else.'

Jang nodded.

'What's his name?'

'Sak.'

'Where did you meet him?'

'At the bus pick-up point, on the way to college.'

'So, he works in the power plant?'

'Yes.'

'Same place as Dad, you better watch out!'

'He's in a different department, Dad's at the coal mine, he's in the power plant building.'

'Where does he live?'

'He rents a room just down the road from us.'

'But, you said, you met him at the bus pick-up point, if he lives down the road why would he take a bus?'

'He used to live in the city centre, he moved there after he met me.'

'That's very sweet of him, he must be in love with you.'

'Yes, I'm his first love, and he's my first.'

'Have you slept with him?'

'Yes.' Jang replied shyly.

'What did it feel like?' I asked curiously.

33

'We kissed.'

'Where? On the lips?'

'Yes, we slept together.'

I remember, one evening Dad came back from work, he went straight to speak to Jang.

'Have you got a boyfriend!?'

Jang was frightened, she was afraid to tell the truth, but she did not want to lie in case she got into even more trouble.

'Yes.' She replied quietly.

Dad grabbed her hair and banged her head against the wall. Jang was screaming, blood ran down her face. He continued to smash her head against the wall.

I was terrified. I knew if I intervened, he would hit me too. I ran to my next-door neighbour. 'Can you stop Dad; he's going to kill my sister.'

'I can't, it's not my business, but I saw your Mum in the market.' She replied.

I ran to the market for Mum. 'Hurry! You need to stop Dad, he's killing Jang.' I was crying.

Mum ran back home and managed to separate Jang from Dad. She took her to the doctor. She needed stiches in her forehead.

'You tell your boyfriend to bring his parents to see me.' Dad said to Jang when she came back from the doctor.

Jang and Sak had an arranged marriage a couple of days later. Jang still continued with her education, but she had to it keep secret from the teachers, otherwise she would be expelled.

One day at college, Pirom, my classmate asked. 'Are you coming to my 18th birthday?'

'What day, and what time?'

'Next Saturday night, at the community hall, about twenty minutes from your house. You could ask Toi for a lift, she's coming too.'

'I would love to, but I'm not allowed out at night.'

I never went on a night out until I was eighteen.

I decided to ask. 'Mum, can I go to my friend's 18th birthday party next Saturday night?'

'Well, if it's at night, you'll have to ask your Dad.' She replied.

I waited until Dad back was home from work, I made sure he was in a good mood.

'Dad, can I go to my friend's 18th birthday party next Saturday night?' I asked him politely.

'No, it's not safe to go out at night.'

'My friend will give me a lift.'

'I don't want to discuss it anymore, it's a no.'

I told Pirom the next day I could not go to her party.

'Your Dad doesn't need to know you're going.' She said.

'How?' I asked.

'Just sneak out of the window!' She was joking.

Dad was on night shift that weekend, finishing at midnight.

'Mum, I'm tired and going to bed now.' I said to mum at 20:00

I sneaked out of my bedroom window. I was wearing black trousers with a fancy red top and soft pink lipstick. I danced like no one was watching at the party. I do not think I talked to any boys because I was so scared of Dad. I had a great time at the party. It was my first night out, ever.

'We need to leave now, it's 23:00. I need to get back home before my Dad.' I said to Toi.

'Another thirty minutes, there's a bus at 23:30.' She replied.

We caught the bus at 23:30, unfortunately it broke down after fifteen minutes. My heart sank. I knew what would happen if Dad arrived home before me.

The driver managed to get the bus started fifteen minutes later. I arrived home at 00:30. Dad was waiting for me at the front door, he looked angry.

'I said no! Why didn't you listen to me!?' He shouted.

I kept silent. He slapped and kicked me, then threw me into my bedroom and locked the door. That was the first time he hit me.

'You treat your children like animals.' Mum was crying.

I was upset, crying in my bedroom. I desperately wanted to leave the house, but I did not have any money to take care of myself.

I kept telling myself, in one more year, I would finish my college course and then there was a good chance for me to get out.

There was no university in my city, therefore I had to go to university in Chiang Mai, about two hundred kilometres from where I lived. I intended staying in a student apartment.

SEVEN

In 1985, I was nineteen when I started the four-year Bachelor of Business Administration course in Chiang Mai University.

Chiang Mai is a city in mountainous northern Thailand. The landscape around the city is full of wonderful natural attractions.

Chiang Mai is most famous for its beautiful temples. It is a cultural and religious centre; the Old City areas still retain vestiges of walls and moats. It is the second capital of Thailand.

Mum and Dad helped me to move into my apartment. Dad was happy with all the rules.

It was a female only apartment, TV was not allowed in bedrooms, no males in bedrooms, the meeting area was downstairs, only. Alcohol was banned, and the gate closed at 23:00. I shared a room with another girl in her second year.

'Come back home every weekend.' Dad told me before he left. Mum gave me five hundred baht (twelve pounds sterling) per month, for food.

I felt strange at first, sharing a one-bedroom apartment with a stranger was a big change for me. Our room was small, just big enough for two single beds, and a shared table for eating and studying.

However, I had freedom, I could go wherever I wanted, and did not have to worry about being late back.

If I knew I would be later than 23:00 I stayed over with friends who had apartments outside the university.

It happened a few times after nights out, but I did not go out much, I had to be careful with money. I did not drink; I was too scared Dad would find out and hit me.

We wore uniform at university, female students wore a short sleeve, solid white blouse, with the front open from top to bottom with five silver metal buttons bearing the university seal.

The blouse had to be tucked neatly inside the skirt, with a university pin attached to the left breast. A navy blue or black knee length skirt in a polite style, with a black leather belt and silver buckle, of a rectangle shape, bearing the university seal. We wore plain low-cut shoes.

Male students wore a solid white shirt with pointed collar-tips, with the front open from the top down with small white buttons, a pocket on the left breast with short (or long folded) sleeves. The shirt length was long enough to be tucked neatly into the long trousers, which were black or navy blue, the belt was the same as the females. They wore plain low-cut shoes and socks.

We wore uniform during the day, except when we had sport or a workshop, then we would wear a suitable outfit for the activity.

Nowadays, every Friday, the students may put on a traditional Thai style outfit.

My university was massive, some buildings were thirty minutes' walk apart, most of the students rode motorbikes or cycled between the buildings.

Most subjects were in different buildings. I could not ride a motorbike or a bicycle, but my classmates gave me lifts. I wished I had continued with my cycling lessons, after the accident.

Business Management was my main subject. I liked the idea of running my own business one day. I did not know anything about computers before my course.

I was amazed with what could be achieved on a computer. I used to type my assessments with a typewriter, if I made a mistake, I had to retype the whole page again, with a computer I just used back space or delete.

Nowadays, there is automatic grammar and spelling checks. Our assessments were much easier to complete on a computer.

Schools and colleges had many rules, punishments and examinations. University was more about accepting responsibility. If you chose not to attend a class, it was fine, as long as you handed in your assessments on time and passed your exams.

After I graduated, I did not want to go back to my house. I missed Mum, and I loved her cooking. But, I was twenty-three, I did not want to go back to my Dad's rules and punishments.

'Why didn't you come here and stay with me for a couple of weeks.' Prang invited me to stay with her family in Bangkok. I enjoyed being adventurous, so I decided to go.

Bangkok is the capital city of Thailand. I was not sure that it was my dream place to be. It was dirty, crowed, and polluted. It had hectic city roads, some with seven or eight lanes on each side, full of people, without helmets, riding motorbikes. You would see little kids sitting on the front of motorbikes, sometimes, as many as four or five.

People ran across busy roads in front of traffic, people jumped on and off buses before the bus stops. Some sidewalks had gaping holes, the subterranean pipes running under the city were visible.

There was electric wires and cables hanging from the poles, which lined every road.

I decided to stay a bit longer, and look for a job, it took me a few months to find one.

I had some interviews for admin work, but every one of them asked me for a twenty thousand-baht (five hundred pounds sterling) cash deposit if they gave me a job.

I explained to them that it was my first job, so I did not have savings. I asked why there was such a large deposit. They explained it was in case I damaged office furniture or left and gave company information to a competitor.

They offered to return my deposit after three months working with them. I was unable to take the job offers because I did not have the deposit.

After these disappointments, I saw an advertisement for a hotel receptionist in the five-star Ambassador Hotel on Sukhumvit Road.

'Qualifications: - Bachelor of Business Administration. Female. Single. Age 23-25. English required. Applications must be completed in English.'

I applied and was thrilled to receive a letter inviting me for interview. I was extremely impressed when I first walked in, I thought it would cost more than my months wage to stay for one night.

A few weeks later, I received a job offer from them, I was over the moon.

I loved my new job, I loved meeting people, most of the guests were foreign tourists, I enjoyed using my English.

Understanding the different accents from around the world was really difficult. In comparison, reading and writing English was straightforward.

One nightshift, I looked up, there was a slim, white western man with blue-green eyes, about five feet nine tall with thinning dark brown hair.

'Good evening, I would like to check-in please.' He seemed friendly, with a warm smile.

'Of course, can I have your booking reference number please.'

Bob was thirty-four, from Scotland. He was on a business trip, staying in Bangkok for five days.

Every day he came around to the reception area and tried to chat me up.

'When will you finish work today?' He asked on his third day.

'I'll be finished at 20:00 tonight.' I replied.

'I wonder; could I buy you dinner after work?'

'20:00 is a bit late, maybe next time, thank you for asking.'

'When do you finish early?'

'I'll have to check my rota.'

He came around the next day. 'I'm catching a flight back to Scotland tomorrow night. Can I buy you a coffee before you start tomorrow?'

'I suppose you can, how about the coffee shop opposite the hotel at 11:00?'

'That would be great.' He replied with a big smile on his face.

I met Bob at the coffee shop before I started work. He explained he really liked me and would like to get to know me better, unfortunately he was leaving that night.

He left me his business card and asked if he could call me sometime. I agreed.

He called me every day, he said he was coming back to Thailand, for a holiday, in six weeks' time.

'Who are you on the phone to every day?' Prang asked.

'Someone I met at work, he's Scottish.'

'Wow, that must cost him a fortune, he must like you.'

'I guess so, he's coming to Thailand next month on holiday to visit me.'

A month later, Bob was back in Thailand. He saw me every day during his stay, he stayed at the hotel where I worked. We met outside it every day, before or after work.

'Would you like to go to Koh Samui with me for a week before I head back to Scotland?' He asked.

'It's not easy, I'll have to find someone to cover for me, and see if it's ok with my boss.'

'It would be great if you can find out today so I can go ahead with the booking.'

I arranged cover; my boss agreed I could have leave. I told Bob the next day. He was excited and made the booking.

I had never been to Koh Samui before, but I had heard so much about it, I could not wait to go. It is the second largest island in the South of Thailand. It is known for stunning beaches, edged with palm trees, and crystal-clear water.

Bob showed me a brochure containing the five-star hotel accommodation he had booked. The air ticket cost the same as my monthly wage.

I had never been on a plane before. I was worried in case something went wrong.

'Can you get me a separate room? If I share a room with someone, it means he's my last, that's the way I've been brought up.' I said to him.

'Yes, no problem.' He replied, he seemed confused.

I had a great time at Koh Samui. I loved the place, but I was uncomfortable to be seen with Bob. He was white and I was Asian, I felt people looked at me as if I was a prostitute. It was worse because I did not have a wedding ring

Sometimes, people made nasty comments, such as, asking to keep my ID in case I caused trouble with the other guests.

I often refused to walk next to him, I did not want anybody to know I was with him.

'If it's difficult for you to have a holiday in Thailand with me, why don't you come to Scotland?' He asked.

'It's not as easy as you think.'

'Why not?'

'I would have to quit my job; we only have two weeks' annual leave and I've already used a week. I can't tell my Mum and Dad because you're white, and I'm Asian.'

He nodded.

'If I ask them, they won't let me go.' And the most important reason is, I've never been abroad before, it's the other side of the world, another language. It's scary.' I replied.

'If you come, I'll get you an open return ticket, so you'll feel free to leave anytime. I'll do anything to make you feel ok and happy.' He made it sound like he really meant it; he was so convincing then.

'Would you like me to meet your parents, would that help?' He continued.

'No, it's too complicated with your culture being so different, if you meet them it means we're getting married.'

'I would like you to come on holiday first.'

'I understand, you don't have to explain, most of my guests in the hotel are white, I understand your culture, it's opposite to mine.'

In Thailand, at that time, it was not usually possible for two people to have a meaningful relationship before marriage.

I knew many Westerners thought, you should live together before getting married, to ensure you got on well together.

After Bob left for Scotland, I discussed going to Scotland with Prang

'I think you should go, he's a nice person and seems to care a lot about you.' Prang said.

'What about Mum and Dad, if I tell them, you know they will say no.'

'You don't have to tell them, write letters to me, I'll change the envelope and post it to them from Bangkok, they'll think you're still here with me!'

'That's a good idea, but I'm still scared. It's a big thing.'

'If you love adventure, then you should go. I would if I had the chance.' Prang said.

I started to hate Bangkok traffic and how busy the city was. It took me an hour to get to work, even though it was not far from where I lived. The traffic made it seem ten times further.

I hated the heat, and the smell of sweat on the bus. Often, the seats were full, and I had to stand all the way. I thought I should go to Scotland, the grass definitely looked greener.

Bob called me almost every day to build up my confidence about coming to Scotland.

'I have someone here next to me who would like to say hello to you.' He said to me one night on the phone.

'Hello, how are you? My name's Atip.' He spoke Thai.

'I'm good, thank you. Who are you, and how do you know Bob?' I asked.

'I'm a doctor in Rama hospital, Bangkok Thailand. I've come to Scotland to continue my Master's degree at Glasgow University. I met Bob at a Thai Restaurant in Glasgow. I just want to tell you that he's a really nice person.'

'I see.'

'He lives with his Mum and Dad, I've already met them, and they were very nice too. He has two Hi-Fi shops, in Glasgow and Edinburgh. You'll be ok and safe here if you come on holiday.'

'I'm still thinking about it.'

'I've given Bob my card and my address, and also my sister's business card, he'll post it to you. You can call my sister in Bangkok anytime; I've told her about you.' Atip continued.

I was less worried about going to Scotland after speaking with Atip, and the girls in the Thai Restaurant where Bob often had dinner.

Bob sent me documents from his solicitor and his bank manager to support my visa application at the British Embassy. My tourist visa was accepted.

Prang saw me off from Bangkok Airport. I gave her Bob's business card, his home address and phone numbers, also Atip and his sister's business cards, and their home addresses.

'Call me when you arrive safe and sound.' She said.

'I will.' I replied nervously.

'Don't worry, if I don't hear from you within three days, I'll take all these addresses to the British Embassy, to find you.' She gave me a cuddle, and I walked off for my flight.

I was worried, but I hoped I had made the right decision. I could not turn back now, I was on my way, hoping for the best.

I put my trust in Bob, and his promise to look after me.

EIGHT

I flew with Thai Airways. I was so scared; it was my second time on a plane. This plane was much bigger than the plane on my first flight to Koh Samui.

It was my first time to the other side of the world, I was nervous, but looking forward to learning more British culture and language.

The plane had two levels, I was in economy class, on an aisle seat, two other females sat next to me in the middle and window seats.

It was an eleven-hour flight to Heathrow. I arrived at 06:30, on the 8th December 1989. Bob met me there and we caught a connecting flight to Glasgow at 09:30 that morning.

We flew with British Airways to Glasgow. The plane was much smaller than the Thai international plane. I looked out of the window and wondered why it was still dark.

'What time is it?' I asked Bob.

'It's 09:30.'

'Are you sure? It looks like 06:00 to me, the sky is so grey and dull.'

'We've short daylight hours in winter, between 08:30 – 15:30, and longer day light in summer, roughly 04:00 – 10:00, depending how far north you are.'

'That's really strange, we have the same hours of daylight all year round in Thailand.'

'Our time moves back and forward, one hour, between summer and winter.'

'I'm confused, what do you mean?'

'The clocks go forward an hour at 01:00 on the last Sunday in March, and back an hour at 02:00 on the last Sunday in October.'

'So, when the clocks go forward, you lose an hour in summer and when the clocks go back an hour you have an hour extra in winter, am I right?'

'Yes, you're right.'

I wondered how I would get used to these time changes. In Thailand, I used to look at the sun in the sky and guess what time it was, I couldn't do that in Scotland.

I wondered if I could sleep in summer when there was sunlight at the window.

In winter, I would be leaving for work in the dark, and coming home in the dark.

My thoughts were interrupted. The plane was shaking madly, I was so scared.

'I feel like we're going to crash.'

'Don't worry, it's just turbulence.' Bob held my hand.

'The sky's so dark, it looks as if there's going to be a storm.'

'We'll be fine, if it's not safe, they won't let the plane take off. They check the weather frequently.'

'Who are they?'

'ATC, air traffic control.'

It did not make me feel any better. I could not help thinking if the plane crashed, no one would survive.

The plane landed safely at 10:30. We disembarked and walked into the terminal. I was shivering in the cold wind. I had never felt this cold before in my whole life, my breath was steaming out of my mouth. I felt much warmer inside the terminal waiting for the suitcases.

Bob took me to his car, an auto sky blue BMW 535. He drove me to the three-bedroom flat in Ibrox where he lived with his parents, Liz and Robert. It was on the third floor, an old tenement building with no lift.

Liz had a full figure, five feet tall, short silvery-white hair, pale skin, blue-green eyes. Robert was a few pounds overweight. Small too, five feet, balding, grey hair, fair skin, blue-green eyes.

Bob introduced me, they were both friendly, and pleased to meet me. His dad shook hands and gave me a cuddle, his mum gave me a cuddle and a kiss on both cheeks.

47

I felt uncomfortable because that is not the way we greet each other in Thailand. I returned the greeting by bowing slightly and putting the palms of my hands together.

'That's the way Thai people greet each other.' Bob explained.

They tried to do the same back to me, it was nice of them. I walked into living room, there was a fire, it warmed me up right away.

I was confused. 'Where do the flames come from, I can't see any wood?'

'It's not real, it's a gas fire.' Liz replied.

'Gas? I don't see any gas cylinders.'

'The gas is piped under the floor.'

'I see. In Thailand, we use gas cylinders for cooking, we never have any heating installed in our houses, it's hot all year. All we have is air conditioning. I don't think gas pipes exist in Thailand.'

'We also have radiators for heating.'

I walked down and touched the radiator; I could feel the heat. Now I knew how they kept the room warm. Occasionally in Thailand, if it was cold on winter mornings or evenings, we would burn wood outside in the yard and sit around the fire.

Liz made a meal of roast chicken with boiled rice, but without any sauce. I was not that keen on it because I was used to food being cooked in a sauce. I found, unfortunately, it had no flavour, and was dry and hard to swallow. I did not want to hurt her feelings, I pretended I really enjoyed it and tried to eat as much as I could.

It was served on one plate, the chicken breast was whole, and there was a knife and fork for me to use.

The only problem was, I did not know how to use a knife and fork! Thai food is always cut up. The spoon is always held in your strong hand, and the weak hand holds the fork, which is used to scoop food into the spoon.

We have one plate for rice, then we all share the side dishes of meat or fish.

'Would you like a cup of tea and some biscuits?' Liz asked, after I finished my meal.

'I don't drink tea in Thailand.'

'It's cold here, you should have a hot drink to keep you warm.'

'Okay, thank you, what are biscuits, I don't know what they are.'

She gave me some cookies.

'They're cookies!' I said.

'Here, we call them biscuits.'

I could not help noticing that the tray she served me with had a picture of the queen on it.

'Is this a picture of the Queen?' I asked.

'Yes, Queen Elizabeth.'

'Is it okay in the UK using trays with a picture of the queen?'

'Yes.'

In Thailand, our King and Queen's pictures can only hang up on the highest part of the wall, or just below Buddha. We respect our King and Queen, and our Thai flag. It is enshrined in our laws. You will not see our Thai flag printed on anything worn below your waist, such as shorts, trousers, and especially not on shoes or flip flops. You could be locked up in prison if you wore skirts, shorts, trousers or shoes printed with the Thai flag!'

Later, I was almost in shock watching a comedy on TV where the actors portrayed the King and Queen, and the Royal family. This would not be permitted in Thailand. I kept thinking the police would break the doors down and rush in and arrest us!

I walked into the kitchen, I thought the kitchen units and work tops unusual because I was used to my Mum cooking outside on the floor.

I watched Liz washing the dishes, she soaked them in the sink, squeezed on some washing-up liquid and brushed it off the plates. It looked like a toilet brush to me! She dried them off with a dishcloth.

'Don't you rinse them under tap water first before you dry them off?' I asked.

'No, this is the way we wash dishes here.'

'Well, if you don't rinse them under tap water, I believe that the chemicals in the washing-up liquid will still be on your plates.'

'If that was true all the Scots would be dead by now.' She laughed.

I could never get used to that. Every time I used her dishes, I always rinsed them under tap water first.

When I went to the bathroom, I was really surprised to see a carpet on the floor. My bathroom was a wet room, you could not carpet it.

In Thailand, there is a shower head attached to every toilet cistern and we use it to wash ourselves instead of using toilet paper. I couldn't help it, but I felt dirty using toilet paper, so every time I used the toilet I had to go into the bath to wash myself before I used tissue. It took me a month to adjust to using toilet paper!

Later on, that day, Liz spoke to Bob. 'I've to go out for messages, do you want me to get anything for Nuch?

'It's ok, Mum. I'll take Nuch to a Chinese supermarket in town tomorrow.' Bob replied.

'Is your mum going to the post office to collect a letter?' I asked Bob.

'No. What makes you think that?'

'She said, she's going for messages.'

'Messages here means food shopping.' Bob laughed.

Now, I realised, we had used American English in school in Thailand, not British English.

Later, Liz made a bed for me in the spare room, she switched on an electric blanket for me. I had never seen or heard of such a thing before.

'Remember to switch the electric blanket off before you go to sleep, in case it goes on fire.' Liz reminded me.

I switched it off when I got into bed, but as soon as it was off, I was freezing! I was so tired and cold, I slept with my hat, gloves and socks on!

The next day Bob took me to his shop in Glasgow city centre. The shop was filled with Hi-Fis of different makes and models. There were five male staff on the shop floor. His office was on upper floor, with two female's administrators and a male accountant.

In the afternoon, I wondered around the shopping centre while Bob was working. I did not like the clothes fashion here, they were too dull and boring. I could not help noticing lots of hoodie tops, something you never see in Thailand, I did not understand the reason for this at first, now, I realise, it was because of the cold weather.

After work, Bob took me to see Atip and the girls in the Thai restaurant.

'It's nice to meet you in the person, Bob talked a lot about you and I was the one who translated your letters to him.' Lek introduced herself.

'My letters were in English, why did you have to translate them?' I asked curiously.

Lek and the other girls looked at each other and then changed the subject.

I suppose, I should have realised something was seriously amiss at this point, but I never suspected a thing. I just put it down to a misunderstanding, I trusted him.

The next day, I enrolled myself in an English as a second language class in Anniesland College, in Glasgow West. There were twenty-five students from around Europe in the class, except Nok, who was from Thailand.

She was nineteen, five feet tall, average weight, long black wavy hair, black eyes and dark skin. I assumed she was from Eastern Thailand from her skin tone, and the fact she was a loud, fast talker. Northern Thailand people are quieter and more reserved.

It was hard with foreign students in the class because we all had different accents. I thought this is not going to help me improve my communication skills. I decided that, next year, I would enrol myself on a different course with Scottish people.

I found learning English to a high standard very hard. In Thailand, our grammar, tenses and the use of adjectives is completely different. We say car red, in English, it is red car.

In Thailand, we do not have plural words, it is understood from the numbers. We do not have tenses. This is also understood from words such as yesterday, tomorrow, next week etc.

I was lucky English was a compulsory subject at school, and because I was a graduate my English classes had continued in university, otherwise I would have really struggled.

I sat with Nok at lunch time in the canteen.

'What part of Thailand do you come from?' Nok asked me in Thai, it was easier for us to speak Thai together.

'Lampang, North of Thailand. What about you?'

'Buriram, North East Thailand. Where are you in Glasgow?'

'I live in Ibrox, near the Rangers Stadium, what about you?'

'In Glasgow city centre, you can come back to the flat with me after the class, if you want to.'

'That's great, I'd love to, thanks. Bob can pick me up after his work.' I replied happily.

Nok told me on the train to Glasgow that her husband, Steve, was a lawyer. They married in Thailand before she moved to Glasgow.

'Where did you meet your husband?' She asked me.

'We're not married. I'm here on holiday to see if I would like to live here'.

'What type of visa did you have?'

'Six months' tourist visa.' I replied.

'I tried with a tourist visa, I didn't get it, so we married, and I applied for a visa to follow my husband.'

'Where did you meet your him?' I asked.

'I met him in a bar on Sukhumvit Road in Bangkok where I worked. My family were poor, I had no education, only as far as primary four, just enough to write and read Thai.' She said.

'So, you can't write and read English at all.'

'No.'

'How did you manage on the train if you can't read the name of stations, how do you know which one to get off at? I asked.

'My husband tells me how many stops.' She replied.

I thought that it must be pretty hard for her to keep counting stops. I could not help thinking, what if she missed one?

Nok made me dinner at her flat, she was a good cook, unlike me. I could only cook a basic meal, Bob and I ate out most of the time.

In Thailand, you can go to a restaurant anytime when you are hungry. The restaurants are open all day, and there is plenty of street food all night, unlike the UK.

I found it strange, that at that time, in Scotland, the restaurants often opened for lunch at 12:00 – 14:30, then 17:30 for dinner. Nowadays, the restaurants in the shopping centres are open all day.

I started to like living in Glasgow. I loved speaking English, I found English was sweet and polite.

British people use the word 'love' all the time, before they got off the phone, when they see each other, when they leave each other. I do not say to my mum and dad, or my sisters that I love them, but I still love them.

In Britain, you can never say please, thank you or sorry too often. British people always say thank you, when someone holds the door open for you, or to the bus or taxi driver when you finish your journey. In Thailand, we do not say thank you on these occasions, nor do we ever hold the door open for you!

British people say thank you when someone gives you something, no matter if it was for free or you paid for it. In Thailand, we do not say thank you if we pay for it, we only say thank you when we get something for free. But, it does not mean we are rude! It is just a different custom.

I remember smiling to myself when I went back to Thailand. I said thank you to the cashier at the check-out in supermarket. She looked surprised, mum told me that I did not have to say thank you because I had paid for my shopping!

Because I love speaking English, I tried my best outside college to improve my communication skills. I read children's' books because I found it easier to pick up kiddies' words. In the house I would read anything I could find.

If I was in the toilet, I would read the words on toothpaste tubes, soap, shampoo, mouthwash etc. If I was in the kitchen, I would read labels on sauce bottles, food packages etc. If I watched TV, I would put subtitles on. I worked hard!

I am not keen on some British customs. In Thailand, we do not hug or kiss in public We do not hug each other at all. Instead, we give a quick little pat on the back, at an emotional time, such as, where we console someone who is sad or grieving.

I do not hug my parents or sisters, but it does not mean I do not love them. Men and women do not hold hands in public, and kissing in public is seen as strange, or even offensive.

I remember, once in Thailand, Bob forgot, he held my hand along the road, we had a disapproving look with nasty comments. It made me cry.

I could never get used to kissing in public. I found it disgusting when I saw British people tongue kiss in public. In Thailand, we do sniff kiss, it is a way to show affection. It is an expression of love, warmth and care. It is also used to show gratitude and appreciation

I looked out at the window one evening in February 1990, it was snowing. I was so excited

'Snow, it's snowing.' I kept shouting. It was a dream come true.

I ran outside wearing only a onesie and running shoes, jumping, and spinning around. I was so excited I forgot my jacket. My neighbours looked at me as if I was crazy.

My first experience of snow! I saw little flakes of white snow, falling down from the sky. It was floating in the air like a feather and slowly touched my skin. I was so excited to touch the snow. It was like flour in my hands, it was soft and had a powdery texture. It was one of those memorable moments of my life which I will always remember.

When I was a kid, I thought snow must be edible and taste like cotton candy, but now I found it tasted like ice! I had always wanted to live where it snowed.

It might not be a big deal for British people because they see it so often. For me, coming from a humid climate, I had only experienced rainy or sunny weather. Snow was something I always wished to see and experience.

Later on, I discovered that a mixture of rain and snow is called sleet. Snow that partially melts as it falls toward the ground, then refreezes into small ice pellets, after passing cold air, is called hail or hailstones.

I do not like sleet, it is damp and can be dangerous when it makes the roads or pavements slippery.

Bob worked six days a week, but one of his Sunday's off, he drove me around the Scottish Highlands.

He had a large motor launch on Loch Lomond, it had a sleeping berth and a galley. Sometimes, we took it around Loch Lomond. He also had a much smaller speed boat which he kept at Cameron House, Loch Lomond.

'You're clever; it didn't take you long to learn to handle a boat.' He said.

'It was easy enough.' I replied.

'Have you steered one before?'

'No, I can't ride a bicycle, never mind driving a car or boat.'

'Why can't you ride a bike? Kiddies here learn to ride bicycles at two or three.'

'I had a bad accident learning to cycle when I was twelve. I never went back on one since. Bicycles were for transport, not for fun.'

'I think you should learn to drive, I'll book some lessons for you.'

'My mum said, if I can't ride a bike, then I can't drive.'

'It's not true. Actually, driving's safer then riding.' Bob booked driving lessons for me three days per week after I finished college for the day.

Three months later, Bob said, 'I've got a ten-day business trip in Sardinia, Italy, with Pioneer, at the end of May.'

I could see he was excited. 'Sounds great? Will I still be here? I asked.

'No, I would like you to come with me, I have an invitation for two.'

'What about getting a visa to Italy?'

Bob called the British Embassy in London the next day. The Embassy informed him that I could not go because Italy would be the third country on my visa. I had to go back to Thailand to apply for a tourist visa to Italy. It was not going to be easy because Bob was British, and he could not support me for a visa to Italy, unless we were married.

After much thought, I decided it would upset my parents too much to arrive home and tell them, at that point, that Bob and I were living together, unmarried. This would be completely against their culture.

I was worried my parents might try to stop me returning to Scotland, but they would not do this if we were married. If I asked my parents for permission to marry Bob, I knew that the answer was going to be no. I thought that Mum and Dad would be worried people would think I was a prostitute, because he was white. At that time, the assumption was, that if a young Thai girl was with a western white guy, then she must be a prostitute.

We decided to get married in May 1990. We had a small wedding, with Bob's family and a few friends, in the registry office, in Glasgow city centre.

I wore a simple knee length white dress. Bob wore a black suit. His brother, and sister in law were our best man and bridesmaid. A traditional white wedding car took us to the registry office.

Later on, I found out, Bob owned the wedding car! He did not mention it at the time, I thought he had hired it. He was very secretive about his business dealings. Unfortunately, I only found this out later.

We had our wedding photo shoot in Bellahouston Park. The weather was kind enough, to us, on our wedding day. We had our reception in a posh Chinese restaurant in Rouken Glen Park.

I felt quite sad that none of my family were there, they didn't even know that I was getting married.

After the wedding, Bob and I spoke about our future, and he approached his parents.

'Mum, Dad, now we're married we're going to move into our own home.'

'Where are you moving to?' asked Liz.

'I don't know yet, I'll look for a flat.' Bob replied.

'Why don't you stay here until you get a house, I don't want you to waste money on renting.'

'I don't want to rush to get something. We want to take our time to find something that we both really like. Now that we're married, we want to sleep in the same room, in our own place.'

I was pleased that Bob talked to his parents about moving out. I loved them, they were nice people, but sometimes I just wanted our own space. I wanted my own kitchen, I wanted to learn to cook.

Three days after the wedding, we went on business trip to Sardinia, an island to the west of Italy. Pioneer, the electronics company, paid for the honeymoon suite. It was very kind of them. The suite was fantastic, spacious, with lovely furnishings and decoration.

But, it was not a honeymoon or even a holiday to me. The hotel was full of business people, talking about work, and to an extent, I was left out because I did not understand anything about the business, at that time.

Unfortunately, as time went on, I found that Bob never shared many aspects of the business with me, especially, anything to do with his finances.

One day after a business lunch, Bob and I were relaxing at the beach, sitting on deck chairs. I noticed he was spending ages with his telephoto camera, zooming in and out.

'What are you looking at? I asked.

'A woman who's topless, she looks very nice, but she's with her boyfriend.'

'You're trying to take pictures of a topless woman on your honeymoon!' I could not believe what I had just heard. It was beyond belief.

'I'm not taking pictures; I'm just looking through the lens.'

'What's the difference?' I was too upset to stay with him. I walked back to the room.

I met Mark and Julie, another couple we knew through business, on my way back to the hotel.

'Are you okay?' They could see that I was upset.

'Yes, I'm fine, thanks. I'm just going back to the room, to keep out of the sun.'

'Where's Bob?' Mark said.

'He's at the beach. Julie, can I ask you something?'

'Of course, you can.'

'How would you feel, if Mark sat next to you on the beach, staring at topless women through his telephoto lens?'

'I would kill him!'

'Bob said, I was over reacting because he was only looking, not taking pictures!'

'You're not over reacting! He's a creep doing it anytime, but on your honeymoon, I can't believe it. You're so lovely!'

I nodded, still in disbelief.

'Come with us to the beach.' Julie offered.

'Thank you, but I'm going to go back to the room for a while, catch up later.'

I tried to forget about it, I decided not to mention it again, and make the best of the honeymoon.

After Sardinia, we visited Rome and Pisa, before heading back to Scotland. I very much enjoyed our time alone in Rome. I loved the leaning tower of Pisa. I remember the tower well, because the guide told us it was the last day you were allowed inside, it was shutting soon for internal visits.

After we got back from our trip, we rented a two-bedroom flat in Glasgow West, a posh area.

I was still in college in the morning, in the afternoon, I helped Bob in his office. He made me an employee in his company.

Ann, the office accountant, helped me learn basic accounting, stock management and invoice processing.

I noticed that I missed my period for 2 weeks. I bought a pregnancy test kit, it was positive!

I was excited, but I was slightly worried because my English was still not very good, and I knew it would be hard to explain any medical issues to the doctor, but then I thought that Bob or his parents would help.

I could not wait to tell Bob when he came in from work. He was not happy. 'Look you can't speak English properly. You can't have a child yet, how can you look after a child on your own when I'm at work. You need to learn to drive before you have a child.'

He made an appointment and persuaded me to go to the doctor with him. He asked the GP the time limits for abortion. The GP told us it was up to the sixth week of pregnancy.

At that time, I was six weeks' pregnant, so Bob arranged for me to have an abortion at the Nuffield private hospital.

I was traumatised, I do not believe in taking life, but I felt I had no choice. I was completely dependent on Bob for everything.

I felt scared, but I went along with it. In my culture and religion, you do not kill anything which you are not going to eat.

I felt I was going against my culture and religion.

Bob made me promise not to tell any of his family but, I told his brother later on because he and his wife had been trying for ages to have a child. Sadly, when his wife was pregnant, she miscarried.

They were really upset, I tried to comfort them. I told them that I knew how they felt and explained what had happened to me when I was pregnant.

They were both very shocked and upset. I asked them not to tell Bob, because he had told me not to tell anybody. Fortunately, later on, they did manage to have two children.

After that Bob and I used condoms, I tried to be careful, but sometimes he would not bother. I suppose, he thought, he could just make me have another abortion.

Every Tuesday, I met up with Thai friends, from the restaurant in Glasgow, for a Thai meal and chat. Not often at mine, because I could not cook well then.

Later on, I stopped going to the weekly get together, because unfortunately, I found that it became very gossipy.

I was closest with Nok, from my college class, sometimes I went back to her place after college.

'When did you start work at the bar in Bangkok?' I asked Nok one afternoon at her place.

'I was fourteen.' She replied openly.

'Fourteen? That was very young.'

'Yes. One night in my home town I had a few drinks, I was only fourteen. I was drunk, and six boys raped me. Then, because I had already lost my virginity, and no one was going to marry me, I went to work in a bar in Bangkok.'

I was shocked. I was not allowed out of my house at that age, never mind go drinking.

I knew what had happened to Nok was not unusual in Thailand. At that time, if you were poor, and had no witnesses or other proof, the police would do nothing about rape. I imagine, and hope, it is different now.

'Did you go to the police?'

'No, I didn't, I thought it was my fault because I was drunk.'

'I'm sorry for what happened to you.' I knew Nok would have had little or no chance of getting married if she was not a virgin. She would be regarded as worthless, and probably also felt like that too.

'It's okay. It doesn't bother me now.'

'Do you mind if I ask, what did you do in the bar?'

'I worked in a Go-Go bar. I wore a sexy outfit for pole dancing. If the clients liked me, they would ask me to have drink with them.'

'How did you make money?'

'From the drinks they bought, and if they liked me, they would take me back to their hotels.'

'How much did you get paid? I'm sorry if I ask too many questions. I'm just trying to understand another side of life, if you don't want to talk about it, don't worry.'

'No, it's okay to talk about it. They paid three hundred baht for a short time and five hundred baht for an overnight.'

'What do you mean by a short time?'

'For an hour in the upstairs room.'

'You mean, at the bar where you worked?'

'Yes, and sometimes I performed sex on stage too.'

'With a guy?'

'Yes, sometimes in a group of three or four.'

'I don't understand, how you could perform while people were watching.'

'We all took drugs.'

I was shocked by what she said about drugs and group sex. I was sure she had not enjoyed selling herself, especially at fourteen. I knew It was because she felt worthless because she was no longer a virgin, so little chance of marriage, and no education to get a job.

I felt I should not have asked her so many questions about such a terrible experience, but she seemed okay and talked openly.

Prostitution is illegal in Thailand, but for decades' lawmakers and police have turned a blind eye enabling the sex industry to thrive.

Rape and sexual abuse of women is common in Thailand, with little protection from the police and judicial authorities. This, in turn, can often lead women to prostitution, such as happened in Nok's case.

The sex tourism industry encourages many to turn a blind eye, to what is, essentially, abuse of women. Drug dealing and organised crime groups, thrive in such an environment.

For years, the authorities have appeared to do little about this, and from recent visits home, that still appears to be the case.

After hearing about Nok's experience, I was glad my father had been so strict, he knew this was commonplace in Thailand and was simply protecting us.

TEN

After our marriage, we were busy managing our shops in Glasgow and Edinburgh. Luckily, it was only forty minutes' drive between them if we avoided the rush hour.

Searching for a house took up a lot of our spare time, but I was worried about Bob's parents. 'Bob, I can't do this. It's not right, we're looking for a house in the most expensive area of Glasgow, and your parents are living in a third floor flat with no lift.'

'What do you want me to do? We've got to live our own lives.' He replied.

'I know you can afford to buy a house for your parents. In my culture, parents come first, without your parents, you wouldn't be here today.'

'That's not true, I left school at sixteen, I built up my business by myself, to where I'm now. My parents didn't have any money, I rented a basement until I saved up enough open a shop.'

'Your parents brought you up and looked after you throughout your childhood. You should be grateful for that. I want you to buy a house for them first, then look for our house afterwards.'

In May 1991, he finally agreed with me, and bought his parents a three-bedroom bungalow in Paisley. He bought it for them with cash.

A month later he bought our five-bedroom house in Whitecraigs, the most expensive area in Glasgow. His business was doing so well, he also bought this with cash.

Our home was a traditional detached villa with a formal lounge, modern family room, a traditional dining room, a stylish modern kitchen, and a conservatory with sun terrace. There was an integrated double garage with a remote-control door, private monobloc driveway, private gardens back and front. Upstairs, there was five bedrooms, one en-suite, and a family bathroom. I was thrilled! There was even a toilet in the garage!

Three days after moving into our new home, we flew to Florida on a business trip. I had heard so much about Disneyland. I was so looking forward to our visit, I hoped I was not too old for all the rides and attractions.

On arrival, I enjoyed meeting Micky and Minnie Mouse for the first time!

We visited Universal Studios, Sea World, then flew to New Orleans for five days, before heading back to Glasgow.

It was like a dream come true, that every woman would wish for, a loving husband, beautiful home, expensive car.

We were healthy, and well off. But sometimes, I wished we could have more time alone together. Most of our time was spent with other business people.

After we got back from the trip, I found out I was two months pregnant. It was an unplanned pregnancy, because I could not take contraceptive pills, they made me ill.

I thought about what had happened last time. 'Bob, I'm pregnant again. I'm not having another abortion, if you don't want a child, I will go back to Thailand.'

He was silent a few seconds. 'Okay, I'll make an appointment for us at the doctor just to make sure you're pregnant.' He did not look either happy, or unhappy.

I was still taking driving lessons, and hopefully I would pass my test before the baby arrived. I worked hard, and after thirty lessons, passed on my first attempt. Bob bought me a dark red BMW 540, automatic.

I thought it was the time to tell my parents that I was married and two months pregnant. I was nervous, but keen to go home. I missed Thai food, especially Mum's cooking. There were lots of dishes that I wanted mum to cook for me.

Scottish food was not appetising for me. I prefer stir fried, crisp vegetables. The Scottish custom was to boil them until they were soft. I could not enjoy food cooked like that, I found it overcooked.

I was worried and nervous, because I was not sure what would happen when I told mum and dad that I was married to Bob.

Robert, my father in law rang me one afternoon.

'Did you get the letter that I gave to Bob to give to you?' He asked.

'What letter?'

'The letter from Thailand, it was delivered to the shop.'

'When did you give it to him?'

'A couple of days ago.'

'No, he never gave it to me.'

'I knew he would forget, that's why I rang you.'

'I'll ask when he's back home, thanks for letting me know.'

After I got off the phone, I was excited because I thought the letter must be from one of my family. I often got letters from Prang because it was so expensive to phone.

I was too excited to wait for Bob to come home. I thought he might have put it away somewhere and then forgot to give it to me. I looked through his drawers and found it.

I saw that it was not my sister's handwriting. Strangely, it was not addressed to me, but to Bob. The envelope had been opened, so I decided to read it. The letter was in Thai.

Dear Bob,

I have not heard from you for ages, I just wondered how you are. My brother starts school in two months. You promised me you would send me money so he could go to school, and I do not have to go to work.

I am looking forward to hear back from you.

Lots of love as always,

Nee

I was really upset, I had been in Scotland for just over a year and was newly married. Already, I had caught him cheating on me.

I wondered when he met her, was it before me or after me? Or was he seeing us both at the same time?

'Who is Nee?' I asked him as soon as he came in the door.

'I don't know what you're talking about.' I knew he was lying.

'The letter from Thailand.'

'Are you looking through my stuff? You shouldn't look through my stuff.' He was angry, trying to divert the conversation, because he had been caught.

'I didn't plan to look through your stuff. Your Dad called me, asking if you had remembered to give me the letter from Thailand.'

'He shouldn't have rung you, it's not his business.'

'Well, he didn't do it for badness, he thought it was for me. Don't give him a hard time about it. Anything you would like to tell me about this person'

'I met her in Bangkok.'

'Before me or after?'

'Before.'

'Where did you meet her? I know you said in Bangkok, but where in Bangkok?'

'In a massage place, not far from where you worked.'

My heart missed a beat. 'Let me get this right, you stayed in my hotel because it was close to her work, and at the same time you chatted with me every day?'

'No. I met her on a previous trip to Thailand before I met you.'

'Tell me about her work, I would like to know.'

'I already told you, she worked in a massage place.'

'Well you need to give me more details about the place, and what made you go there in the first place?'

'I stayed in your hotel, but I never saw you on my first visit. I went for a walk after dinner and a hotel taxi guy asked me if I wanted to go to a massage place. I was curious to see what it looked like, so I went.'

I was not that gullible. 'And what did it look like?'

'There was a glass showroom filled with girls with numbers on their chest. Then they asked me what number I liked.'

'So, you picked her?'

'Yes.'

'How much did you pay for her?'

'It was three hundred baht for an hour in the room upstairs, and five hundred to take her out. I didn't pay her, I paid her boss.'

'Did you go upstairs or take her out?'

'I took her back to the hotel.'

'When I worked in a five-star hotel, I never saw a policy where prostitutes were allowed in. I know that in cheap hotels they don't care.'

'I avoided reception, the security guy, at the lift, let her in.'

I didn't know wither to believe him or not. 'How old was she?'

'She was fourteen.'

I was disgusted. 'You make me sick, how could you sleep with a girl fourteen years old.' I couldn't believe what I was hearing.

'I didn't sleep with her. I took her back to the hotel so I could find out more about her, and why she worked in that place at such a young age.'

'Yeah, whatever. And what was her story?'

'She said, her family was really poor. Her parents didn't have money to send her and her brother to school. One day, a rich woman came to the village and gave money to her mum, twenty thousand baht, and she said she would take her to Bangkok to work and pay off the debt.'

'I know that people who have no education can't speak or read and write English. Are you telling me this conversation was in English?

'No. I paid the hotel taxi driver to translate.'

'How old was she when she was sold?'

'She was twelve. When I met her, I paid off her debt, then I went to meet her parents in the village in Chiang Rai.'

'Why did you go to her parents' house? Were you getting serious with her?' I related this to my own experience, my parents were worried people would think I was a prostitute, but she was taking Bob to meet her parents. I assumed this could only be because they knew she was a prostitute and would be happy she had met a rich Westerner and could possibly marry him.

'No, I wasn't thinking about marriage. I was curious. I have only stayed in five-star hotels and been to tourist places. I wanted to see the other side of Thailand.'

'You wanted to know about prostitutes?'

'No, just the other side of life.'

I did not want to believe he was lying. 'So, if you hadn't met me, you would've married her instead.'

'No, I'm a businessman. I couldn't marry her; she's nothing like you. Her family was really poor; her house was very basic. The toilet was outside, just a hole in the ground.'

'Were you sending her money?'

'Yes, if I hadn't, she would have had no choice but to go back to work as a prostitute.'

'There's plenty work.' I noticed he made no reference to her age.

'She had no education.'

'Well, you're married now. I don't think it's right that you still keep sending money to another woman. I've written a letter to her, told her who I am, and asked her to stop writing to you.'

'You shouldn't have told her that. She'll be upset, she'll have gone back to work in the massage parlour again.' Bob said angrily. 'I think she will be broken hearted, I'm sure she loved me.'

I looked at him in disbelief, he was talking about a fourteen-year-old.

'Well, it's her choice, you've paid off her debt, I can't see how she could fall in love with you in these circumstances!?'

'Her mum will sell her again. You're so cruel sometimes, not everybody has had a chance like you.'

'Don't you talk to me like that! My Mum and Dad worked hard to send their children to school. I worked hard in school, and university!'

'Okay, I'm sorry.'

'Is there anything else I should know?'

'What do you mean?'

'Did you use a condom?'

'I told you, I didn't have sex with her.' He looked nervous. I should have realised he was a liar.

'I'm expecting. I don't want to take any risks with sexually transmitted diseases. I'll go for tests.' I could hardly believe what I had just been told.

I remembered when the girl in the Thai restaurant said she had translated letters from me. I wrote to Bob in English, I thought it was really odd at the time, but I was in love, love is blind.

I realised they were not my letters, they were from this young girl who he met in the massage parlour.

I was so confused. I did not really know what to think. I did feel sorry for that young girl if she had been sold at twelve, especially when it was her parents who sold her.

She had been forced into prostitution, from a sense of duty to pay off the money loaned to her family. It was, very likely, a case of, take the money or her family would starve. This type of exploitation of poor people is quite common in Thailand.

People were so poor; this amount of money can make a huge difference to their lives. It can be the difference between life and death.
Sometimes, the money is used for hospital bills, sometimes, it is just for food. There is no state provision, if you have no money, you can starve, or die from common ailments which are treated as a matter of course by the NHS, in the UK.

I was still in elementary school when I was twelve. I did not have a clue about sex. I could not imagine what that girl had been through and was still going through.

At the time, I thought it was very kind of Bob to pay off her debt. In my naivety, I did think that he could not save everyone, and it was not right to keep sending money to another woman behind my back. But, I did not think it was any worse than that.

I did start to wonder if there was anything else, I did not know. I just wanted to go back to Thailand and get away from him. But, I just could not imagine what my Dad would be like if I went back home single and pregnant.

I knew my father might throw me out because it would be so shameful for him. It was possible he would kill me, or seriously assault me. I felt frightened and trapped.

My parents would normally receive a dowry of 100,000 – 300,000 baht for me because I was a middle class, university-educated, young woman. The dowry price falls drastically if you have been previously married, already have children, or are not a virgin. Nobody wants to marry you.

After much thought, I decided to forget about what Bob had done, and concentrate on being a mother. It was my first child in another country. I wanted to concentrate on doing the best for my baby, learn English and a new culture.

None of my family were here in the UK to support me. It was too much for me to think about it. I decided to go back home to tell my parents that I was married, and two months pregnant.

I called my sister and asked her to write to mum explain about Bob, so they knew what to expect on our arrival.

ELEVEN

We went back to Thailand in mid-August 1990. Mum and Dad wanted us to get married again in Thailand, even though, we had been married in Scotland four months previously. They were worried there might be gossip about me if we did not get married locally in Thailand, because Bob was white, I think they thought that people would not believe we were really married. I wanted to do this too, so I could pay my respects to my parents and family.

We had a wedding ceremony on the 1st September 1990 at home. Mum organised everything.

I wore a pink and gold traditional Thai costume. I paid for someone to do my make-up. I rarely wear make-up and was not sure about doing it myself. Bob wore a black suit, despite the heat.

Some of the normal marriage ceremony stages were missed, such as, the proposal, because Bob's parents were not in Thailand. They would normally ask my parents if their son could marry me. My parents would then negotiate the *sin sod,* dowry money.

It was common for Thai people to arrange their children's marriages. Even if it was not an arranged marriage, it was very important that the parents of the bride and groom were all consulted.

 In this case Bob parents were not able to travel to Thailand. We all worked in the family business and Bob's father could not be off on holiday at the same time as Bob. I asked my neighbours to act on behalf of Bob's parents.

Most often, before any important event, a Buddhist will pray to call good things into our lives. There are a few ways to make merit, such as the release of a captive animal, or donating money to a temple.

I was not keen on the idea of putting an animal into a cage, just to release it. It seemed pointless to me.

Usually, for a wedding, my parents would invite monks to come and bless the marriage at home. There should always be an odd number of Buddhist monks invited to a Thai wedding ceremony or party, usually three, five, seven, or more commonly, nine. But never more, Mum invited nine.

The monks chanted and offered life lessons. In return, my family served dishes of food. After the ceremony, my parents gave each monk some money in an envelope.

Mum placed the traditional headpiece, *Mong Kol,* on my head, and then on Bob's head. Both *Mong Kol's* were joined together by ceremonial string. This string headpiece, previously blessed by monks, must be made from one piece of cotton. It will join Bob and I together during the rest of the ceremony, and symbolically for the rest of our lives.

Bob and I sat next to each other, the bride sits to the left, with our hands folded in a prayer position. The guest began to line up and tied pieces of white string, *Sai Sin,* around our wrists.

Each guest gently poured holy water, from a conch shell, over our hands to wish us happiness. This is known as *rod num.*

These *Sai Sin* were meant to be kept on our wrists, for at least three days, to allow us to benefit from the good luck they bestow.

After the ceremony, we had a photo shoot in a beautiful park near the power plant. It was an extremely hot afternoon, and Bob was overheating in his suit. We had to take the photographs as quick as we could.

Our neighbour, acting on behalf of Bob's parents, presented the 100,000 baht dowry to my parents at the reception. The dowry is given for the loss of a daughter, and to demonstrate that the future husband is financially capable of taking care of his wife.

The wedding reception was held in our garden, at 18:00, with two hundred guests. Mum hired a live band, rented dining tables, and her friends and neighbours helped to prepare and serve the food. It went really well with all the helping hands from her friends and neighbours, she was very popular.

Bob and I greeted each guest as they arrived. The guests presented us with a gift, normally, money in an envelope. In return, the guests received a small memento of the wedding day.

After the wedding, we spent a few days with my family, then flew to Phuket to meet Mark and Gordon, our friends from Glasgow.

They were in Barley Indonesia on holiday and wanted to meet up with us for a couple days in Phuket before they headed back to Glasgow.

We were all looking forward to visiting and meeting up, none of us had been in Phuket before.

It is a mountainous island, covered by rain forest, in the Andaman Sea of Southern Thailand. There are many popular beaches, situated along the clear waters of the western shore.

Phuket is home to many high-end seaside resorts, spas and restaurants. Phuket City, the capital, has old shop-houses and busy markets. At that time, it was relatively unspoilt by tourism. Unfortunately, nowadays, it is very commercialised. I went back in 2019 and was shocked and disappointed by the commercialism.

We stayed in a resort on Karon Beach, on the west coast of Phuket. This beach is generally quieter than the neighbouring beaches. It is popular with families and couples.

One night, the four of us walked along the beach after dinner. There were a few *Tuk-Tuk,* three wheeled taxis, driving by. The drivers kept shouting 'Patong Beach'.

'What's Patong Beach?' Mark asked me.

'I've not got a clue; I've never been here before.' I replied.

'Why don't we just get on the taxi and find out?' Bob suggested.

'Don't just jump on, they'll charge you a fortune, when you're all foreigners. You have to barter the price first.' I said.

'We don't speak Thai, you do.'

'I'm not good at bargaining; I'm too soft. I can only ask; can you give us a lower price?'

'Ok, I'll do the bargaining, you just translate to Thai.' Bob said.

'How much?' I asked a taxi driver.

'Four hundred baht.' He replied.

'How far from here to Patong Beach?'

'Fifteen, twenty minutes' drive.'

'Can you give us a lower price if it's only a fifteen- or twenty-minutes' drive?'. I said.

'How much does he want? Bob asked me.

"Four hundred baht.' I replied.

'Two hundred.' Bob said to the taxi guy.

'Three hundred.'

'Two hundred, that's it, if not, we're going to take another taxi.' Bob said. We started walking away.

'Okay, two hundred baht.' The taxi guy shouted to us.

We all jumped in the taxi. Bob was good at bargaining. I did not think, I could have managed to get that price.

The taxi dropped us off in Patong Beach. Bob gave the driver three hundred baht.

'Thank you very much.' He looked confused.

'Why did you waste your time bargaining in the first place if you were going to give him that, anyway?' I asked.

'I don't like to be ripped off, just because I'm a tourist.'

After paying the taxi driver, we started walking along Bangla Road. I could not believe my eyes. The whole street was full of pole dancing bars, and pubs with women dancing on the bar. It was a very noisy place, with live music blasting out from the various pubs. I hated it so much, it was too noisy, crowded and touristy.

I felt awkward, walking with three white guys. I felt ashamed to be Thai because this street was full of Thai prostitutes. They shouted at every man that passed to go into their bars. Some of them even grabbed Bob, Mark and Gordon to go into their bar.

'Which one is your guest?' A girl at the bar asked me. I was speechless.

'I'm sorry; I can't handle it any longer. I'm leaving now.' I said to Bob.

'How will you get back to the hotel?'

'By taxi.'

'It's not safe to get in a taxi by yourself at night.'

'I know, but I'm not staying here any longer, it's embarrassing!'

'Okay, I'll come with you.'

'You don't have to, you can stay with your friends or you can just come in the taxi with me, and then come back after you drop me off.'

'No, I'll just tell Mark and Gordon that we're leaving.'

This street reminded me of Pattaya. It was exactly the same, noisy and overcrowded, full of go-go bars, and prostitutes. I visited Pattaya once with my friend, I never went back.

Next morning, I was having breakfast with Bob in our hotel restaurant. Gordon, Mark and a Thai girl walked over to our table. I assumed one of them had picked up the girl from a bar last night.

'Can we join you?' Mark asked.

'I'm sorry, Mark. You need to sit somewhere else. Bob and I are hiring a jeep to drive around the island after breakfast. You and Gordon can join us if you want to.' I was embarrassed, I knew Mark's girlfriend, Julie, well.

Mark gave me a heavy look, but, in the end he and Gordon joined us.

'You put me in awkward position.' I said to Mark. 'I know Julie well. How am I supposed to look at her when we get back?'

'Please, don't tell her, just pretend you know nothing.'

'Shame on you.' I felt I could not face Julie when I got back to Glasgow

We drove around the island and discovered that there were more than thirty beaches in Phuket. A few were crowded, many were quiet, some were hidden, and some were still secret. There were so many beautiful beaches where you could walk alone for miles, even during high season.

We stopped at Patong beach. I was sure that there were more things to see than whatever I saw last night. It was large, probably the largest and the busiest beach in Phuket. There were lots of activities with vendors offering rental deck chairs, umbrellas and a variety of water sports. The beach was lined with cafes, restaurants, bars and massage parlours.

TWELVE

After we saw Mark and Gordon off at Phuket airport, Bob and I stayed on for a couple of days.

Bob loved water sports, and he wanted to explore Phuket more. He booked tour groups for snorkelling, scuba diving and jet skiing over the next two days. I told him I did not want to go because I got seasick.

That was the true, but deep down, I did not want to go with him because I felt people looked at me as if I was a prostitute because I was with a white guy. I tried to explain this to Bob.

'You shouldn't care what other people think, I'm your husband, you should only care how I feel.' Bob complained.

It was true, I should not have cared about what other people thought, but it was difficult.

'Shall we try parasailing?' Bob asked, when we were at the beach.

'Well, I've never done that before, I'm not sure.'

'I've not tried it either, that's why I want to give it a go.'

'If you look at it, you are relying on the operator and his equipment. Your safety is entirely in their hands. We don't know how often they check their equipment.' I was apprehensive.

'Would you like to give it a go, one thousand, three hundred baht.' The operator asked.

'Is it safe?' Bob asked.

'Of course, we do it every day, and have never had any accidents.'

'How often do you check your equipment?'

'Every morning before we set off.'

'Okay, I believe you. How long for each flight?'

'Ten – fifteen minutes.'

'Okay, I'll go for seven hundred baht.'

'Eight hundred, please, we can't really go any lower than this.' The operator resisted Bob's offer.

'No, seven hundred.'

'Just give them eight hundred, there are four or five people in the team.' I agreed with the operator because I knew it was hard for them to make a living.

'You're meant to be on my side.' Bob was not happy.

'They have to make a living; I know you can afford it. What are you trying to do, improve your bargaining skills?'

Eventually, Bob agreed with me.

'Are the weather conditions ok today?' I asked the operator.

'It's not suitable if it's cloudy or windy. Today is perfect, sunny and calm.'

Bob went for it, I was too apprehensive! I took some pictures when he was flying above me. It did look great, so, I gave it a go after he landed safe and sound. Unfortunately, I got air sick, it ruined the rest of my day, but I was proud I had enough courage to try it.

After Phuket, we flew back to Bangkok and spent a few days with Prang. I did lots of clothes shopping because I found fashion in Scotland so boring. Unfortunately, later on, I was unable to wear them because the fabric was not warm enough for the low temperatures in Scotland.

I could not stop eating Thai food, I went out constantly with Prang for street food or to restaurants. I missed my food, I knew I would not get to come back next year, it would be difficult to travel with a baby, so I made the most of it.

'How is life over there with Bob?' Prang asked me during one of our meals.

'It was great until I came back to Thailand.'

'I don't understand. What do you mean?'

'Bob is white; I could tell people thought I was a prostitute when I was with him. That upset me, and sometimes I was in tears with nasty comments, especially in expensive hotels. They were presuming that I was a local and there was no way I could afford to stay in their hotel. They were talking to me like I was dirt.'

'What makes you think that?'

'Yesterday, I was thinking to have lunch at the restaurant in Hilton Sukhumvit where we were staying. Bob was at the swimming pool and I asked the waitress if she had a table for me. She looked at me from head to toe and said that she had a table, but only had an English menu for me.'

'What did you reply?'

'I said, I'm well educated and have no problems reading English.'

'I didn't realise that you were in this situation, it must be awful.' Prang looked upset.

'I suppose you don't know because you have never walked around with a white guy, especially in a tourist town. I didn't realise this either, until I came here with Bob.'

'Next time when you come back with your baby, it will be a completely different reaction, people will have positive, happy view of you.'

'Bob and I are meeting John, our friend from England, tonight for dinner. That means I will be hanging out with two white guys. It will be even worse!'

'You can tell me all about it tomorrow when I see you off at the airport.'

I did some shopping and went back to the hotel. We all sat down for dinner, John loved speaking Thai, and I loved speaking English.

'Can I have a glass of still water?' John ordered his drink in Thai. The waitress brought him a coconut juice. I killed myself laughing.

'I asked for *Nam Plow,* still water, not *Nam Ma Prow,* coconut juice.' He said to the girl, he was not willing to give up.

'It's okay, I will have it, can you bring still water for my friend, please.' I said to the girl.

'No Nuch, you don't have to have it. Tell her to take it back.'

'It's okay, John. If she takes it back, that coconut juice will come off her wages.'

John ordered his dinner in Thai. I spoke Thai to the girl making sure she understood what he ordered.

'You don't have to repeat my order.' John was a little disappointed.

'I just want to make sure she had the right order.'

'Shall we go to Soi Cowboy after dinner?' John said to Bob and me.

'I've heard about that nightclub. I don't think that I will feel comfortable in there, especially with white guys. Why don't you two go, I'll just go up to my room.'

John and Bob left and I walked up to my bedroom. I was not sure if I wanted Bob to visit night clubs, but at the same time, I wanted him to have a nice time with his friend on his holiday. I hoped I could trust him.

'How was your night?' I asked him when he came back to the room at two in the morning.

'It was okay.'

'So, it was good then. Where did you go?'

'We had a few drinks in the bar.'

'What kind of bar?'

'It was a Go-Go bar.'

'So, you two had a few girls around you, did you buy them drinks?'

'Yes, John was chatting with them in Thai.'

'Where is he now?'

'Back in his hotel room with a girl from the bar. He told her that he didn't want her and he didn't have money. She said it was okay and went with him anyway.'

'What about you?'

'Her friend jumped in a taxi with us. I told her, I didn't want her, that I have my wife in my room.'

'Nice to know that you've got a wife in your room.'

'She didn't want to get out of the taxi. She told me she needed money to buy milk for her baby.'

'And?'

'I gave her two thousand baht for the milk and asked her nicely to get out of my taxi.'

'Okay, I think you've seen enough of this side of Thailand, there are plenty of other places you haven't seen.'

I went back to bed and wondered what would have happened if I was not here.

I did not like Bangkok; it was such a touristy area. I thought, if we were in Thailand next year, I would spend our time visiting less popular places. In some ways, I was glad to be going back to Scotland tomorrow night.

THIRTEEN

I was still at college and also working in Bob's office until I was seven months pregnant. I started feeling perpetually stuffed, and slightly out of breath. I thought it was the time to stop running around and doing too much.

I felt the baby kicking, punching, stretching and rolling in my tummy. The feelings were becoming more distinct and stronger.

The first time I experienced the baby's movements was when I was four or five months pregnant. I felt as if there were small bubbles inside my tummy.

I started a childbirth education class every Tuesday, at seven pm. Bob was meant to come along, but rarely made it, he was too busy with work. I was keen for him to go because people think it can help you and your partner focus on your pregnancy and prepare for labour and the birth.

The class helped me to build up confidence in my ability to give birth, through the presentations in the class. It helped me to understand how to cope with pain, by promoting comfort, relaxation techniques, movement and massage.

I also read lots of baby books and tried to improve my English as much as I could. I thought I better be well prepared because I did not have any of my family here to support me.

Bob's shops opened every day in October – January, this was the high season for us. He worked seven days a week. Sometimes, I felt I was on my own, I never saw him.

We decorated the baby's room with gender-neutral colours, such as yellow, green and white. I thought, orange was a fitting choice for boys and girls alike. Red was too strong a colour for babies. I knew that we could find out the baby's gender, but we wanted it to be a surprise until the birth.

We were quite well off financially. We had decorators come to our house with nursery room brochures. In fact, for every room in the house, we just picked what we wanted from the brochures, and the decorators followed suit.

I bought a baby's name book to help us make that important decision. I could not help but notice that there were lots of people with the same name in their families.

"Why do a lot of people here have the same name in their families, like the father is called Robert and the son is also called Robert? I asked Bob.

'Because, in the past, people liked to give their child the same name. Usually, a first son is called after his father.'

'How weird, if the mother is talking about Robert, how are people supposed to know which Robert she is talking about, husband or son?'

'Well, most people would say, young Robert, for the son, and old Robert for the dad.'

'How does it work with criminal records checks, with people having the same name?'

'Obviously, by date of birth, and most people have a middle name, after a granny or a grandad.'

'So, if we have a son, his middle name will be your dad's name and if we have a daughter, her middle name will be your mum's name?'

'He or she doesn't have to have a middle name, but it will hurt my mum and dad's feelings if they don't.'

'I don't want to hurt their feelings. We should give our child a middle name, if that's the case.'

'I don't like my Mum's name. It's too old fashioned.'

'We should concentrate on the first name.'

I looked through the name book. I found it tricky for me to understand, because, at first, I was not sure the pronunciation. I wanted a name that my Thai relatives could pronounce easily, and I wanted something meaningful.

In Thailand, people usually give their baby a name which is unique to their child. Every person has a first name, and a nickname, in addition to a formal, given name.

Nickname in Thailand has a different meaning from the UK, it is not a nickname, it's just a short name.

I made a note of five girls' names and five boys' names that I really liked the sound of. Of course, they were not too long, and not too hard for me and my family in Thailand to pronounce.

During my pregnancy, I started to get quite worried when Bob was away from home on business so often. He was away at least one or two nights a week. This continued, it came to a head when I was eight months pregnant.

In 1991, he had only two shops, one in Glasgow and one in Edinburgh. He was due to be opening another one in Manchester soon.

'Why do you want to open another shop? You already make lots of money.' I asked Bob.

'I just want to expand my business in England.' He replied.

'Remember, you can't drive up and down between Glasgow and Manchester on the same day.'

'We can afford to stay overnight in a hotel.'

'We? Have you forgot, I am expecting.'

'If you can't go, I will only stay one night.'

'You know, it's not going to be only one night. I still don't understand why you need to open another shop. You've made plenty of money in your Glasgow shop. You are the second biggest customer in your branch of Bank of Scotland. You've got a house, without a mortgage, in the most expensive area in Glasgow.'

'It is not about money. It's about achievement. I want to be a success in the UK, not just Scotland. I left school when I was 16, I worked in a Hi-Fi shop. I thought, one day, I will own my own shop. I rented a basement when I first started my business. I started from nothing building up to where I am now, and I will keep going.'

I nodded. I was disappointed that he would not listen to me. He went ahead and opened another shop in Manchester.

I suggested to him that his business was too big now for him to run on his own. He had three shops, and one of them was one hundred and eighty-three miles, three and a half hours drive from Glasgow. He was never at home after that.

I put my foot down and explained to him that I thought he stop the overnight stays because I only had a month to go and could give birth at any time.

Bob agreed, I was so happy because I was getting really worried on my own, at such a late stage in my pregnancy.

Then, one night, after this discussion, Bob's parents knocked on my front door.

'Hi Nuch, we are here to stay overnight with you because Bob called us, he won't be back to Glasgow tonight.' Liz told me.

'He agreed not to stay away overnight after I was eight months' pregnant, anything could happen.'

'I know, that's why we are here.' Liz said, she looked sympathetic, but it was awkward for them.

I was still worried even though Liz and Robert were there, neither could drive. I knew I could call an ambulance, but that was not enough reassurance, I needed my husband with me.

I felt unsupported, and I wished he would just not expand his business any further, but he just kept opening more shops, spending less and less time at home.

On the 5th March 1992, at three in the morning, my waters broke. I could feel fluid coming out in a burst, contractions were becoming more frequent with strong pains in my tummy.

Fortunately, Bob was at home and called the hospital, the midwife asked him to take me in right away. He drove me to hospital in Paisley. Luckily, there was not much traffic about. He drove through a red light because he was panicking so much!

The midwife examined me, 'How many weeks pregnant are you?'

'I'm not sure, but the baby is due next week.'

'Have you had any problems during pregnancy?'

'Not that I can think of.'

'When did the contractions start and how frequent are they?'

'They just started since the waters broke at home, just about an hour ago, at most.'

She checked the baby's heart rate and measured my contractions. 'I think we'll just take you to the labour ward, everything is fine with the baby.'

'Thank goodness!'

I changed to a hospital gown before she took me to the delivery room. An obstetrician came in to check if I was ten centimetres dilated yet.

The mid-wife said to the obstetrician. 'She's only six centimetres dilated.'

'Okay, we'll give it a little longer.' He replied.

It seemed to go for ever, but I did not reach ten centimetres dilation. They asked me to push, I listen to my doctor's guidance. He told me when to push hard and when not to push so hard.

I kept pushing as hard as I could whenever he told me. I was in labour progression for twelve hours, from three in the morning till three in the afternoon. I was so weak I could not keep my eyes open.

I could hear the doctor talking to Bob. 'It's taking too long now. She has a small frame and the baby is too big. I don't think, she will reach ten centimetres. Her cervix has stopped dilating, it's still six centimetres. The baby's heart rate is going down and your wife is too weak to push.'

I could hear Bob crying. He was probably thinking about what I told him, if he had one life to save, then save the baby. I thought it was better to save the child, I was terrified.

'What are you going to do now?' Bob's tone was shaky.

'I will give her an emergency C-section.' The doctor replied.

The doctor gave us two options. One, a general anaesthetic, where I was completely unconscious. I would see the baby when I woke up.

Two, an epidural, this would numb my body from the waist down. I could stay awake all the way through the procedure. A curtain would prevent me from seeing the surgery itself.

'You won't feel any pain.' The doctor said.

I thought about it. 'I will have the epidural; I want to see my baby when he or she first comes out.

During the C-section, I could feel some pressure, pushing and tugging as the doctor made the incision and guided the baby out.

I could hear the baby crying for the first time. It was amazing.

'It's a girl.' Bob said to me.

'Is she perfect?' I asked, it was the first thing I wanted to know.

'Yes, she is absolutely perfect.'

After the doctor cut the baby's cord, Bob had her for a few second in his arms next to me. I looked at her, she was absolutely perfect, all I wished for. I still keep her cord, twenty-eight years later.

The mid-wife took her into a warmer room, to be assessed and stabilised.

The doctor started to stitch up my tummy. I remember, Bob told me later on, that there were a few layers to be stitched up, not just the outer skin on my tummy.

Now that I knew the baby was fine, I was relieved and fell asleep. I woke up in an intensive care unit (ICU) with ICU bedside monitors. Bob was next to my bed with a nurse.

'Is the baby okay?' I asked Bob.

'Yes, she is fine. She needs to be kept separate from you, she is not allowed in this room.'

'Where am I?'

'You're in intensive care.'

'Am I dying?'

'No, you'll be fine. You just need special care till you get better.'

'When will I see the baby?'

'When you're out of intensive care.'

I tried to get up, but it was too painful. I called the nurse over. 'I'm in so much pain around my incision. I can't get up.'

'Don't worry, rest today, I'll help you get up tomorrow.' The nurse replied.

'I'm supposed to be breast feeding.'

'Don't worry, we'll just give her a bottle just now.'

My parents in law came to visit me the next day. I was only allowed two people per visit. Bob waited outside the room while his parents visited.

'How are you? Liz asked.

'I still can't get up, I'm in pain when I try to get up.'

'It takes a few days because you were so weak before the C-section.' Liz held my hand, I could see tears in her eyes.

'Have you seen the baby?' I asked.

'Yes, I saw her yesterday when you were asleep, but we weren't allowed to see you. She is absolutely beautiful and perfect. She's a big baby.'

'What weight was she? Bob never told me.'

'She was a ten-pound baby. Considering you are only five foot three and very slim, it's no wonder you were struggling to push her out.'

'My goodness! Has Bob given her a name yet?'

'Not yet, she has a name tag 'baby Smith' on her wrist.'

I still have her name tag today. After three nights in the intensive care unit, I was moved into a private recovery room. Bob and I agreed we would call the baby Nicola.

I was so looking forward to see my baby and holding her in my arms.

Shortly afterwards, I saw a nurse approaching with Nicola wrapped in her shawl. The nurse smiled and handed her to me. I was overwhelmed to have her in my arms at last.

She had lovely chubby cheeks, fluffy jet-black hair. Her eyes were green- blue, she had tiny little hands and feet. I remember all the details of those first moments, with Nicola, as clearly as yesterday.

I felt some soreness around the incision. The nurse gave me pain killers and checked my wound. 'Don't lift anything heavier than your baby and take showers regularly until you heal up and there's no more bleeding.'

'It's not just about the wound, I am also sore in my tummy, and feel so uncomfortable.'

The nurse pressed my tummy, 'Your tummy is hard, can you pee?'

'No, I can't.'

'Ok, we will have to sort you out with a catheter just now, until it all returns to normal.'

Shortly after that I had a catheter inserted, linked up to a bag.

'I also can't poop.'

'The C-section can make your muscles sluggish; everything is shut down temporarily. You will be ok after a week when your bowel starts moving normally again.'

'How can I relieve the constipation?'

'If you are able to move around, just do that several times a day. Drink a glass of warm water with lemon juice every morning, and plenty of fresh water throughout the day. Eat prunes, they help alleviate constipation. Eat iron rich foods.'

'Okay, thank you.'

The mid-wife came visited and helped me with breast feeding. Nicola had become used to being fed with bottles while I was in intensive care.

'She doesn't want my breast.' I was worried.

'Don't worry, we'll keep trying. We'll give her your breast, before the bottle, every time we feed her.'

'How long will it take for her to accept my breast?'

'It won't take her long to get used to her mother's body again.'

Eventually, after six attempts, she started sucking my nipples. I did not feel any pain in my breast or nipples, although, she sucked strongly with her first few attempts.

I looked at her carefully, I could tell when she was swallowing. She sucked a few times, then swallowed, then I could hear a soft sound of swallowing and I noticed a pause in her breathing.

I looked at her blue-green eyes, similar to Bob's. 'The eye colour may change during the first year.' The nurse said.

She had sprinklings of black hair, which she definitely took from me. Her skin was pale, she looked like her grandad.

The nurse also showed me how to change a baby's nappy 'Changing a nappy is an important skill.'

'I hope I can manage.'

'Don't worry, you'll get the hang of it after the first few days.'

'How often do I change her?'

'Very frequently, especially when she poops. You'll be surprised how many nappies they go through in a day. Never leave your baby alone on the changing table. In case they fall off. Always wash your hands before or after changing your baby's nappies.'

My sisters' babies in Thailand were nappy-free, I had never seen nappies in Thailand, babies just wore baby clothes. Mothers washed frequently, but clothes dried quickly. I could see why this would not work in the Scottish climate.

No sun to dry the washing. The temperature is too cold for the babies to be wet, even for a few seconds. In Thailand, our wooden furniture and floors are easily to clean. The Scottish norm of carpets and soft furniture is easy to soil.

I was meant to stay in a private recovery room for seven days, but on the fifth day, the nurse asked me. 'Nuch, do you mind if I move you to another ward, you will have to share the room with other mums and babies?'

'Do you need my room for someone else?'

'Yes, a woman just gave birth, sadly, she lost her baby. We don't want her to share a room with other mums and babies.'

'That's very sad. Of course, I don't mind moving.'

I moved to the shared a room, it was ok during the day, we kept each other company when there were no visitors. But, I could not sleep during the night, it was always noisy, the babies never stopped crying. They took turns, one was asleep, one was awake!

I was in hospital for ten days. It felt like ten months, I could not wait to go home.

FIFTEEN

It was strange to be back home with a baby. I missed my mum, I wished she was here.

Liz visited me the next day. 'I will stay with you for a couple of days.'

'I'll be fine, we'll manage.'

'You've had a C-section, there are a few things that you're not allowed to do. I could stay until Bob comes back.'

'If you wait till Bob is back in, there'll be no trains for you to catch back home. He's always late back.'

'Don't worry, I'll get a taxi.'

'You can catch the train at 17:00, honestly, I'll be fine. Thank you for coming.'

It was very nice of Liz. I did not want her to travel back and forwards, it was an hour's journey on public transport. It was too much for a sixty-year-old woman. I knew, she did not mind, she loved to spend time with her first grand daughter.

My family doctor visited me, at home, to take out my stitches, and check the wound. It did not hurt, but it felt uncomfortable.

I cleaned and dried my wound, carefully, every day. I felt it was more comfortable wearing cotton, high-waist pants, and other loose clothing.

It was really uncomfortable to cough, laugh, or do anything that required my abdominal muscles.

After Liz left, I was thinking of bathing Nicola for the first time. The nurse had showed me how to bathe a baby before I left hospital. I remember she said the water should be warm, not hot. She talked me through and it helped me the first time.

'Check the temperature with your elbow, mix it well, so there are no hot patches. Hold her on your knee and clean her face with a warm, wet cloth. Wash her hair with tap water, supporting her over the bowl. After you dry her hair, take off her nappy, wipe off the mess then gently lower the baby into the bowl or bath using one hand to hold her upper arm and support her head and shoulders.'

I went back through the conversation in my mind, but I was not sure that I could handle this all by myself the first time. It seemed so complicated. I decided to wait until Bob was back home and he could give me a hand.

My sisters in Thailand washed their babies by laying the baby down between their upper legs, supporting the baby's head between their knees. They bent the knees up a little bit and just poured water over baby's body, they were soaked too, but n such a hot country, it did not matter.

Nicola slept in a Moses Basket on a stand next to my bed. Every noise she made woke me up. I suppose, it is a mother's instinct.

One Sunday, Bob took me out for lunch with Nicola. 'I want to buy you a present for giving me such a beautiful daughter.'

'That's very thoughtful of you, thank you.'

'I'm thinking of buying you a watch.'

'That would be lovely, I use a watch every day.'

Bob took me to the Rolex shop in Glasgow city centre. 'You can pick any one you like.'

'This's a very expensive shop.'

'I know, but I can afford it.'

I picked a gold Rolex with diamonds around the face. 'I love this one, I hope it's not too expensive.'

'It's £15,999.00.' The shop manager said.

'How about £15,000.00.' Bob offered.

'I'm sorry, it's too much discount to drop £999.00. I could give you it for £15,500.00, that's the best I can do.'

'I'll pay with cash if you take the offer. If not, I'll leave it just now. I own shops, I know how things work. I think that's a good deal for cash. Actually, I bought a £2,500.00 wedding ring from your dad last year.'

The shop manager was silent for a few seconds. 'Okay, you've got a deal.'

I was over the moon. I had never owned a Rolex before. It wasn't just a plain Rolex; it was studded with diamonds. It was a stunning!

Two months after Nicola was born, Bob asked me. 'Would you like your parents to come here to see Nicola?'

'That would be great. Nicola's too young to travel for twelve hours on a plane, to Thailand. It would be great if my parents could come here instead.'

'That's what I was thinking. I really like Tann, she could come too.'

'Yes, she would love to go abroad. She'll be so excited to go abroad at eight years old.'

I was so excited, I called Mum the next day. 'Mum, would you and Dad like to come here to see Nicola'

'Wow, that would be amazing to see Nicola and see where you live. Your Dad will be over the moon.'

'It's not only you and Dad. Bob said, Tann could come too.'

'She would love that, I'll tell her when she gets back from school.'

'You'll need to sort out your passports, let me know when you're organised.'

Two and a half months after Nicola was born, my parents and Tann, my niece, were due to arrive, May 1992. I was so excited, I kept counting the days until they arrived.

The night before they were due to arrive, I spoke to Bob. 'I'm worried, I hope, they manage to get on the plane okay.'

'Don't worry, they'll be fine.'

'I can't help worrying. They've never been abroad before; I hope they manage in the international airport.'

'Is your sister taking them to airport?'

'Yes, my sister and my brother in law are taking them.'

'They'll be fine, your sister and her husband will help them to check in and take them to the departure.'

'I know, but they're on their own after they pass security. Will they manage to find their gate?'

'Tann's a clever girl, your parents also. I'm sure, they'll ask someone for help if they can't find it.'

'What about problems on the plane?'

'It's Thai Airways, they can speak Thai to the staff on the plane.'

'What about the connecting flight from London to Glasgow? They don't speak English, how are they going to answer all the questions at immigration? How will they know where to get their suitcases? How will they know where to check in for their flight to Glasgow?'

'I paid extra for staff in Thai Airways to take care of all these issues.'

'I know, although I'm Thai, in some situations I don't trust Thai people, especially when they've been paid up front. Sometimes, they just take the money and do nothing. It's never a good idea to pay up front in Thailand.'

'Get some sleep, you'll see them tomorrow.' Bob was tired of all my questions and worries.

I only managed to sleep for three hours and woke up just after 04:00.

'Let go to the airport.' I asked Bob, as soon as he got up

'Their flight's arriving at 11:00. It's too early to go now, it's only 9 o'clock.'

'I know, but I'm worried, I just can't sit here and do nothing.'

'It's only thirty minutes' drive from our house to the airport. How about we leave at 10 to give us plenty of time?'

We arrived at Glasgow Airport at 10:30am. I ran to the British Airways help desk.

'Could you please check if the Yawong family were on the flight from Heathrow at 10:00.'

'Just a moment, I'll check that for you. Yes, good news, the three of them are on the plane, they'll be arriving at 11:00.'

'Thank you so much.'

I ran off and told Bob the good news. I could not keep my eyes off the arrival gate.

I saw them as soon as they came through, they looked tired, but had huge smiles as soon as they saw me.

'How was your flight?' I asked Mum and Dad when we finished our hugs.

'We really struggled because we don't know any English words.'

'So, the Thai Airway's staff, they didn't take you through to the connecting flight?

'No, no one took us. We just followed the passengers on the same flight to immigration. Of course, we couldn't answer any questions. They announced for Thai Airway's staff to help, and one of them came to translate for us.'

'What happened next?'

'She looked at the information board and told us it was belt number 23 to collect our suitcases. Then we went through 'Nothing to declare' then followed the sign 'Terminal 3'. When we reached Terminal 3, we looked for British Airways and gave them our tickets.'

'Are you telling me, you did all this by yourselves?'

'Yes! She wrote instructions on a paper for us, 'belt 23', 'Terminal 3', 'British Airway'. We just followed the note.'

'You three did so well, despite the fact you haven't got a clue about English. You can't even say one word.'

I laughed but was really pleased they had all managed so well. 'I'm really sorry for putting you through all of this. It must have been very stressful.'

'Tell them, I paid extra to Thai Airways to take care of them until they checked in to the connecting flight.' Bob was unhappy that no assistance had been given by Thai Airways.

'I told you, I don't trust them when they receive money before the job is done.'

'Ask your Mum if they had special meals on the plane?' Bob said.

'No, Mum said their meals were the same as everybody else.'

'I'll call Thai Airways when I get home. I paid extra for special meals for them, and so they would be served first and didn't have to worry about the menu.'

Bob called Thai Airways straight away and made a complaint. Their customer services said they would investigate and get back to us, but we never heard anything.

'British Airways were really helpful, they knew we didn't speak English, so a staff member took us through everything until we were on board.' Mum told me happily.

Bob called British Airway to say thanks to them and sent them a lovely bunch of flowers.

SIXTEEN

Tann, my niece, ran up and down the stairs checking out all the rooms in my house. 'Wow, your bathroom is so beautiful, and it has a carpet on the floor! Can I sleep in your bathroom tonight?'

She was used to wet bathrooms in Thailand, so the carpet in our bathroom was amazing to her.

Later on, I almost collapsed after because Tann decided to swim in the bath, the carpet in the bathroom was soaking, water was splashed all over the floor.

Not only that, my Dad had a shower without closing the shower cubicle door!

'Dad, you can't take shower without closing the glass shower door.'

'I'm sorry, I didn't know that I have to close the door.'

'Tann, you had to be careful, no splashing water over the bath.'

'I'm sorry Auntie, I thought that's what the bath was for.'

'I know; you're all used to a wet bathroom in Thailand. There's no wet bathroom in Scotland, that's why there's a carpet in the bathroom.'

I tried to calm myself down. I remembered when Sang visited us in our hotel in Bangkok, and had shower, there was water everywhere afterwards.

'Why didn't you keep the shower curtain closed over the bath when you had your shower?'

She replied, 'I've never had a foreign husband, how am I supposed to know!'

My Mum did not like my kitchen. She would have preferred to cook on a charcoal burner on the floor outside!

'I don't know how to use your kitchen.' She complained.

'I'll show you how to use the cooker, it's quite simple.'

'Where's your fridge?'

'It's in the cupboard.'

'In the cupboard? I've never seen a fridge in a cupboard before, in my whole life.'

'Here it is.'

'It's amazing how it's fit in there. I don't see any Thai herbs in your fridge.'

'I'll take you to the Chinese supermarket in town tomorrow, but you might not get everything you need.'

Nicola started to cry.

'I think she's tired, mum. She wants a little sleep.'

'I'll take her for a nap. Where's her swinging bed?

'There's none here, mum.'

'How can you get her to sleep?'

'I rock or nurse her till she gets drowsy, then I put her down in her cot.'

'Well, she won't sleep long without a hammock.'

At home, my big sisters would swing their babies to sleep in swinging hammocks, the movement helped them to fall asleep, and they slept longer.

At night, after their babies fell asleep in the hammocks, they would transfer them to a bed fitted with a waterproof sheet.

My big sisters had ten babies between them. The way they looked after them was completely different from Scottish traditions.

I showed Mum Nicola's nursery room and cot. 'Does she sleep here by herself?

'Yes, that's what this room's for. I know that, in Thailand, the babies sleep in the same bed with their parents but it's not the same here, Mum.'

'I disagree! It should be the same everywhere. How are you supposed to know what happens to her during the night? And what if she needs you?'

'I've got a baby monitor.'

'What's a baby monitor?'

'If she cries or if she makes any movement, I'll hear her through the baby monitor and the light will also flash.'

'It's still not right. She needs your body heat, and she wants to feel your love.'

'Mum, she has slept on her own since she was a month old. I'm not going to move her into my bed now.'

'You're cruel.'

'Mum, it's not about cruelty. The doctors here do not recommend bed-sharing between parents and infants, because it increases the risk of sleep-related deaths, including sudden infant death syndrome.'

Mum went on and on about it for ages, she did not agree with the western way. I did see her point. For starters, not everybody in Thailand has a big house with their own bedroom. It is hot all year round, there are no concerns about room temperature.

But, I did agree with the UK doctors. I did not want to go to sleep and worry that I would roll over on top of her, or pull my blanket over her face, so she could not breathe.

Some of my nieces and my nephew in Thailand are over twenty, but they still share a bedroom with their mum.

Now, I think that's madness. Their house has enough bedrooms for everybody to have their own. They keep sharing because they been brought up that way and will continue to do so.

I remember walking into my big sister's bedroom in Thailand. I saw two king-size beds and one single bed. There was not much room left to walk about in the bedroom because it was so full of furniture and beds.

She explained. 'The children and I sleep together, their Dad's the only one with his own room.' I did not know wither to laugh or cry.

Bob and I drove my parents and my niece to London to show them around. We stopped overnight in different cities on our way.

Bob showed my parents his shops in Leeds, Manchester and Newcastle. It was spring, but they all still had thick jackets, winter hats and gloves on.

Nicola was two and half month's old, so we left her with Bod's parents and a babysitter.

We thought it would be too much for her to travel around with us. I did not want to leave my baby but at the same time I wanted to give my parent the best holiday they ever had. They had worked hard all their life, and they deserved it.

They all loved their holiday with us. One evening Bob's brother came round to meet them all. He gave my Dad a whisky to drink, Dad then promptly asked my Mum to make some *Tom Yum* soup.

Dad had a drink of whisky with each spoonful of soup! It was the custom in Thailand, but Bob and his brother thought it really odd, at first.

EIGHTEEN

The three-week holiday with Mum, Dad, and Tann passed far too quickly. I was incredibly sad when it was time for them to go. I saw them off at Heathrow Airport. 'I'll see you next year when Nicola was a bit older.'

I could see Mum, Dad, and Tann were all really upset to be leaving us.

Before she left Mum asked me to shave Nicola's head because this is the custom with Thai babies. Their parents shave their babies' heads when they are about three months old, because they believe that this will make their hair grow back thicker.

'I think it is time to shave Nicola's head.'

'Mum, Nicola's not a hundred percent Thai. I can't see that Bob and his parents will agree with this Thai culture.'

'It's a good traditional culture. A baby 's birth hair is very fluffy; she's bald on the back of her head. Shaving allows it to grow back thicker and stronger.'

'I believe you, Mum. If you shave any part of your body, hair grows back thicker. I'll leave it just now, though, until I mention it to Bob.'

I did mention it later Bob and his parents. There was no issue with Bob and his dad, but his mum had a few issues.

'What about if her hair never grows back?' Liz looked worried.

'Don't worry, before you know it, her head will be covered with hair again.'

'Bob's bald, so is Nicola's grandad, and I've got thin hair myself.'

'That's why I want to do it, so it grows back thicker, stronger.'

Liz was still strongly disagreeing with me. I thought, Nicola is my baby. This was a decision was for Bob and me. I would not suggest shaving her head unless I had a good reason.

I decided to shave Nicola's head a few days later on Sunday. Bob woke up for his breakfast, he was shocked.

'Oh my gosh! What did you do with our baby?'

'Well, I did mention it to you, you seemed okay with it.'

'Yes, I was okay with it, but you didn't tell me that you were going to do it today.'

'What's the difference?'

'If I knew ahead, I would have been prepared.'

Bob settled down a few days later. We took Nicola to visit her grandparents. I put a lovey pink, girly, hat on Nicola. Liz took it off and burst into tears when she saw Nicola's bald head. She went off to cry in the kitchen.

'Don't worry, before you know it, her head will be covered with hair again.' Grandad said.

I remember, not long after my parents went back to Thailand, Bob came to speak to me. 'I've been offered a weeklong business trip to Malaysia, and a week in Hong Kong.'

'I don't want to leave Nicola to go to the other side of the world. She's only three months old.' I was really sad at the thought, I loved spending my time with her.

'It's only two weeks. She'll be fine with my parents and a babysitter.'

'We've already left her, almost a week, when my parents here, and now we're leaving her again.'

'Yes, and she was fine.'

'But this time is different, you're talking about the other side of the world. What about if something happens to her, we may not be able to get a flight back straight away.'

'Nothing's going to happen to her.'

'You can't be sure that nothing's going to happen. I'll be worried about her. I can't see that I'll enjoy myself, I'll miss her too much.'

'I don't want to go by myself. If you're not going, I'll take someone else.'

'Who are you going to take?'

'I've not decided yet, but that's not your problem.'

I felt that I had no choice other than to go with him. I went, but I could not sleep, I cried every night on the trip.

I called my mother in law everyday asking about Nicola. There was no free call apps or mobile phones, at the time. Sometimes, when she answered the phone, I did not know what to say, I could not speak. I just cried on the phone.

'I'm not going on any business trips with you again. It's not worth me being ill or sick worrying about our baby. It's not fair on Nicola either.' I said to Bob.

I thought he understood this time. He could see that I could not sleep and cried often. I had to pretend to be happy in front of other people. It was only two weeks, but it felt like two months. I could not wait to be back home with Nicola.

I was not a single mum, but I felt like I was a single mum. Bob was always late back home. I felt that I was looking after Nicola on my own.

After I had Nicola, our marriage slowly started going downhill because Bob was always demanding that I came out with him for dinner, three or four nights a week, just as we had done, when we had no children.

I really did not want to go out at all. It was not the way I had been brought up. I wanted to look after my baby myself, not leave her in the house with a babysitter.

I could not understand why Bob did not feel the same.

I refused to go out for dinner more than once a week, this annoyed Bob, he started giving me a hard time.

'I miss going out for dinner. I really enjoyed eating out before we had Nicola.' He complained.

'It's not just about us anymore. We have a baby now.'

'My mum and dad don't mind looking after Nicola. They love having their granddaughter over the weekend. I can afford a babysitter to help out as well.'

'It's not about the fact you can afford a babysitter. I don't want to miss seeing her grow up.'

'You won't miss much.'

'Yes, I won't miss much if we're out once a week. I don't mind going out with you once a week. But you're demanding three or four times a week.'

'I'm a businessman. I've got business dinners or trips more than once a week.'

'You could go without me sometimes.'

'But the invitations are for two, and you're my wife!'

'I'm sure people will understand that we've a three-month old baby. I can't just run around with you all the time.'

'You're spending more time with the baby than me.'

'That's what most normal mothers do. You're talking about our baby.'

'Yes, and I'm your husband. You have to spend half of your time with your husband too.'

'I can't believe you're complaining about my time with our daughter.' I started to walk out of the room.

'Well! I've got plenty money, it's not hard for me to find someone to go with if you won't come.' He shouted after me.

I was so upset. I could not believe what I had just heard. He reminded me of Ken, his business friend. Every time, I met Ken, he was always with his secretary.

When I first met them, I thought they were a couple because they stayed overnight in the same room. We often ate out together. I found out later, Ken was married, his wife and two kids were down in England. He was having an affair with his secretary.

I felt that Bob put me in difficult situation, making me choose between, keeping him happy, and looking after our daughter.

I did not think he was nasty or selfish enough to go off with another woman just because his wife wanted to spend time with her baby daughter. I was wrong, unfortunately.

He was always back home late, he had seven shops altogether, one in Glasgow, one in Edinburgh, two in Manchester, one in Newcastle and one in Leeds. He never got back home before 21:30. We started to argue more.

'I feel, I'm a single mum. You're never at home'.

'Just in case you've forgotten, I've seven shops!'

'Of course, I know you've seven shops. Although, you've ignored my opinion about doing that.'

'I've only tried to secure our daughter's future.'

'She's too young to think about her future, just now she thinks about when she will see her dad.'

'I work hard so you have plenty money to buy whatever you want to buy.'

'I'm not looking for money. I'm looking for a husband and a father to our daughter.'

'I don't want to argue anymore. I'm not coming home tomorrow. I'll be staying in Manchester over the weekend. I've to go and sort something out in the shops.'

'Why are you only telling me now?' It was Friday.

'Because if I told you three days ahead, then we would be arguing for three days until I left. But if I tell you a day before, then I only have one day's argument before I leave.'

I did not know what the right thing was. I kept questioning myself, did he love me? Did he want to spend time with his daughter? I felt his work was more important than his family.

Sometimes, I felt embarrassed looking for him in his shop. I remember ringing him at work one day. 'Hi Rosemary, can you put me through to Bob, please.'

'I'm sorry, Nuch. Bob is not here.'

'Do you know when he'll be back?'

'He won't be back in. Didn't he tell you that he is away to Germany?'

'Oh yes, he told me, I completely forgot.'

'Can I help you with anything?'

'No, thank you. I just couldn't find something in the house that's all.' I did not want her to know that he had not told me.

I was shocked that he had gone to Germany and not told me. I was unhappy that our relationship had deteriorated so much, that now he was going abroad in secret.

How sad and embarrassing it was. I was his wife; I did not even know what country he was in.

He was back in at 23:30. 'I'm sorry, I'm late.'

'It's ok, you are always late anyway, maybe you should keep it and say sorry when you are early.'

'You better stop the sarcastic comments! I'm too tired for an argument.'

'Are you telling me that I have no right to be upset that you went abroad without telling me? Oh, by the way, when were you planning to tell me? Tomorrow? Or next week? Or would I find out when the plane crashed?

'I already said sorry. What do you want me to do?

'Sorry no longer means anything to me because I hear that word too often. You better do something about it if you want to save our marriage.'

He grabbed me, shaking me madly, squeezing my wrists hard. 'Don't you dare tell me what to do, ok!'

I was so upset, I could not stop crying, I slept in the spare room. Both of my wrists were bruised the next day.

That was the start of the domestic violence. At the time, I thought it was a normal thing for a husband to do, because I often saw my dad abuse my mum, my sisters and me. I no longer knew what the future held.

I wanted to go to Thailand for a break. I thought, if Nicola and I are not here, when we come back from Thailand, maybe he will appreciate our time together more.

I needed his agreement to apply for Nicola's passport. I called the Thai Embassy to see if Nicola could have a Thai Passport. Unfortunately, she could not because she was born in Scotland.

'I am taking Nicola to Thailand for a holiday next year.'

'That's good. When are you thinking of going?

'I'm thinking of when she is over one year old, but I need to sort out her passport first.'

'I can put her on my passport.'

'I don't think that's a good idea. because you are travelling all the time. I think it's better she has her own passport.'

'Yes, you're right, I agree with you.'

I was really happy and looking forward to going to Thailand. None of my sisters had met Nicola. It would be good for her to meet her aunties and Thai cousins.

Bob took Nicola and I out for Sunday lunch, he started a conversation. 'I've been thinking.'

'What's about?'

'It will be too much for you to travel to Thailand on your own, with a baby. There's lots of stuff to carry with you on the plane, such as a push chair, a baby changing bag, Nicola's food, her bottles and spare clothes etc.'

'Yes, you're right, I forgot all about that.' I thought it was really generous of Bob to think about me.

'I am thinking of getting your sister, Sang, to come over here for three weeks holiday. She can go back to Thailand at the same time as you. She can help you with Nicola on the plane, and we could have more time together when she is here.'

'Yes, that's a good Idea, thank you, it's very nice of you.'

I thought it was really sweet of Bob to be concerned about my twelve-hour flight with Nicola. He had also thought about my sister, and how she would love a holiday here.

Sang, my second sister, was a single mum with two kids, Tann was the eldest. Tang, her son, was 3 years younger. The children were born to different fathers, both of whom left as soon as Sang was pregnant.

Neither father wanted anything to do with their children. The situation is different in Thailand, there is no means to force fathers to make a financial contribution to their children, such as have here in the UK.

That is also why women have to put up with really bad behaviour from their partners, because otherwise they could be left on their own, with no means to support their children. This can mean starvation, or at least, a very difficult life for the mothers and their children.

My sister brought up her children without any help from their fathers, with no state benefit whatsoever. As well as no state help for single mothers, there is no free NHS. She had a very tough life, I thought she deserved a holiday.

Nicola started eating solid food when she was five months old. I called Mum for advice.

'Mum, Nicola is starting solid food now. What should I feed her?

'Well, the main food here is rice soup, you can mix minced chicken or pork in it. Make sure you cook it on low heat for over an hour, so it's tender to swallow.'

'I remember Jang fed her baby a bowl of rice soup, with minced liver.'

'Yes, that's fine too, it's easy to prepare. But do not give her it more than once a week because liver does have a high concentration of vitamin A.'

One night, Bob after was back from work, he looked at the kitchen sink. 'What was the black stuff in the pot?

'I cooked rice soup with chicken's liver for Nicola.'

'What were you thinking of? Liver has too strong a taste for a toddler.'

'She seemed to like it, I did ask my mum first if that is okay. Mum said, it was okay once a week.'

'I don't want you to feed her with liver at all, not just once a week. I don't care what Thai babies eat. Nicola is not a Thai baby. Don't you ask your mum; ask my mum what western babies eat.'

I did not understand why he was so mad. I did not mean to do any harm, especially with my baby. I called his Mum the next day.

'What do people here feed their babies with?'

'There are plenty of jars of baby food in the shop.'

'I don't want to give her jar food. I believe they contain preservatives; I think you are best to avoid those.'

'The main food for babies here is mashed potato with butter.'

'What about meat?'

'White meat is the most easily digested.'

'You mean fish?'

'Yes, fish or chicken.'

'Okay, thanks. Bob was angry yesterday because I gave Nicola minced chicken liver. I thought, it was okay, my sister fed her babies with it.'

'Might be okay with Thai babies, but I think it's too strong for babies here.'

I wondered what the difference was between western babies or Thai babies. Maybe I should have asked, but I did not want to upset anybody.

NINETEEN

In June 1993, Sang arrived in Scotland for her holiday. When Bob was off on a Sunday, he drove us to see different places. Nicola was fourteen months old, she had already started walking.

During the following weeks, Bob often took my sister into work with him.

'I will take your sister into work with me so she can look around Glasgow City Centre while I am working.'

'And, how will she get home?'

'I'll take her back.'

I was worried. 'She might get lost on her own. Glasgow is a big city and she doesn't speak English. You're always late; she might get bored waiting for you finishing work.'

'She's not a kid, she'll be fine. You're worried for nothing.'

I asked my sister. 'Do you want to go to town with Bob?

'Yes, I'd love to.'

'Will you be ok on your own?'

'I will be fine, it's better than staying in the house all day.' I wanted to say, 'Are you not happy to spend time with Nicola and I?'

Instead I said. 'Ok, Bob will take you into town with him, when you want to go home, you can meet up with him in the shop.'

They were back in late most nights. Bob was always late, but I thought he would come back earlier when he had my sister with him. One night they were back in at 23:30. I decided that was enough.

'Why you are always back in late, especially so tonight, it's nearly midnight?

'Ken visited me in the shop, so we went out for dinner.'

'I don't want you take my sister out anymore. You told me you were inviting her over here to help me, not to leave me in the house every day on my own. I've had enough of it.'

My sister did not know any English, but she could understand what was being said from our body language. She was upset and walked upstairs into her bedroom.

'You've upset your sister.'

'Is that all you care about? What about me? Do you care how I feel?

'You're jealous.'

'Of course, I'm jealous. She was to come here to help me with Nicola, so you and I could have more time together, was that not your idea in the first place?

'Yes, but I thought it wasn't fair that she looks after Nicola every day.'

'You know it's not every day. We always take Nicola out over the weekend, if I go out during the week, I always take Sang with me.'

I was not sure who to blame, was it him, was it my sister or was it me. I hate to say now that I hoped it was over soon. I just wanted to go back to Thailand.

Three days before we were due to go to Thailand. Bob said to me. 'I am sorry; I couldn't get a ticket for your sister to go back to Thailand with you.'

'What do you mean, you can't get a ticket? I thought you bought her a return ticket?'

'Yes, but it was an open return ticket. There's no seat available for her to go back on the same date.'

'When did you call the airline?'

'Yesterday.'

'No wonder, it's not available. You called four days before she was meant to go back!'

'I'm sorry.'

'It's not good enough. She's been here almost three weeks. You knew well enough when she was meant to go back and you did nothing about it. From the start, you never told me that you bought her an open ticket. Why did you buy her an open ticket in the first place?'

'I don't know; I wasn't thinking.'

'Yes, you weren't thinking! You booked my tickets and Nicola's two months before you booked my sister's ticket. You knew exactly that she was meant to go back at the same time as us. That's the reason she was here, to help me with Nicola on the plane.'

'I'm sorry.'

'Just please stop saying sorry. I have had enough of that word. Anyway, what date did you manage to get her a ticket? Let me guess, the same time as you?'

'Yes, there was a seat available three days before my flight and also the same day as my flight, so I just booked hers at same time as mine.'

'That's good you've got company. Don't worry about me and your daughter, or how I will manage with a fourteen-month old baby on a twelve-hour flight.'

I could not stop crying. I was so upset and disappointed. I was worried how I was going to cope with a baby on the plane.

What if I wanted to go to the toilet, who would keep an eye on her? How would I manage to carry her and all her stuff?

I booked a taxi to the airport. 'I'll take you to the airport.' Bob said.

'No. I'm taking a taxi. I don't want you to waste your time taking me to the airport.'

'How will you manage with a taxi? I want to see my daughter off.'

'Oh, you worry how I will manage with a taxi? It's only twenty minutes' drive from our house to Glasgow Airport. It's not something like twelve hours on the plane plus the connecting flight. It's not going to kill me, don't worry.'

118

I was crying on the taxi all the way to airport. I tried to pull myself together for Nicola's sake.

'Is everything okay? The taxi driver asked.

'Yes, I'll be fine, thank you for asking.'

'If I can help you with anything, just let me know.'

'I will, thank you.' I wished Bob was as considerate as the taxi driver.

I arrived at the airport. I struggled to cope with Nicola, a push chair, handbags and a suitcase. Bob turned up with my sister, she was crying.

I was crying too 'Do me a favour, you two just get out of my face. It upsets me more if you two are here.' Nicola started to cry. I walked away without turning back.

Prang was waiting for me at Bangkok Airport. 'Where is Sang?' Prang asked.

'I don't want to talk about it, just now.' I started to cry.

'Did they arrive safe and sound?' Mum called Prang to see how we were.

'Yes, Mum. Nuch is here with the baby.'

'What about Sang?'

'I don't know Mum. Sang isn't here.'

'Let me speak to Nuch.' Prang passed the phone to me.

'What's happening?' Mum asked.

'I don't know, Mum.'

'Is she still in Scotland with your husband?'

'Yes, they're coming back together in two weeks.'

'I'll kill her when she gets here. She's exactly liked your dad. I'd like to kill them both.' My mother had to put with years of domestic violence, and numerous affairs, from my father. Unfortunately, a situation that was all too common place in Thailand. It was starting to look like Bob and my sister were, even worse than my father.

Mum no longer put up with my Dad's violent, adulterous, behaviour because we were no longer dependant on him for financial support.

Jang had rung me about a violent incident between Mum and Dad a couple of months before I arrived Thailand. 'Nuch, you need to speak to mum.'

'What's going on?'

'You know how Dad was always involved with other women. Mum found out, she was going to kill dad last night.'

'Well, he deserved it.' I said light-heartedly.

'It's not funny, Mum could have ended up in prison.'

'Tell me what happened?'

'Last night, I heard a loud argument between them. I ran over to their house, I almost had a heart attack when I saw what was going on.'

'What...?'

'Mum had a gun pointed at dad, he was crying and shaking with fear, begging for his life and saying that he won't have any more affairs. I tried to stop Mum, but she wouldn't listen. I shouted to Yoy to run for help. He found a security guard nearby and he came back to the house with Yoy. '

'Thank goodness.'

'That wasn't the end of it. Mum scared the security guy off. She shouted at him that it was a husband and wife thing and nothing to do with him. She threatened to shoot him too, so he ran off.''

'Did you manage to take the gun from Mum?'

'No, I freaked out too. Then Mum fired the gun at Dad.'

My heart sank. 'Was he okay?'

'Yes, he was lucky, the bullet went out of the window because mum has never shot before, it must have just missed him.'

'Oh my God.'

'I had to stand in front of dad, I told her that her daughter and her grandchildren were all here, and that she could shoot us accidently. Eventually, Yoy managed to take the gun off her.'

'That's good no one was hurt.'

'Yes, but that's not the end.'

'What do you mean?'

'Dad had a gun on him the next day. He said to mum if she shoots him, he'll shoot her back.'

'For God's sake! Where did they get guns from?'

'Just bought them off the black market.'

'I'm not worried about dad; he's not brave enough to use a gun. I'll speak to mum.'

'I know what you're saying, but dad might use it to defend himself.'

'Okay, I'll speak to them both.'

I told mum that it was not worth it, and that she could end her life in prison. If she was unhappy with dad, she should just get divorced. I would help her financially, and Jang lived next door, and would also help out. She would not be alone, or starve to death, if she divorced.

I called my parents in law in Scotland the next day to let them know that Nicola and I had arrived safely in Thailand.

'I'll call and let Bob know that you two arrived safely.' Liz said.

'Is my sister ok? I called the house yesterday no one answered.'

'Bob took her to Ireland.'

I was speechless. Bob tried to ring me, I did not answer and I have never spoke to Sang since then. It was heart breaking, she was my sister.

Two weeks later, Bob and Sang arrived in Thailand. Mum spoke to her angrily. 'What were you thinking about?'

'I did nothing.'

'Don't you dare tell me that there was nothing going on. She's your sister! You're just like your Dad. He slept with my best friend. In fact, you're worse than your dad, because you are her sister!'

'I didn't sleep with him.'

'Why didn't you come home with your sister? You were meant to be there helping your sister with the baby.'

'There was nothing I could do about it. I didn't buy the ticket, it was her husband. Why don't you give him a hard time about it?'

'Don't you be smart with me.' Mum was furious, and hugely disappointed.

'What do you think people thought when you got off the plane and cried? Sang turned to me. I could not believe that she was accusing me of doing something wrong.

I did not enjoy my holiday in Thailand. I could not pretend that nothing had happened. Nicola had two cousins a couple months younger than her. I did my best to make sure that she had a nice time with them.

TWENTY

After I got back from Thailand, I slept in the spare bedroom most of the time. I would never forget about him and my sister.

I kept myself busy with Nicola. I had a routine for her almost every day. We went to a mother & toddler group once a week.

We had a mother & toddler swimming class once a week, sometimes twice per week. Nicola loved swimming. I took her to the park if it was dry. I took her to soft ball play if it was wet. She had a busy life.

Bob and I were not getting along, we were argued all the time. If he did not get his own way, he became violent towards me.

I remember one incident well, it had become quite heated, I knew it was time to get out of the way, I knew what was coming next. 'I'm going upstairs to my bedroom now. I don't want to argue with you.'

'Come back here! I'll tell you when you can leave the room.'

'I don't want to argue with you. I'm going to bed.' I continued walking out of the living room. He grabbed my arm, he pulled me back into the room.

'I told you, you can leave when I say so, not before!'

I kept silent in the room. I did not say anything otherwise; he would hit me and I would have bruises on my wrists, arms or neck.

I had a chance to get out of the lounge, I ran upstairs as fast as I could. I locked myself in the bathroom because it was only a room that had a lock. Unlike Thailand, where every room had a lock.

He ran upstairs, trying to catch me. 'Open the door! Open the bloody door!' He kept shouting and banging the door.

'No, you're mad. You need to calm down first.' I was frightened. There was no way I was going to open the door. He could kill me! I was terrified.

'I will smash this door in if you don't open it!' He was kicking the door hard. He kept kicking and kicking. The door was straining, but it was a good solid door and lock.

The noise woke Nicola up. She was frightened, crying, screaming.

'You better stop your violence; you are frightening your daughter.'

'I won't stop till you open this door! You're the one who is frightening her. If you hadn't locked yourself in there, this wouldn't have happened!' He kept kicking the door until the lock broke.

He walked straight towards me, gripped my jaw, squeezed it really hard, forcing me to look at him. 'Don't you dare do this again! You'll do whatever you're told!'

'Let me go, if you don't, I'll call police.' I thought he would kill me if I didn't do something.

'If you call the police, I'll make sure you're dead before the police get here.'

Nicola was still crying, screaming loudly. She was frightened by his shouting.

'Let me go, I need to see Nicola. She is frightened.' Eventually, he loosened his grip on my jaw.

I walked to Nicola's bedroom and opened the door. She was standing in her cot holding the cage-bars crying. She was only eighteen months old. I lifted her up in my arms and said to him. 'Get out of her room, don't you dare put your hands on me in front of her.'

I knew how it felt watching your dad hitting your mum when there was nothing you could do about it.

I slept in the single bed in Nicola's bedroom. I felt safe in there.

Liz phoned me the next day. 'Can I come to see Nicola today?

'Is it ok tomorrow or the day after?' I did not want her to see the bruises on my chin.

'I'm not free tomorrow, I have an appointment to see the doctor. My friends are coming to my house the day after.'

'Okay, it's fine, you can come today.' I decided to put a put a jumper with a high neck on rather than disappoint her. I knew Liz had a brain tumour, I did not want to upset her.

She noticed the bruise on my chin almost as soon as she arrived.

'What happened to your chin?' She asked.

'Oh, Nicola accidentally hit me with her toy.'

'What was it?'

'A wooden shaker.'

'She must have hit you hard.'

'Yes, she gets stronger every day.'

'Just get her plastic toys in case she hits herself on the head.'

I knew that if I told Liz the truth, she would be upset and would probably get headaches. She had enough to cope with.

In 1994, when she was two years old, Nicola started a private nursery school. It was twenty-five pounds a day, the most expensive nursery in Glasgow. She was picked to be on the television one day. It was a programme about what you learned in nursery school. I was really proud of her.

One of my Thai friends rang me one day. 'Nuch, I'm not sure that I should tell you this.'

'Well, you've already made the call, you better tell me.'

'I went to the Chung Ying supermarket this morning.'

'And?'

'I saw your husband with an Asian woman. I was not sure if she was Thai or Chinese.'

'Didn't you say hello to him?'

'No, I walked away. I wasn't sure what to do.'

'Next time, just say hello.'

'Are you okay with this?'

'I put up with it for the sake of my daughter. She's British, I can't just leave her and go back to Thailand.'

'I'm sorry.'

'It's ok. Thanks for letting me know.'

I felt trapped in a foreign country, I had no choice but to stay in the UK. I was forced to put up with his behaviour.

I was scared to report him to the police after he said I would be dead before they arrived. I did not know how I would manage financially with the children if I did report him. I was frightened and confused because in Thailand, at that time, there was no help for abused or divorced women.

I do not know if it is much different now. I hope the situation has changed to help women suffering domestic abuse.

I enrolled myself in an English class to try and become as fluent as possible. I missed the first-year exam because I was on business trip with Bob. I tried to keep myself busy while Nicola was in nursery school

I was driving home on the motorway one day, after picking Nicola up from her nursery school, I noticed a familiar car in front, I realised it was Bob. I could see there was a front seat passenger.

My curiosity got the better of me, I decided to overtake. I saw the passenger was an Asian woman. I was not sure if she was the same one my friend told me about it. I beeped the horn and gave them a wave when I was alongside. Bob looked surprised but did not acknowledge me.

I felt so sad, not because I still loved him. How I could possibly love him? I felt sad because Nicola was in the car with me. Luckily, she was too young to know the other side of her father.

'Who was she, the woman in your car?' I asked him when he arrived home.

'A customer. She bought lots of stuff in the shop, over a thousand pounds' worth. I just delivered the stuff to her house.'

'That's strange. She could afford to spend over a thousand pounds in a day, but she didn't have a car. Did she take a bus or a train to your shop?'

'I didn't ask.'

'Did you take her to do food shopping too?'

'No, that's a stupid question.'

'My friend told me a couple weeks ago that she saw you in Chinese supermarket with a woman. I didn't say anything to you because I didn't see it with my own eyes.'

'Well, if your friend really saw me why didn't she say hello?'

'She didn't want to embarrass you.'

'I don't think that's the case.'

'Anyway, why don't you just give me a divorce and you can go to see whoever you want to see.'

'You just want a divorce because you after my money! You know British Law, if we get a divorce you could have half of what I have.'

'Thanks for telling me that. I wish I knew more about British Law. I will take a course with Scottish Students to find out more. Maybe, I will find out more about British Law, and organisations that can help me out of this awful situation.'

'Don't you be smart with me! I brought you here from Thailand with nothing and you'll leave with nothing! I'll divorce you when I'm ready, not when you're ready, okay!' He gripped my chin and squeezed hard, forcing me to look at him while he was shouting at me.

I wondered how someone could change so much. When I married him, he was fun and kind. In such a short time, he had become quite violent, especially when he was angry or did not get his own way.

Nowadays his affairs and leaving me for days on my own with Nicola, his behaviour with my sister, and the threats to kill me, would all be considered mental torture.

Unfortunately, because I was from Thailand, where this behaviour was accepted at that time, I knew no better. I was so naïve, an easy target for abuse.

I kept all his bullying and violence from everybody, especially my family in Thailand. I did not want them to worry about me. I was on the other side of the world. They could not help. It would only make them feel pain and anxiety, especially my mother who had been through it all herself.

I saved every month to give money to Mum to build a house for me on my Mum's land. Hopefully, one day when Nicola was older, I could go back to live there again. The thought of this made my situation easier to deal with, I felt I had an escape plan.

We had separate bedrooms, but sometimes, he came into my bedroom.

'Get out of my bedroom, please.' I asked him.

'It's my house. I can go to any rooms, I want.'

'Get out of my bed, if not, I will call the police.'

'You're my wife! I can sleep with you when I want to. Don't make a fool of yourself, there is no such a thing as a husband raping a wife.' He forced himself on me. I was in tears, hurt emotionally and physically.

The phone rang one night. 'Hello' I answered.

'Hi Nuch, it's Martin here. Is Bob there?'

'No, he's not here. If you want to speak to him, you will have to call after midnight.'

'Is he always late?'

"Yes, he probably has another house and woman somewhere.'

'Are you okay?'

'I don't love him anymore, so I don't care, who he sleeps with. But I hate it when he comes into my bedroom.'

'Are you telling me that, he forced you to have sex with him?'

'Yes.' I started to cry.

'You have to call the police.'

'He said that there was no such a thing as a husband raping his wife.'

'That's bullshit. He knows you know nothing about British Law. You have to call the police, at least his name will be on record.'

'He said, he would make sure I was dead before the police arrive.'

'Just call, don't tell him that you're going to call. If you need any help, don't hesitate to call me. I know, he's my friend, but I don't like the way he treats you. I'll help you if I can. I don't care if he doesn't speak to me again.'

'Thank you, Martin.'

I felt a bit better after that phone call. But, I was not sure if it was true. I did not trust any men at that time. I did not know, at that time, if Martin was saying that for any ulterior motives, or not.

At least now, I was able to talk to him about it. I could not talk to my Thai friends, they just thought how lucky I was because I had a big house, expensive car and plenty of money. I could not talk at work, because he was the boss.

I could not talk to my neighbours because I did not think anybody would believe me.

One day, I took Nicola to visit his mum. 'Bob, told me that you're sleeping in a different bedroom.'

'Yes.'

'I don't think it's right that you have a separate bedroom from your husband. Maybe, that's the cause of the arguments?'

'Did you ask your son, why his wife's in a separate bedroom?' I was so disappointed by what I had just heard. 'Remember, when I had a bruise on my chin. I kept telling you that Nicola hit me with her toys. No, that was a lie. It was your son, my husband. The bruises were not just on my chin. They were on my wrists. I covered them with long sleeves.' I tried to hide my tears.

'I don't believe you. He's not that type of person.'

'You don't believe me because he's your son, he's your blood. My mum's not here for me to cry on her shoulder. That's why I'm crying now with you.' I started to cry, I could not hide my tears anymore.

'I'm so sorry to hear this.' She was crying too. It became too much for her and she went to bed with a headache.

'What's going on? Robert asked me when he saw Liz had gone to bed.

'I just told her the truth about why I had bruises. I kept it secret before because I didn't want to hurt her feelings or make her ill. I told her now because I felt I had no choice.'

Robert picked up the phone, I assumed he spoke to Bob. 'If you don't stop hitting people, you'll end up in prison!'

'I called him, but he says he hasn't got a clue what you're talking about.' His dad said to me.

'Maybe, he never hit anybody else. You should have used the word 'wife'.'

'I'm sorry; I'll call the police myself if he does it again.'

I was feeling guilty about Liz being ill after we spoke. I should have kept my mouth closed.

Bob started shouting at me as soon as he got home. 'Don't you dare say anything to my Mum again. She can't cope with it, you know she's got a brain tumour. You're killing her.'

'Are you suggesting that I should put up with your violent behaviour for the rest of my life?'

'I'm the father of your daughter. You can't cut me off. Where are you going to live? How are you going to feed Nicola? You can't go to work and look after her. You can't afford a baby sitter. You can't pay all the bills.'

He was right, I could not pay all the bills. I could not take her away from whatever she had. I kept telling myself, I am a mother, I should sacrifice my happiness for my daughter.

I almost collapsed one morning when I found out I was expecting my second child, completely unplanned.

I rang him at work. 'I'm expecting. I'm telling you now, don't you dare come in my bedroom ever again! Don't you dare put your hand on me. If you do, I'll call the police. You can kill me if you want to!'

I could not tell how I felt. I had mixed feelings. I was happy Nicola was going to have a baby brother or sister. I had no doubt that I would love him or her very much, no matter what.

But, I was terrified by the whole situation. I did not know what to do. I could not really go back to Thailand as a single mother of two children.

The situation here in the UK seemed to be getting worse. My husband's behaviour was becoming more and more violent, in terms of both physical and verbal abuse. One thing I knew; I was determined to stop it.

I remember, one day, he asked me to go to court to support him. 'I sacked Annemarie, the girl in the office.'

'She seemed a nice person to me.'

'Yes, but she didn't do a good job, so I sacked her. She was mad about it and she sued me.'

'For what? It can't be racism because she's Scottish.'

'For sexual harassment. But, I never touched her.'

'If you never touched her, how can she sue you for sexual harassment.'

'It's for badness because she wasn't happy that I sacked her. She wanted to get back at me.'

'What did she say about sex harassment?

'She said I touched her leg when she had a mini skirt on.'

'Did you?'

'No, she's fat and not my type.'

'Why are you telling me this?'

'I'm going to Court on Wednesday. I want you to go to court to support me. People can see that I don't need her because you're much more beautiful than her.'

'Sorry, I'm not going to court to support you.'

'Why not? I'm your husband.'

'You gave me the wrong answer when you said she was fat and not your type. You should have said, you're married, a husband and a father. You forced yourself on me. That's good enough reason to me, for not going to support you in court.'

'That'll make me look bad! You're my wife! You must support me, especially in this type of case. If I lose the case, who will run the shops? Have you thought about your children's future?'

'Nicola's the only reason that I'm still here talking to you. Just remember, I didn't ask you to touch her legs!' I started to walk away. 'Oh, don't you ever think about pushing me back into the room. Bear in mind, I'm expecting! I won't put up with you if you harm my baby.'

I still could not believe that he tried to blame me for not going to court to support him. In fact, I was worried, but I did not want to show him any weakness. I thought about the consequences if he lost the case, if he lost his business. His business was my children's future.

I went to see a family doctor for a normal pregnancy check-up. 'I could see from your file that you had a C-section with your first child.' The doctor said.

'Yes, I had a C-section with my first child.'

'It looks like you will have the same issues.'

'You're saying, I can't give birth naturally?'

'Yes, that's right.'

'I'll have a C-section when I'm in labour.'

'You might not need to go into labour, if you do, it will be a very short one.'

'I don't understand.'

'I will arrange for a C-section when your thirty-nine weeks pregnant.'

'What if I am in labour before this?'

'We'll give you a C-section straight away, so you won't have to go through the pain again.'

'That's good. I was in pain for more than twelve hours with my first child, before the C-section.'

'You don't have to go through that this time. You might not need to go through labour at all. Let me check the date.' She was counting on a calendar. 'Ok, I will give you four days, pick a date between 28 – 31 January for a C-section.'

'I'm not sure, what date is the best, let me think.'

'My birthday is 31 January.'

'Wow, that's great. I choose 31 January, your birthday, to give birth!'

'Are you sure?'

'Yes, I would love to give birth to my child on your birthday.'

'That's great. I'll arrange it for 31 January.'

It was funny when people asked me. 'When is your baby is due?'

'It's 31 January.' I could give the exact day.

When I was expecting Nicola, I was mad about roast duck. I had to eat crispy roast duck, with pancakes, from the local Chinese take away, every day.

The owner of the Chinese take- away called me one evening. 'Nuch, you just come to the shop and pay the bill at the end of each month!'

'Ok thanks.' I think he made the offer because sometimes I couldn't find enough change for the delivery driver.

When I was expecting with my second child, I could not eat or smell Asian food. It made me sick, I had to clear out all Asian herbs and sauces in my kitchen. It was the complete opposite to how I normally am. I loved eating some Scottish food which I had never enjoyed before, such as cheesy, creamy, or buttery tasting food. Normally, I hate them!

When I was pregnant it was hard trying to chase after Nicola, who was, by now, over two years old. She was into everything.

I was not keeping well during the first stage of pregnancy. I suffered from morning sickness. He was always late coming home, I could only talk to him on the phone if I needed his help. I felt I had no support from him.

I rang him one night before I went to bed. 'I just want to let you know that I have an appointment to go for a scan tomorrow morning, to make sure all is okay with the baby.'

'That's great, what time is it?

'10:30 Do you want to go?'

'Of course. We'll just go to the hospital first, then I will drop you off back at the house before I go to work'

'I think I will take Nicola too, it would be nice for her to see her sister or brother in my tummy.'

'Yes, that's a good idea. She will love that'

'Okay, good night I'm going to bed now.'

We went to hospital the next day. When we arrived, there were two couples before us. There was no waiting room, we just sat on chairs in the corridor.

Bob's phone rang while we were waiting for the couple in front of us to be seen. 'I need to answer the call.' He told me, as he disappeared around the corner, phone in hand.

'Mrs Smith, would you like to follow me.' The nurse came for me.

'Mummy, where is daddy?' Nicola asked me.

'He's busy on the phone.' I was so disappointed. We walked into the scan room, the nurse noticed that he was not there. 'Where's your husband?'

'He was talking on the phone.'

'Would you like to wait?'

'It's ok, there are a few couples waiting after me, so please carry on.' I did not want anybody to have to wait longer because Bob was too busy to come in. I wondered why I bothered to invite him.

The nurse placed some gel on my belly and rubbed the scanner handset on it. We could see an unborn baby on the monitor.

'Mummy, is that a baby in your tummy?'

'Yes, that's your baby brother or sister.'

'How long will they stay in your tummy?'

'It's about thirty-nine weeks altogether.'

The nurse gave Nicola a picture of the baby scan. She was so happy and told everybody that she had a picture of her baby brother or sister.

'Daddy, where were you? You didn't see a baby in mummy's tummy.'

'I'm sorry, I had to take a call.'

'Let's go, I don't think she understands why a phone call was more important, to you, than seeing a baby in her mummy's tummy.' I was disappointed and upset. I tried not to get upset because I believed the baby in my womb could feel my emotions. I knew they could pick up my feelings.

If I was depressed, I believed that could affect how the baby develops after it was born.

Nicola was a great baby. She slept through the night, I never had any problems with her sleeping. She only cried when she was tired and wanted to sleep, or when she was hungry.

When I was expecting her, I had positive emotions. I felt love, I felt care, I felt affectionate, I felt optimistic. I was happy, I believed that was the reason, Nicola was a happy baby.

I knew my feelings were different this time. I tried to focus only on the positives to ensure the baby had the best chance of being happy too.

Late one night the door belt rang. It was one of our employees. 'Oh, hi David, Bob's not here.'

'I know, that's why I'm here. Bob stayed overnight in Manchester, he asked me to stay overnight here with you.'

'That's very kind of you. I'm ok, you don't have to.'

'I already said to Bob that I would be here with you.'

David worked in our Glasgow shop. I felt awkward that somebody had to stay over because my husband was unable to come home.

I rang him. 'Why did you send David here? You know he's got his own family.'

'I know, but I couldn't make it home tonight.'

'Next time, don't send anybody. I don't see the difference, anyway, wither you are in Glasgow or not. I still feel like a single mum.'

There was no reply from him.

TWENTY-TWO

The next morning at 10:00, I packed my suitcase to stay overnight in Paisley Hospital for the C-section. I was not allowed to eat or drink after midnight. Nicola stayed over with her grandparents.

Bob was at home for once, he dropped me off at the hospital. 'I'll come back tomorrow morning for the C-section.' I believed him.

When I got settled in the ward, I asked the nurse. 'How long will I have to stay in hospital? They kept me for ten nights with Nicola, my first child.'

'It depends, if everything goes well, we might keep you for five nights. You were so weak, before the C-section with your first baby, that you had to stay longer. But this time, you're much stronger and fitter. You'll recover quicker this time.'

I was pleased to hear that. I went through a tough time with Nicola. I did not want to go through that pain again.

Bob was still not here at 09:30. I was not surprised. Sometimes, I thought that he was living some sort of double life. I never saw him from one day to the next, neither did Nicola. I tried not to dwell on these thoughts, too much, in case they affected the baby.

The nurse took me down to the operating theatre. I was so disappointed Bob had not come.

The nurse gave me the spinal block at 09:45. The doctor arrived the theatre at 09:55. I could hear the doctor asked the nurse quietly. 'Where's her husband?'

'He's not here yet.'

'When did you give her the spinal block?'

'09:45.'

'The medicine begins to take effect in ten to twenty minutes. I have to start the procedure at 10:00.'

Tears were in my eyes. At 10:00 the doctor started the procedure. The nurse whispered in my ear. 'Don't worry, your husband is already here. He's getting changed.'

I still could not believe it, I was in tears, because of my husband, until the last minute of my pregnancy.

It was a girl, she was perfect. Her weight was ten pounds. I could see my face on her face. The doctor finished stitching up my tummy and I fell asleep.

I woke up in intensive care with bedside monitors clicking away beside me.

'Is the baby okay?' I asked Bob anxiously.

'Yes, she's perfect.'

'Why am I here? I was okay before or during the C-section.'

'You lost too much blood.'

The male nurse was changing my sanitary pad every five minutes.

'Can you ask for a female nurse for me. I'm uncomfortable with a male nurse cleaning and changing my sanitary pad.' In Thailand, at that time, male nurses would not perform intimate procedures on women. In fact, I had never seen a male nurse in Thailand.

Bob, and the male nurse, explained that this was quite normal in Scotland.

Bob started chatting with him and found out that they both had the same surname. Bob give him his business card and offered him a job if he ever fancied a new career!

I could not believe what I heard. I was in an intensive care unit with three different specialist doctors, an obstetrician, a cardiologist, and a haematologist. I was bleeding heavily, my heart rate was increasing and Bob was boasting about how good his business was.

The haematologist came in to check on me. 'I think your wife is losing too much blood.'

'What makes you think that?'

'It came right through her sanitary pad in five minutes. It's dark red with a few lumps.'

'What causes that?'

'Some women have problems with blood clotting which makes it hard to stop bleeding after any type of cut, tear or bruise.'

'Is she going to be okay?'

'She needs a blood transfusion. If she doesn't have it, she will get dizzy or unconscious.'

'Where does the hospital get the blood from?'

'From people who have donated their blood.'

'Has the hospital checked where people who donate their blood come from?'

'Of course.'

'Do you mind if I ask, where do you originally come from?'

Although I was only half awake, I could not believe my ears. I was afraid the doctor would walk out or ask Bob to leave.

'No, I don't mind, I'm from South Africa.'

'Which country did you qualify in, here or South Africa?'

I was squirming, I was so embarrassed by Bob.

'Cambridge University, England.'

'How long have you been working in a hospital?'

'Two years.'

'I'm sorry if I ask too many questions.'

'It's okay, I understand.' The doctor finished his examination and left. He was very professional, he displayed no trace of annoyance at Bob's behaviour.

'Why did you ask him all those questions?' I asked.

'I was worried about his qualifications, I have got the right to ask.'

I thought my husband was a racist. 'Would you ask all those questions if he was white?'

'Well, maybe not.'

'That's your answer. You're a racist.'

Bob did not answer, or even look annoyed. I can only assume he knew he was a racist and did not care.

I had the blood transfusion, it was one bag, but I never found out how much was in the bag. I continued to bleed heavily for the next three days. I was in intensive care for three nights. I then moved to a private recovery room for five days.

I called our baby girl 'Teresa'. I found it was easier with the second baby in terms of looking after her, because I knew what to do this time around.

I remember my family doctor advised me everything would be fine because they already knew about the problems, I experienced giving birth to my first child. I never thought, I would wake up in intensive care again.

I was back home after eight days in hospital. It was hard work looking after Teresa. She was always crying. I had to carry her in my arms most of the time, because if I put her down, she would scream madly.

I blamed myself because I had so many negative emotions when I was expecting. I did not feel love for my husband or feel loved by him.

I was always crying and upset, that is why I think Teresa was affected by my negativity.

I hardly had time for myself with Teresa and Nicola. Nicola was three now, she was very mobile and with an enquiring mind, so she was into everything if she got half a chance. I had to watch her constantly.

I had no support from Bob, he was away straight after breakfast and I would not hear or see him until at least 9.30 pm, usually he returned between 11pm and midnight.

The children and I were already in bed by the time he was back home. The only time they saw him was for ten to fifteen minutes during breakfast.

I knew our lives could not go on like this, but I was frightened of him. I actually thought he was capable of seriously hurting me, killing me, or paying somebody else to do it for him. I thought the latter would be more his style.

I decided to approach him with a few conditions if life was going on like this. First, I wrote to my close friend, Nellie enclosing a letter for the police if anything should happen to me.

TO THE POLICE

10 Feb 95

If anything should happen to me, it is my husband who is responsible. He has threatened to kill me if he receives any letters from my lawyer for divorce, he says he will kill me.

He puts his hands on me if he does not get his own way, he beats me and shouts at me all the time. I have reached my limit now, I cannot take any more, and I am going to ask him for a divorce. I do not know what will happen. He should be your first suspect if anything happens to me.

Nuch Smith.

I talked to him one Sunday morning. 'I would like to make a deal with you.'

'What is it?'

'You say you're not ready for a divorce, that's fine. But I've a few conditions if we're going to keep living like this.'

'What if I don't accept your conditions?' I could tell he was turning nasty.

'I'll find a lawyer for a divorce. I've already written a letter to my friend to give to the police if anything happens to me.'

'Don't you be smart with me.'

'I'm not playing games with you. I'll stay under the same roof with you for the sake of our children. We'll live our separate lives. You do whatever you want to do. See whoever you want to see. I do whatever I want to do and see whoever I want to see.'

'Ok, if that's what you want!'

'It's not about what I want, it's what you're already doing! I want you to take the children out every Sunday, if not, you won't get to see them at all.'

'Okay, I'll take them out on Sundays.'

'Why do you never come home before midnight?' At that time, I thought he had another house somewhere because I knew he could not be at work till mid-night.

'I thought, we just agreed that we'll live separate lives.'

'I'm just trying to find out what to say to the children when they ask about their dad.'

'I'm working.'

'Are you telling me that you're working till midnight every night?'

'Not every night, I just visit my friend if I finish early.'

'Is it a male friend or a female friend?'

'Male.'

'It's must be a close friend then if he lets you stay till midnight every night.'

I knew he was lying as usual, but I did not care who he was with. I just felt sorry for our children and I did not know what to tell them when they asked about their dad.

I did not want to lie to them, at the same time I could not tell them the truth.

He kept up the Sundays with the kids, not every Sunday, maybe half of them, until Teresa was two. Sometimes he remembered their birthday, but not always.

I supposed no one would believe me if I said, he only had a meal with them once or twice a year. One of those would be at Christmas or New Year.

My Thai friend called me one Sunday afternoon. 'Hi Nuch, I'm sorry, I've to ring you.'

'Are you ok?'

'Yes, I'm fine. I was in Chinese restaurant on Bath street. I saw your husband having lunch with an Asian woman. I only saw her from the back and I thought she was you, so I went to say hello.'

'Thanks for calling. Are they still there?'

'I think so, they were on starters when I went to say hello. I just walked out afterwards.'

'Why did you walk out?'

'I didn't want to embarrass him.'

'I don't think he would feel ashamed. Thanks for letting me know.'

I was really angry, not because I loved him. It was because, he was too busy to take his children out for lunch on a Sunday as he promised.

I sent him a text message.

I am giving you twenty minutes from now to stop having lunch with whoever you are with and take your children out for lunch instead. If you do not get here within twenty minutes, I am going to see a lawyer tomorrow morning.

Bob arrived within twenty minutes. 'I'm glad that you're back within the twenty minutes. I don't care who you were having meal with. Do you know why I'm mad?'

'I don't.'

'Because it's Sunday. I asked you to take your children out for lunch every Sunday. You agreed. You said, you were too busy with work to take them out for lunch, but you managed to have time for lunch with someone else!'

Bob said nothing, he just took the children out for lunch, but he did not take them the next weekend. He told the children that he was too busy, unfortunately, or perhaps fortunately for them, they believed him.

I did not tell them otherwise; it would only upset them. I never told the children any of what was going on.

'Hi Nuch, is Bob there?' Martin rang me one night. He was looking for Bob but he was not in as usual.

'No, he's not here.'

'Okay, I'll try later.'

'Make it after midnight.'

Martin called me on my mobile phone just after I got off the land line with him. 'I called the land line just to make sure he was not in. Why don't you just get a divorce, Nuch?'

'I want so much to get a divorce, but I can't take the children away from everything they have. I'm working in a Thai restaurant Thursday to Saturday to make ends meet. Thank goodness their grandparents look after them.'

'You must be tired out.'

'I drop them off before I go to work, then go back there to sleep because I'm so exhausted. I go home in the morning. I can't afford to give them a comfortable life. Bob's really controlling with money now, I want to get out and be independent.'

'I don't know if you're aware but if you get a divorce in this country, you're entitled to 50% of whatever he has.'

'I know, it might sound stupid to you and everybody else, but that, and fear of his violence, are the reasons I don't push for a divorce.'

'I'm not sure what you meant and yes, it sounds stupid to me. Everybody would be happy with 50% of what he has.'

'It's about his business, I feel it's my children's future. How will it work out if he has to split half of his business with me? I'm scared he will go bust, and there will be nothing for the children's future.'

'Nuch, you're too kind. If he can't split his business, the court will order him to give you money to the value of 50% of his business. Remember, you're still entitled to half of the house. Your house is valued at over £600,000. You can get a very good house for £300,000.'

'I don't think he'll accept that.'

'If you're waiting for him to accept a divorce then you might not end with much, it's not going to be easy. He's a businessman, and very underhand, if not downright criminal. The more time you give him, the more he'll try to hide his assets. Just to remind you, he's my friend, but I can't support the way he treats you and the children.'

'Thanks, Martin. I know you're trying to help. It's still not easy for me, because none of my family is here to support me. Where am I going to live during the divorce process? I can't see that we can live under the same roof. I won't be able to sleep, he'll kill me. He threatens to kill me.'

'Nuch, you need to see a lawyer.'

'He said, he'll kill me if he gets a letter from a lawyer.'

'You have to see the police too. Do you know why I called you back on your mobile phone?'

'No, why is it?'

'He paid for a private investigator to follow you. He also tape records your land line phone conversations.'

'Sounds like the movies!'

'That's correct, that why I said, you can't wait till he's ready to get a divorce.'

'He must have plenty money to pay for a private investigator. What is he trying to get from that?'

'He thinks you're having an affair with a Korean guy who works in the Thai restaurant with you. He's trying to get evidence for the court, to help his divorce.'

'Well, he can keep trying as long as he likes because he won't get anything from it. What's a bloody joke. How dare he! Thinking I'm having an affair, in fact, he's the one who is having an affair.'

'I know, that's why I called you, I saw him doing food shopping with a Chinese woman in the Chinese supermarket.'

'I know Martin, someone told me that already. I did see him with her once myself, she was in his car.'

'I'm sorry, I feel guilty.'

'It's nothing to do with you. I'm not waiting around for him to take me to do food shopping, otherwise, my children would starve to death.'

'That's not what I meant. I was the one who introduced her to him on my son's birthday party. She knows my wife, she lives her illegally and will do anything to find someone to help her stay here legally. That's why I feel guilty'

'It's not your fault, she's not the only one he sleeps with. You don't know the whole story. It's not a nice story, for me, or the children, unfortunately.'

'I was shocked when I saw you working in the restaurant. You're probably the only person who lives in Whitecraigs and works as a waitress.'

'I had no choice, when I was working for him in our shops, he started to shout at me in front of his staff, it was happening all the time. He was pretty rude and nasty to me in front of them.'

'Oh dear.'

'It was really embarrassing, I'm his wife, not just one of his staff. I spoke to him about it and asked him to speak to me privately if he had an issue and not to shout at me in front of his staff. It was getting so bad I was scared to go into work.'

'Yes, I know what he's like. I know he has had physical fights with staff members in his shops.'

'I know, his behaviour is unbelievable, he came home once with a ripped shirt after he had been fighting with a young lad in the shop!'

'Yes, he's quite violent.'

'This evening job suits my time commitments. I have to get the children ready for school, and then collect them afterwards.'

'Can't he just get children ready for school? It's his own business, he can start anytime he wants.'

'I did ask, he said that I'm a mother, it's my responsibility. He also refuses to come home early before I leave for work in the restaurant. I have to drop the children off at their grandparents before work.'

'He's a nasty person. I feel, he doesn't want you to go to work so you have to depend on him for finances, then he can control you. He doesn't like you becoming independent. He also tries to cut you off from meeting other people, for the same reasons, it's all about control.'

'Yes, I'm going to look for a college course, it'll help me start over.'

Martin's view did make sense to me. I started looking for a course at the college with other Scottish people. It would give me more chance to get to know more of British culture, find any organisations to help me out of this awful situation, and understand what the law could do to help me, and, of course, improve my English.

TWENTY-THREE

In 1997, Nicola was in Primary one. Prang phoned me one morning. 'I just called to let you know that Sang has cancer. She's already on the last stage, we've just found out. She's got six months to live.'

I almost collapsed with the news. I could not stop crying. I had not spoken to her since she went to Ireland with Bob four years ago. But, at the end of the day, she was still my big sister. I was devastated.

I booked an open ticket to Thailand as soon as I could. I did not know how long I would be there. I did not know how long she would live. I wanted to spend as much time with her as I could.

I was worried about the fact that the hospital system in Thailand is completely different from the UK.

There are two systems, you pay in both. One is called the public hospital, but you still pay, but it is much cheaper than what are known as, the private hospitals.

In the public hospitals, there are long queues, and you just wait in the queue irrespective of what is wrong with you. There is no prioritisation of patients, you just wait your turn.

When you are eventually seen, the doctor will tell you how much your treatment will cost, you must pay the bill before you can have the treatment.

I rang my mother in law. 'Liz, I've received bad news from Thailand.'

'What's happened?'

'Sang, has cancer.'

'I'm awfully sorry.'

'She's on the last stage, she has six months left. I'm going to Thailand to be with her. Can you take care of Nicola and Teresa, after school, until Bob gets back from work?'

'Of course, no problem at all. You just stay in Thailand as long as you need to.'

'Thank you.'

I flew to Thailand three days later. I went straight to the hospital; my Mum was already there.

I was shocked when I saw Sang. She was thirty-five, but she looked like a sixty-year-old woman. She was so skinny, I could see the bones under her skin, but there was a big solid lump in her tummy. It was the tumour.

She was losing her hair due to chemotherapy. I tried my best to hide my tears. 'Hi, how are you feeling today?'

'I'm not too bad.'

'Prang called me, I came as soon as I could.'

'Who's looking after your girls?'

'My parents in law, they said I can stay as long as I wish.'

'Just stay a fortnight, there's nothing you can do about this.'

I stayed with her all day until 16:30. Mum said. 'Maybe you should go home now. Sang's children will arrive home on the school bus at 17:00. Maybe you could look after them?'

'Okay, what about their dinner?' I asked Mum. I wasn't sure what they liked. Tann was thirteen years old, and Tang was ten.

'Just buy something for them at the market on your way back home.'

'What about you?'

'Don't worry about me, I'll just go downstairs and get something later.'

'What time are you leaving, how will you get back home?'

'I sleep here with Sang every night.'

'Where do you sleep? There's no bed here for you.'

'I sleep on a mat on the floor, next to her bed. I have to stay just in case your sister needs something or she wants the toilet.'

'What about the nurse?'

'They don't come around to check patients very often.'

'There's a button to call them.'

'Yes, but your sister doesn't like to trouble them.'

'It's their job, mum and we pay the hospital.'

'I know, but your sister would prefer me to take care of her, especially, going to the toilet.'

'Mum, you're fifty-four. It's not good for you to lie on such a hard surface every night.' I loved my sister, but I knew this would be hard for Mum.

I understood Mum wanted to comfort Sang as best as she could. I could not swap with her because I had problems with my back. I could not lie on a hard surface. Otherwise, I would have gladly swapped.

I saw the doctor the next day, to discuss my sister's treatment. 'How long she does she have?'

'She's on the last stage. The cancer started in her intestine, by the time we found out, it had spread everywhere. There's nothing we can do about it. She has six months, at most.'

I was sad when I heard that, Sang had been to the hospital much earlier because she was having a sore tummy so often. The doctors gave her pain killers and told her that it was caused by her irregular eating habits. In fact, it was cancer.

I turned my mind back to what was happening now, there was no point in dwelling on the past, we had the future to deal with. 'How much less could her time be?'

'Three months, to be honest. There is no point wasting your money paying for hospital every day. You should take her home.'

'Thanks, I will talk to Mum.'

I did not know what to do. I knew my sister felt safe in hospital, but I did not want to see Mum on the floor every night. I was glad the doctor had been so honest, but I was worried how to explain this to Sang.

Mum, 'I just saw the doctor, he advises not to waste money paying for a lengthy stay in hospital, there's nothing more they can do.'

'I agree; she's been in hospital three weeks now. It is five hundred baht per night for the bed, one hundred and fifty baht for each painkiller injection. We would be better keeping the money for her children's education.'

'The doctor said, he would give us painkiller pads to decrease the pain, and a morphine drip to take home.'

'That's good. Our neighbour across the road is a nurse.'

'I've a friend who is a nurse too.'

'I'm getting a sore back; I don't know how long I can keep sleeping on the hospital floor at my age. If she comes home, I'll be able to cook for her, too.'

'I'm not sure, how Sang is going to take it. What if she doesn't want to leave hospital?' She feels safe here. I don't think we should tell her what the doctor said, it'll be too upsetting for her.'

'I'll tell her that her children want to be with her, and the doctor said, it's ok to go home.'

Mum explained as best as she could to Sang, but she didn't take it well. She was scared she would be in pain at home.

I explained, 'The doctor will give us all the drugs and medicine to take back home. Mum's too old to lie on the floor every night. She just can't keep that up much longer.'

'I want to be close to the doctor and the nurse.'

'But the doctor's not really close to you. If you think about it, he comes to check up on you at 09:00 every morning. The nurse just comes round for a routine check. Mum's the one who's taking care of you. She feeds you, she helps you move around, she takes you to the toilet.'

Sang was scared. 'You just don't want to help me. You just don't want to pay anymore for my treatment.'

'Don't say that! I do want to help you, it's hurtful. I helped you open your hairdressing business at home. It didn't work out. Then I helped you to finance the restaurant business in the power plant canteen. A year later, you said, running the restaurant was too much work. Then, I bought a school minibus for you to drive. Please don't you say that I don't want to help you.' I was disappointed and hurt.

I helped everyone in my family as much as I could. I was able to do this because of the huge differential in the exchange rate.

My wage per hour in Scotland was the same as my sister's wage, per day. I felt it was my responsibility to take care of them, because compared to them, I was really well off.

If anything happened to Sang, it would be my responsibility to take care of her daughter and son. This meant, I would have to send money to mum and dad every month, to cover all the bills, until both children graduated.

In fact, that was exactly what did happen.

Eventually, Sang agreed to go home. It was much easier for Mum to take care of her at home. Mum could cook for Sang and the rest of us. She could carry on with her gardening and look after six her dogs.

During my stay, one night, there was an incredible display in the sky. We could see millions of shooting stars; this only happens every forty years. My mum, sister, niece and I lay down on mats in the yard and watched as the shooting stars fell to earth. It was absolutely beautiful, something I had never experienced before.

'Aunty, is it true, if I make a wish when I see a falling star, my wish will come true?' Tann asked me.

'Yes, but you have to work towards your wish too.' I couldn't prove that a shooting star could fulfil her wish. Seeing one, in itself, was such a miracle. 'Wish on it with all your heart and work towards your goal.' I thought it was too complicated to explain to a thirteen-year-old.

'I wish my Mum will get better.' Tann said aloud.

'Yes, she's getting better.' It was heart breaking. I just could not tell her the truth that her mum would not get any better.

'Why are the stars falling from the sky?' Tann asked.

'Well, it's not actually a star. It's just a piece of rock burning up as it hits the earth's atmosphere. When they hit the atmosphere, the friction from, travelling through the air so quickly, makes them heat up, then they break up and glow very brightly. They are called meteors.'

'Why are they called shooting stars when they aren't stars?'

'It's just another name, shooting star or falling star.'

The next morning Sang stuck a pain pad on the wall, next to her headboard. 'Why did you stick it on the wall? It's meant to be on your chest.'

'It's not working!'

'What do you mean? Didn't it stick to your skin?'

'It's pointless sticking it on my chest, it doesn't stop the pain.'

'You've an appointment at the cancer centre tomorrow. I'll ask them about it.'

The next day I took Sang for her chemotherapy treatment at the cancer centre. She met a woman who had been in hospital with her.

'Is that you, Sang?' She was excited to see her again.

'Yes, it's me. How are you keeping?'

'I'm not too bad, and you?'

'I get tired easily, maybe it's the side effects from chemotherapy.'

'I know... this is my last chemotherapy.'

'Wow, that's great. Are you clear now?'

'No, I'm not clear, but I don't have any more money to pay for my treatment.'

'I'm so sorry. I don't have money either, my sister pays for my treatment.' They were both crying, cuddling each other and saying good bye.

'I wish you all the best with the treatment.' She started walking toward the exit.

'Hey, I've five thousand baht here in my purse. Keep it for your next treatment.' It was so sad, I handed the money to her.

'It's truly kind of you, thank you. But, I can't take it. You keep it for your sister's treatment.'

'I've still got some money left for her, just take it, please.'

'Thank you so much, you're so kind.' She took the money.

'Don't worry, all the best with your treatment.' I gave her a cuddle.

It was so hard for people in Thailand, if you do not have enough money, you cannot have treatment. If you are poor, you will not last long with cancer.

Scottish people do not realise how lucky they are having a free NHS providing the medical care you need, unlike Thailand, where it is based on your ability to pay.

'You need to lie on your side more.' Mum told Sang when she was cleaning her back.

'It's not comfortable to lie on my side, Mum.'

'Your coccyx has come through your skin because you have been lying too long on your back. You're so skinny you need to turn more frequently.'

I felt so sad, Sang had no appetite and had difficulty eating and swallowing fluids. She was weak and exhausted. She spent most of the day in bed, sleeping or resting. Her body was shutting down.

She was always calling and looking for Mum and Dad. She did not look for her children.

'She's dying that's why she's looking for me and your Dad for support.' Mum told me.

I was in bed upstairs during my second week in Thailand, at 03:30 Mum shouted for me 'Nuch, come down to see your sister.'

'I'm here.' I ran downstairs to her bed and held her hand. Mum and Dad were there too.

'Should we call Tang and Tann?' I asked Mum.

'No, they're too young, she didn't ask to see her children.'

'I can't breathe...' She whispered.

'Take a deep breath, in and out slowly.' I held her in my arms.

'Will you promise to look after my children.'

'I promise, I'll take good care of them, I'll love them as my own.' I tried my best to hide my tears. I knew her death was minutes away.

'Please forgive me.'

'I forgive you.'

'I love you all.' It was her last sentence. She passed away with her eyes open. Mum closed her eyes with her hand.

'You're no longer in pain.' Mum was crying and cleaned my sister's body with a wet towel. Mum changed Sang into her favourite outfit. She put a little make up on her face.

Dad tied my sister's ankles and wrists with a sacred, white string. It was a sign to give safe passage to the next life. He placed my sister's hands in a praying position.

Mum placed a lotus flower and incense stick in my sister's hands for good luck, and put a coin in her mouth, in case she needed money to pass into her next life.

In the morning Dad organised a stainless-steel coffin fridge. He and the neighbour placed my Sang's body in the coffin. Half of the coffin lid was a glass; we could still see her inside.

We kept her at home for seven days. The Buddhist monks visited every day to chant at my sister's funeral.

Food and drink are a large part of the Thai funeral tradition. We served large meals with drinks to all the guests, throughout the seven days. Everyone wore appropriate outfits, white or black, or a mix of both.

Mum cooked every night, with lots of help from our neighbours. The common dishes for funerals are green pumpkin soup, vegetable curry, noodles and pork.

The traditional Thai funeral is more like a party, than a western funeral. Our funerals can feature barbeques, music, dance and even some gambling, spread throughout the seven days.

It was common to play funeral songs loudly, so the event can be heard from anywhere in the village. The music was our way to find joy in the funeral process.

It may seem unusual to have people celebrate so festively after a loved one's death, but it is an integral part of the Buddhist belief in reincarnation. Those who have died have not fully passed on, because they are either finding themselves in their next lives or reaching Nirvana.

'Mum, why do we have to play music so loud?'

'It's a joyous celebration of your sister's passing to the next life.'

'It must cost a fortune for the funeral.'

''I know, we give out funeral invitations, usually people will put some money in an envelope to help cover some of the cost.'

'It won't cover all the cost.'

'I know, but we can't think of that, it's our traditional funeral ceremony. Life doesn't stop at death, and that is the reason to celebrate.'

'I understand the food and soft drinks, but I don't understand why people drink whisky and gamble.'

'It's just to help people stay awake as late as they can through the night. Then Sang won't feel she is on her own, she won't feel abandoned.'

I agreed with Mum, but not about the whisky and gambling, but I didn't argue. I knew Mum believed that for Sang to move into her next life, we must follow our traditional culture. It was how Mum would find the best way to comfort her loss, through our culture.

For six nights, Dad, and my brother in law, took turns to sleep next to the coffin, after everybody left. This was so my sister knew she was not alone; we were always with her.

The cremation took place after seven days of Buddhist chanting. It is uncommon to bury our deceased. Sang was moved to a wooden casket covered with her favourite flowers.

Her name, date of birth, the date she died, and her age, was written on the middle of the casket, with her picture placed on a stand next to it.

Her ten-year-old son, Tang, ordained as a novice monk in order to make merit for his Mum. Even though it was only for a short time, he still had to do the full ordination, which included shaving his hair and eyebrows.

On the morning of the cremation there was more chanting, and then food was offered to the monks.

Once everybody had eaten, the casket was carried outside with ropes underneath and placed onto an ornate cart. The rope was then transferred to the cart, and everybody pulled it to the crematorium. I led the way carrying a portrait of Sang. A couple of monks held a white thread attached to the casket.

The casket was then placed onto a high table in front of the crematorium. My family and friends covered the table with a white cloth along with Sang's favourite flowers to honour our love.

The monks prayed during this time to prevent my sister from becoming an evil spirit.

After the Buddhist chant, we walked around the crematorium three times anti-clockwise. The men in the family then took the casket up the steps, placed it in the crematorium, and took the lid off.

A coconut was cut open and the juice poured over my sister's body. It was the last chance to see her and say good bye.

I gave each guest a flower made of wood shavings on their arrival at the crematorium, these flowers were a symbol of the funeral fire.

The monks went up the steps first with their wooden flowers. These were placed under the casket, to help start the funeral fire. Once the monks had finished, it was the turn of my family and the guests.

Most people tapped the casket a couple times with the wooden flower, then placed it in a tray under the casket, some threw it in the casket. I placed my wooden flower inside the casket, 'I forgive you for any wrong doings in the past and please forgive me too'.

After the guests had placed their wooden flowers, one of the monks lit the fire underneath. Some of the mourners left after this, but close family and friends watched until the fire had consumed the casket and burnt away to nothing.

During the fire, I looked around for Mum to comfort her, I saw her cuddling Tang. This was unusual because he was a monk, and in our culture, women do not touch monks. I saw they were both crying and cuddling each other.

We collected the ashes the next day, Mum kept them at home for the 100-day ceremony.

Buddhists believe death is a natural part of the life cycle. We believe that death simply leads to rebirth. We believe in reincarnation, that a person's spirit remains close by and seeks out a new life.

We believe that if you do good things in your life, then when you are reborn, you will have a good life, as a human or animal.

If you do bad or evil things in your life, you will be reborn as an animal with a difficult or hard life, possibly suffering a lot. You could be a human, but it will not be a happy or easy existence.

I went back to Scotland a week after funeral. After Sang's death, I sent money, monthly, to Mum for the children's education and living expenses. I continued to this because it was my culture to do it, until Sang's children were financially independent.

The only reason that I could afford to do it was because of the very high exchange rate, which meant that my wages were much higher than a comparable wage in Thailand.

It is part of my culture to look after your family first, but I felt that I had so many financial responsibilities that I could not concentrate on my own happiness. I say this not because I wanted to spend money on myself, but because these financial responsibilities prevented me progressing my divorce, leaving me trapped in an unpleasant marriage and forcing me to remain in the UK, instead of returning to Thailand.

TWENTY-FOUR

In 1999, two years after my sister's funeral, Bob approached me. 'I've got tickets for you and the children to go to Thailand, when they're off for the summer holidays next week.'

'Are you kidding, we are leaving next week?'

'Yes, here's the tickets. You're going for two months, the whole of the school summer holidays, plus two weeks afterwards.'

'How am I supposed to pack for three of us for two months in a week? The children will miss the first two weeks of the next term. What about the visa?'

'I've booked an appointment for you, for the visa, at the Royal Thai consulate tomorrow.'

'So, if it wasn't for the visa, I guess you would have told us the day before we leave? What about the doctor? Do they need any injections? You need to let the doctor know six weeks ahead, not a week! Some of the inoculations need to be done six weeks in advance.'

'Sorry, I forgot about that. I'll get plenty mosquito cream for them.'

'It's not just about mosquito's, just in case you have forgotten, Teresa has asthma and eczema.'

'I'll see John, next door, who owns the chemist first thing tomorrow morning.'

'He can't give Teresa medicine or an inhaler without a prescription.'

'He has Teresa's medical records. I'll pay him for the treatment.'

'Two months is too long for me to take care of them in Thailand. It's not a holiday for me because I have to take extra care of them. It's quite difficult, Teresa doesn't eat Thai food at all. How am I going to find her Scottish food for two months in a small village?'

'If she's hungry, she'll eat it.'

'No, she won't eat it! The temperature is far too hot for them at that time of year, it'll be over 35 degrees. Teresa can't take the sun, she goes pink.'

'Just keep them in the shade.'

'How will I keep them occupied for two months. Their Thai cousins are in school, they'll have no one to play with. They can't watch telly, they don't understand Thai.'

'I'm sure, they'll be fine.'

'They even can't go to the toilet or shower by themselves because they're not used to the wet bathrooms in Thailand. I have to go with them every time they need the toilet or a shower. I'm not looking forward to it. Of course, I would love to see my family and friends but it's too much work for me to take the girls to Thailand for two months, at that time of year.'

'Don't worry so much, you'll manage.'

Bob was quite friendly when we were discussing this, it was not his usual argumentative style at all. Looking back now, maybe I should have realised he was up to something, but it's my nature to trust people. I thought he was just keen for us to visit family back home.

Ruth, his cousin called me. 'Nuch, are you still okay to meet next Saturday?

'No, Ruth. I was going to call you tonight. Me and the girls are going to Thailand next week.'

'That's great! How long are you going for? I don't remember you mentioning that to me.'

'We're going for two months, the whole of the school summer holidays. I just found out yesterday, that's why I never mentioned it to you before.'

'How did you just find out yesterday, is everything okay in Thailand?

'We just got surprise tickets from Bob yesterday. I've got six days to pack for three of us!'

'I'm speechless; I don't know what to say.'

'Me too!' I was not surprised that Ruth was speechless. It was not normal for a father to send his wife and kids away for two months. I would cry if I didn't see my children for two months.

'Mummy, who will feed our fish?' Nicola looked worried.

'I guess your dad will.'

'Dad's always late with everything, they'll go hungry.'

'There's nothing we can do about it. I didn't want to go to Thailand for so long. Your Dad hasn't given us an option to go for a shorter period.'

'We'll have no one to play with, our cousins will be in school.'

Bob drove us to Glasgow airport. 'Dad, will you come home early to feed our fish when we're in Thailand?' Nicola was still concerned.

'Don't worry. I'll feed them every day.'

'Will you keep your promise?'

'Yes, I promise.'

'Mum cleans the tank and water every week, will you do that too?'

'Don't worry. I'll clean it every Sunday.'

It was hard work travelling with two young kids, aged four and seven. I had to keep them occupied on the twelve-hour flight, they were full of beans.

'You two better get some sleep now.' I was concerned they would be tired if they didn't sleep before we landed.

'I can't, Mum. Teresa keeps annoying me.'

'Teresa, you need to get some sleep now.'

'I don't want to, I'm not tired.'

'We're landing in four hours. I can't carry you if you're asleep when we land. You're too heavy for me now.' I was worried that I would not be able to wake her up if she decided to go to sleep in the last two hours of the flight.

'I'll just stay awake till we land, Mum.'

'Okay, if you think that you'll manage to stay awake. Stop annoying your sister, she wants to get some sleep.'

Eventually, Nicola fell asleep. I pretended to sleep and hoped Teresa would fall asleep too. Just as I feared, she fell asleep two hours before we landed. They slept through the flight breakfast.

I managed to wake Nicola, but not Teresa. She was in a deep sleep. Another passenger helped me to carry my hand luggage. I carried Teresa off the plane into the terminal. I took her to the toilet and washed her face to wake her up.

Prang met me at Bangkok Airport. We stayed with her for a couple of days to break the journey before catching another flight to my hometown, Lampang.

I took them to KFC for lunch in Lampang city centre. Every day, I bought colouring and drawing books to keep them busy.

Their cousins came home from school at 5 pm.

'Mum, why don't my cousins come and play with us after school?' Nicola asked.

'Well, children here spend more time in school and on homework than you do. They get up at 06:00 to catch the school bus at 07:00. They get back home at 17:00, by the time they finish their homework and have dinner it's 20:00.'

'We miss playing with our friends. Dad told us not to play with granny's dogs.'

'I know, your Granny's dogs never have a check-up at the vet.'

'Why doesn't Granny take them to the vet.'

'Because she has to keep money for more important stuff. There's nothing for free in Thailand.'

'I'm bored,' said Teresa.

'Okay, you can play with the dogs, you can touch only two, Numwan and Samlee. They are both friendly. Don't touch the other three, I'm not sure about them.'

I gave hand towels to Nicola and Teresa to play with the dogs. The dogs tried to pull the towels from the girls. Nicola and Teresa were running and dragging Numwan and Samlee. Mumu and Dum, the other two dogs joined in. Dang was a quiet dog, she just watched the others. They were all having a great time.

I remember, one afternoon we went to the street market. There were puppies for sale.

'Mum, we want to buy a puppy for granny.'

'I don't think so; she has five dogs already. I don't think she wants anymore.'

'Dad won't let us have a dog in Scotland. You won't let us have a dog in Thailand. That's not fair.'

'Well, I'll let you have one if it's okay with Granny, because she'll be the one who looks after her.'

As soon as we got back the girls found my Mum. 'Granny, can we have a puppy?'

'I already have five dogs. It costs me a fortune to feed them.'

'We'll send our pocket money every month for her food, please?'

Mum looked at their sad faces. Eventually, she said, 'Okay, if you promise, you'll send your pocket money for her food.' I knew Mum did not want to disappoint Nicola and Teresa. She loved dogs herself, they kept her company. Mum bathed them almost every day.

After she bathed and dried them all, she would look for ticks on their fur. They were all intelligent dogs. They lined up for their bath and tick picking.

They knew their turn, Numwan was always first, then Samlee, Mumu and Dum. Dang was always last, Mum kept shouting for her. She did not like baths, but she didn't mind the tick picking. I thought they were very clever to form a line.

Nicola and Teresa chose a four-week-old Rottweiler puppy. 'Mum, we want this one. He's so cute.'

'That's a Rottweiler pup he'll grow into a massive dog.'

'Yes, we know, we want a guard dog to protect Granny.' It was very thoughtful of the girls. Mum was by herself most of time in the big house. Dad lived in small house on his land ten minutes' drive away. He did not like living in a big house.

'What are you going to call him?'

'We're going to call him, Scott.'

'That's a very nice name.'

'We thought, we live in Scotland, it would be nice to call him, Scott.' Nicola and Teresa loved looking after their new puppy. They had five dogs and a puppy to keep them busy.

One day, late in the afternoon, Teresa had a problem with her breathing. 'Mum, I can't breathe.' She was panicking.

I put her inhaler in her mouth, pressed down on it quickly to release the medicine. 'Breathe in slowly for three to five seconds. Hold your breath, count to ten slowly for medicine to go deeply into your lungs'

'I still can't breathe properly. I'm going to die....'

'Don't cry, it's not helping. You need to stay calm, panicking will make things worse. You're not going to die.' I knew, it was not easy to tell a four-year-old girl to stay calm.

I gave her five puffs, one minute between them. She did not get any better, I took her to a private hospital in the city centre. The doctor saw her quickly, she needed a breathing tube to pump oxygen into her lungs.

While I was waiting for Teresa to finish her treatment, I saw a boy about the same age as Teresa. He was suffering from an allergic reaction, with lumps over his face and body. His eyes were almost closed with the swelling.

I overheard the nurse say to his parents. 'We need to keep him overnight to do tests before we can give him specific antibiotics.'

'What happens if we don't' want him to stay overnight?'

'We can give you general antibiotics but we're not sure that's going to work because we don't know what he's allergic to.'

'How much for a bed to stay overnight?'

'One thousand, five hundred baht.'

'We don't have enough money, we can only afford the general antibiotics.'

'Okay, I'll sort out the antibiotics for you. Can you go to the cashier and pay for your examination and the drugs?'

I could not imagine what I would do if that happened to Teresa and I could not pay for her treatment. It was heart-breaking. I walked toward them after the nurse left. 'Hi, I couldn't help but overhear the nurse's conversation. Here is two thousand baht to keep your son overnight.'

'That's very generous of you, but we don't know when we can pay you back.'

'You don't have to pay me back, I don't need it.'

'Thank you so much.' They had tears in their eyes. They said to the nurse that they would keep their son in overnight. I was happy that I could help them.

'Mum, why did you give money to strangers?'

'Their son wasn't well. They didn't have money to pay for the correct treatment.'

'What happens here if you don't have enough money.'

'They just send them home.'

'Well, they shouldn't tell the nurse they don't have enough money.'

'You have to pay the bill first before they give you treatment, not treatment first.'

'Do we pay for the hospital in Scotland?'

'No, we don't have to pay for hospitals or schools.'

'Wow, we're lucky.'

'Yes, some people in the UK don't realise how lucky they are, they take things for granted.'

After an hour's treatment in hospital, Teresa was getting better. I took her back home.

A week before we were due back in Scotland, Bob called me. 'I've got something to tell you but please don't tell the children till they're home.'

'Let me guess, you were too busy to feed the fish and they're all dead.'

'Yes, the fish are all dead. I fed them every day, or Dad did, if I was not home.'

'They wouldn't be dead, if you fed them every day.' I knew he was lying.

'I'm sorry. Please don't tell them, I don't want to spoil their holiday.'

'I'll leave it to you to tell them.' I felt sorry for those fish, they starved to death.

I could not imagine how Nicola and Teresa would feel when they found out all their fish were dead. They fed and talked to them every day.

He picked us up at Glasgow airport. He started telling them about the fish on the way home. 'I'm sorry, I've got a bad news for you.'

'Did something happen to one of our fish.'

'I'm sorry, they're all dead.'

'You promised us, you would feed them every day.' They started to cry.

169

'I fed them every day. I think, the water was dirty, it looked cloudy.'

'Did you change the water?'

'I did, but sometimes the water just got dirty or the oxygen wasn't working properly. I'm sorry.'

'We've never had any pets. You won't allow us to have a dog. Now our fish are all dead.'

'I'm sorry, I can't say anymore, maybe you can have more fish in the future.'

'That's not the point.' Nicola was not going to let him away with his excuses.

They ran to the fish tank when they arrived home. It was empty, no fish, no water. Nicola walked upstairs to her bedroom. She came downstairs with a piece of paper. 'Mum, could you please post this letter to God for me?'

'Okay honey, I'll put it in envelope and post it for you.'

I read the letter before I put it in the envelope.

Dear God,

Could you please look after Golden, Chocolate and Orange for Teresa and me. We were so sorry that we did not get a chance to say good bye because we were in Thailand.

Dad told us that the oxygen machine was broken that caused the water to become poisonous when he was at work. They were all dead when he arrived home. There was nothing, he could do to save them.

Please tell them that we love them very much.

Nicola and Teresa xxooxx

I was so sad reading the letter. I knew he was too busy to have a meal with his children, never mind feeding the fish.

TWENTY-FIVE

Not long after we came back from Thailand, I had a phone call from Martin. 'How was your holiday with the girls?'

'It was great, the girls had a nice time apart from the heat. It was too hot for them.'

'It was quite a long trip in that heat.'

'I didn't plan it. Bob just booked surprise tickets for us.'

'I know why he sent you and the girls away for two months.'

'Why?'

'He was planning to sell the house when you were away.'

'Are you kidding, right?'

'No, I'm not kidding. He contacted an estate agent to come to see the house during your holiday. Luckily, they can't go ahead without your agreement.'

I was in shock, I could not believe that he was thinking to sell our family home without telling me and the girls.

'Are you thinking of selling our family home?' I asked him after work.

'Yes, I'm just trying to make extra income by selling our house and then buying a smaller one for us. We could buy another house or flat to rent out with the money left over.'

'Don't you think that you should discuss it with me first, instead of doing it behind my back?'

'How do you know?'

'It doesn't matter how I know. It matters to me that you did it behind my back.'

'I just wanted to know how much the house was worth before I told you.'

'Whatever the reason is, I'm your wife, and the mother of your children. You should show me some respect.'

I was upset, I wished he had discussed it with the girls and I, instead of us hearing it from someone else. I knew that he was up to something when he got rid of us for two months, but I never thought for one second that he will sell our family home behind our backs.

His business trouble started in early 2000. He did not have much turnover, and had lots of bills to pay, such as rent, heating, electric, and wages for over fifty staff in seven shops.

'I didn't have such a good turnover over the past couple of years.' He said to me one Sunday.

'I told you from the start that you make more than enough with the two shops in Glasgow and Edinburgh. I knew it would be too much for you to keep an eye on all seven shops, especially with such a huge distance between them. If you had listened to me from the start, you wouldn't be in this situation.'

'I hired a manager for each shop, I thought I could trust them.'

'Maybe, the person you should have trusted and listened to, was your wife. Obviously, you didn't, anyway, why are you telling me now?'

'Because you're still my wife, and I'm looking for a support.'

'I'm your wife, but what about these women you've been seeing? How dare you look for my support after what you've put me through.'

'Because I'm the father of your kids, and will always be, no matter what.'

'That's good, can you tell me what the father's role in the family is?'

'I take care of all the bills.'

'Is it that all, taking care of the bills?'

'No.'

'What's else then? I know, you're struggling to give me more answers. By the way, about the bills, I did offer to help to pay some of the bills, but I asked you to show me how much you made and share your financial information. You refused to do it, you preferred to keep everything secret, which is quite worrying.'

I walked away from the conversation. I was worried but did not want to show my concern. Of course, his business was my children's future. I could not sleep at night.

I started running to try and sleep better. I ran everyday no matter what the weather. It became addictive, and soon I could not sleep without running. It was hard, at first, because I was not good at sports.

I started running fifteen minutes on my first day. I built up ten minutes more, each day, until I could run two and half hours without stopping.

A few months later he confessed to me. 'My business is going bust soon. I need you to go and open a bank account in Thailand.'

'Why?'

'I need to put money away, somewhere safe, as much as I can.'

'How will you get money if your business is going bust?'

'You don't have to know, it's too complicated to explain.'

'Why don't you put it in the children's accounts here.'

'I could only put some in there, I'll put thirty thousand in each of their accounts tomorrow.'

It was too complicated for me to understand when he kept everything secret from me, and had done so, since met.

I went to Thailand and opened a six-month, fixed saving account. I remember, the interest was quite high, thirteen percent at the time. He transferred twenty million Thai baht into my account, about £300,000.

A few months later Martin called me. 'He told me that he's hidden money in your account in Thailand, and some more in the children's accounts here.'

'That's correct, both children's accounts are joint accounts with me.'

'You should take the children back to Thailand. You can live on the interest; you won't have to work for the rest of your life.'

'I don't have the children's passports. He's hidden them somewhere.'

'Just go without them first, then come back for them later.'

'I can't leave them, I can't walk away from them. Even if I had their passports, I can't take them away from their school, their friends, their grandparents, and their dad. It's not right.'

'Listen! The way he treated you is completely wrong! They'll learn Thai and meet new friends there. This is your only chance to go without fighting with him.'

'I know…'

'You've got a life too, don't be stupid. You need to think about your happiness. I'm his friend, I know what he can be like. He has been saying that he'll not let you have a penny from his businesses.'

Martin was right, that was my only chance to walk away from him without fighting for my life. I started searching for the children's passports. The only place I could they might be was in his parents' house. I was lucky enough to find them hidden in a bedroom drawer.

I kept questioning myself, what made me happiest in my life? The answer was, my children.

In the end, I did not go, I just couldn't bear the thought of them asking me, 'Mummy, when are we going home, we miss our dad, our grandparents, our friends.' I sacrificed my happiness for my children's happiness.

A year later his business went bust. Somebody he knew took over the shop in Glasgow, and hired him to run it, but it was no longer his business.

Two years later, in 2002, after everything settled down and nobody was trying to trace his cash, he asked me to transfer money back to his account in Scotland.

He also asked me to transfer money from the children's accounts to his. 'Everything has settled down now. I would like you to transfer the money in Thailand back to my account in Scotland.'

'When do you want it?'

'As soon as possible, I'm looking for a ticket for you just now.'

'Okay, because you're so secretive, I suppose there's no point in asking you, what you're going to do with all the money.'

'Will you transfer the money from the children's accounts back to mine too?'

'Don't you think you should keep it in their account for their future?'

'I need it to start a new business.'

'Okay, I won't waste my time asking you what business?' I never did find out what business he started, such was the level of secrecy he maintained.

The following day, I transferred money from the children's accounts back to his account. I flew back to Thailand for two weeks, and while I was there, I transferred all the money back to his account.

Looking back now, if I had known what was coming, then maybe, I would not have been so quick to transfer every penny back to him. I was too trusting, and too naïve.

TWENTY-SIX

When both children were in primary school, I enrolled on a, one-year, part-time computer course, The European Computer Driving Licence (ECDL), at Cardonald College.

I passed all seven modules, IT user fundamentals, using email and the internet, security for IT users, word processing, spreadsheet software, presentation software and database software.

I was very proud of myself, studying and passing, in my second language, had been hard work.

I wanted to go back to work as a hotel receptionist, so in 2003, I enrolled myself on a two-year course, an HND Front Office course, at the City of Glasgow College.

There were twenty-five students in my class. I had to study harder than the rest, because I was the only one whose English was not their mother tongue.

I was so proud of myself when I received the outstanding achievement certificate after completing my course. I was the only one who passed all the subjects with merit.

I remember, before the college, I searched for a job. It was so hard to get a start somewhere without a previous employer 's reference, and without UK qualifications. Also, the fact, English is not my first language, played a big part in job refusals.

Things were different now because of my outstanding achievement certificate, I received a job offer, as a hotel receptionist, in the Normandy Hotel, Glasgow.

I was so happy with the job offer, I thought it was not a bad start. I was not worried about the job role because I was familiar with it. I was more worried about the working rota. There were three round shifts, 07:00-15:00, 15:00-23:00, 23:00-07:00. I needed help to have the time to commit to it.

I had no problem with the first shift. Bob reluctantly took the kids to school, I collected them after I finished work. For the second shift, his mum or dad collected the kids from school and looked after them till he finished work.

He had to come home before I left for work so I could go to the third shift. I thought, surely, he will not have any problems getting home before 23:00. Especially now it was no longer his own business.

A month later I was proved wrong. 'You need to get a babysitter. I don't want to come home early to look after the children. I make much more than you, so my work is more important.'

'It's not fair, they're your children too.'

'As I said, I don't want to come home early.'

'It's not early, your mum or dad pick them up from school.'

'I don't want to keep them late and I have to take them back to their house.'

'Why don't you get a babysitter?'

'It's your job that affects me, you should be the one who gets a babysitter.'

'It's not right to say that, it's your job too, and your children.'

'You're a mother, it's your job to look after them.'

In the end, I had to give up my job because he refused to come home early to look after the children.

I started looking for a job that finished by 15.00 to allow me to collect the girls from school.

In 2005, he wanted to sell our family home. He handed me the paperwork and a pen. 'Will you sign this paperwork for me?'

'What is it?'

'The agreement to sell the house.'

'I need some time to think about it. It's our children's future.'

'It was my money that bought the house. So, it's up to me, I can do whatever I want.'

'If that's the way you are going to talk to me, then I won't sign any papers.'

He squeezed my jaw hard, banged my head against the wall and threw me back against the table. 'Just sign the papers!' He shouted.

I was crying, shaking, in fear for my life. I signed the agreement.

'I'll leave it to you to tell the children.'

'I'm going to sell our house.' He said to the girls.

'Why do you want to sell it? We love our house. We don't want to move away from our friends.' Nicola was not keen.

'I want to buy a smaller house. I'll use half of the money to buy another house to rent out.'

'I don't understand why you want two houses.'

'One for us to live in, and one to rent out.'

'Why do you want another house to rent out?'

'I want to save up for your future.'

'Where are we going to move to?

'I don't know yet. We'll look around together.'

'I won't see Laura and Nadine again after we move away.'

'Don't worry, I'll take you to visit them, or they can come to visit you.'

It was heart breaking for the girls and me. I felt so sorry for them, but there was nothing I could do about it.

The estate agent came to take pictures for the brochure. There was no for sale sign up in front of the house. The estate agent agreed to only send people who could afford to look at it.

Only three families came to look, one offered £700,000, we accepted. We had to move out within four weeks. I was worried how we were going to find a house within a month, never mind organising the packing.

'How are we going to find a house within four weeks?'

'Don't worry, I started to look a month ago. I think I've found one that is suitable for us.'

'So, you've found one yourself, without involving us?'

'I'm not buying it, it's a rental house. Don't tell the girls that it's a rental house. I don't want to worry and upset them.'

'Are you telling me that you want to waste money on renting every month?'

'Just temporarily until we find somewhere suitable to buy.'

'We? Or do you mean you?'

'Us and the children.'

'I don't believe you. How much for the rent? And where?'

'Newton Mearns, just ten minutes' drive up the road the road. It's £1,200 per month.'

'How many bedrooms?'

'Four, I'll show it to you and the girls tomorrow.'

The next day, he took us to see the house. It was a lovely house with four bedrooms upstairs, one en suite. Downstairs there was a living room, dining room, office, kitchen and washing room.

It had a double garage, with great front and back gardens. I had no doubt that it was going to be a lovely home for us, but I wondered why he wanted to with waste money renting every month.

'Do you realise all our furniture won't fit in this house?'

'I know.'

'What are you going to do?'

'I'll leave some at Mum and Dad's house.'

'I don't know what I should do about packing, now you're telling me that I have to pack for two places.'

'I'll help you as much as I can.'

I started to take some stuff I did not need to the charity shop. There were too many things to pack. It was difficult to decide what to keep and what to give to the charity shop, what to pack for granny's house and what to move to our new house. It was stressful. He never did help, I was not surprised.

A month later, we moved to our new home. I had an en-suite bedroom. He had the smallest bedroom in the back of the house. Teresa chose the pink bedroom at the front, Nicola had a blue bedroom, also at the front.

'Mum, I don't like blue, it's for a boy. Can I change the colour?'

'It's a good question. Why don't you ask your dad? I knew, she could not change the colour because it was a rental house.

'Dad, I don't like blue, I want to change the colour.'

'Why don't you like blue?'

'It's a boy's colour.'

'I don't think so, it's for both boys and girls.'

'I don't mind sky-blue, but I don't like navy-blue.'

'Maybe later on, okay.'

'That's not fair. Mum asked me to let Teresa chose first and I did. She chose the pink one, I ended up with blue. My friends will laugh at me, blue is for boys.'

'Do you want to swap with me? My bedroom is white.'

'No, your bedroom is smaller than mine.'

'Well, you can't have it both ways. You have to wait.'

'It's not fair!'

Nicola was upset, I did not like telling a lie. I wished I could tell her the truth. 'Everything is new to you, just give yourself some time to adjust. How about this, after three months, if you still don't like it, we'll think of something else.' I gave her a cuddle and hoped she would forget about it.

A couple months later I successfully applied for a full-time job, as an office assistant in a family bakery business for Costa in Livingston, about forty minutes' drive from Glasgow. I worked Monday – Friday, 07:00 – 15:00.

I knew it was a long distance from Glasgow and an expensive commute, but I needed to start somewhere, I kept looking for jobs in Glasgow.

I was up by 05:30, which was too early for me to help the girls get ready for school. I was concerned because he was often staying away overnight.

'You never come home before midnight, or you don't come back at all. Where are you sleeping?'

'With my friend.'

'Male friend or female?'

'Male.'

'Does he have a family?'

'Of course, he is married.'

'Is it ok with his wife that you hang out with him until midnight and sleepover most nights?'

'We're close friends.'

'I don't believe you.'

'That's up to you, anyway, we agreed that we'll live separate lives.'

'Yes, I don't care if you come home or not. But, I want you to be home every morning to make sure the girls are up for school, and make sure you give them breakfast too.'

'Why don't you do it?'

'I'm starting a new job in Livingston on Monday. I have to leave the house by six o'clock in the morning. If you can't do it or start not turning up, I'll see a lawyer for a divorce, I had to give up my last job because you were so unreliable. You don't pay nearly enough maintenance, but you won' t allow me to work. It's very controlling behaviour, and it is extremely stressful.'

He did not reply.

Nicola was thirteen and Teresa was ten, they caught the school bus five-minute's walk up the road.

Teresa became friendly with a boy in her class, John, who lived opposite. His mother, Mandy was lovely. 'Don't worry if you're late from work, I'll keep them after school until you're back.' Mandy said to me.

I said to Nicola, 'If I'm not in, it's fine to go to Mandy's house, but if you're here, don't answer the phone, or open the door to anybody.'

'Don't worry, Mum.'

John and Teresa were close friends, he often came around to play, and Teresa also went to his place.

Teresa asked me one day, 'Mum, can John stay overnight this weekend?'

'Where's he going to sleep? We don't have a spare bedroom.'

'In my bedroom, he's got a sleeping bag.'

'I don't think it's a good idea.'

'Why not?'

'He's a boy and you're a girl.'

'I can't see the problem.'

'I'm sorry; boys are not allowed to sleepover.'

'Can I sleep over in John's house instead?'

'No, you can't sleepover with a boy.'

'That's not fair!'

Teresa was disappointed. I knew nothing would happen, but I just thought it was not a good idea.

I was not allowed out after 18:00, until I finished college, never mind sleep overs with a boy!

'Mum, we're not living in Thailand and we're not Thai.' Nicola was annoyed, they both gave me a hard time.

They made even worse comments when I asked them to do the dishes or tidy up.

'You've had a tough life, Mum. It doesn't mean, we have to have a tough life too.'

Honestly, I was not sure wither to laugh or cry, I was proud of my upbringing, and tried to bring up the girls the same way.

Around that time, I came back from work and saw Teresa was in the house alone.

'Where's Nicola?'

'She's not back from school yet.'

'Why are you back before her?'

'I didn't go to school today.'

'Are you sick?'

'No, Dad said, it's okay, I don't have to go to school today.'

'Did he say why?'

'He said, I could take a day off.'

I was curious, I decided to call later to find out why he said that. I took off Teresa's clothes to give her a bath, I saw bruise on her arm. 'What happened to your arm?'

'Dad hit me.'

'Is that why you didn't go to school?'

'No, he said, I could take a day off.'

I called him straight away. 'Did you hit Teresa?'

'Yes, I'm sorry. She was naughty, I lost my temper.'

'You only look after them in the morning before school and you can't handle it. I look after them every day on my own, you're never here to help.'

'I'm sorry. You do a good job.'

'Why didn't you send her to school?'

'She had gym today, I was afraid the teacher would notice the bruise when she got changed.'

'I put up with your violence, but I won't put up with it towards our daughters. If I see any more bruises, I'll take them to the police!'

'I'm sorry, it won't happen again.'

Teresa has a really strong personality. She would answer us back every time. She always wanted her own way. Nicola is the opposite, it is true, you never have two the same.

TWENTY-SEVEN

The girls always wanted a pet. I thought it was too much work for me, a mother of two, and in full time employment.

'Mum, can we have a puppy?' Nicola asked this time, although it was a common question from both.

'It's too much commitment to have a dog. It needs a walk at least twice per day.'

'We'll take it for a walk before school and after school.'

'Maybe, when I see you are ready to take on responsibilities.'

'What about a rabbit? We don't have to take them for a walk.'

'I don't know, I don't like seeing anything locked up in a cage.'

'We can let it out in the garden, sometimes, please?'

'Okay if you promise, you'll clean the cage. If you take responsibility for the rabbit, maybe, one day I'll let you have a puppy.'

'Yes, thank you. We love you.'

I had never had a rabbit before. I did not think it would take too much work to look after it, just making sure it had hay, food and water.

I took the girls to the pet shop at the weekend.

'Mum, can we have one each?'

'No, only one, to see how you get on.'

'You don't want to be by yourself, do you?'

'Listen, if you have two rabbits in the same cage before you know, there will be babies everywhere.'

'We can just have two girls or two boys.'

'But we don't know which one is a girl, which one is a boy. It's hard to tell.'

Teresa said, 'Don't be silly, we just make sure that they're brother and sister.'

'That's enough arguing, you're allowed one, total.'

The girls chose a white rabbit, they called her Avalanche. They also bought a rabbit harness to take it for a walk after school!

Since 2000, I had been running every day after work. I like to keep myself busy, it helped me sleep. Now, I found it hard to go to sleep without running.

I did a race twice a year, a 10 K and a half marathon. Eventually, my ankles became sore, I made an appointment to see the doctor.

'When did you start running?' He asked.

'Six years ago,'

'How often, and how long is each run?'

'Every day, roughly two hours.

'You're forty, running two hours a day is not good. You're overdoing it. If you're going to run two hours a day, three times a week is the maximum you should do to prevent injury.

'I can't go to sleep if I don't run. I have to run every day.'

'You need to do another sport in between, such as swimming.'

I agreed with the doctor, I tried to think of another sport, between my running days.

I was not good at swimming. I could not ride a bike. I was not good at any sports. I failed PE in school every year, I only passed on because Mum bribed the teacher!

One evening I watched a programme about climbing. I saw the climbers were slim and fit. I was slim, I was must be fit too, otherwise I would not be able to run for two hours every day.

The next day, I decided to book an introductory climbing course at the Glasgow Climbing Centre. I remember well, it was on the 6th May 2006. I have been a keen climber since. It keeps me alive; it keeps me going.

Ten months after working in Livingston, I started an admin job in Marks and Spencers, Glasgow. It was full time employment, Monday – Friday, 07:00 – 15:00. I was less tired with the shorter journey to work. I could stay in bed a bit longer, and I was always home before the girls were back from school, it was great.

One day Teresa asked. 'Mum, where are we going for our summer holidays?'

'Don't you want to visit your Thai grandparents and your Thai cousins?'

'We go to Thailand every year. I want to go to Disneyland. I don't remember much about it, when we went last time, I was only four.'

'Yes, you were four and Nicola was seven.' I agreed with her, she could not remember much.

'Can we go again please?'

'I need to ask your Dad first, because I need help, I can't keep my eyes on you both.'

I did not want to spend time with him on holiday. But, I did not have a choice because most of the rides in Disneyland had only two seats. If I sat with Teresa, Nicola would have to sit by herself, or with a stranger.

I asked him the following Sunday, it was the only day in a week that I saw him. 'The girls want to go to Disneyland this summer.'

'That's good, why don't you just take them?'

'I can't go alone with them.'

'Why not? You go to Thailand with them every summer.'

'This is different, Disneyland is always busy, crowded with people. I can't keep an eye on both of them. Also, most of the rides have two seats. I'll sit with Teresa, and you can sit with Nicola. I don't want her to sit with a stranger or by herself, especially on those roller coasters.'

'I'm busy and I don't have any money.'

'You know, I only ask you when I have to. You don't have to pay a penny, I'll pay for everything! If you're too busy for a free holiday with your children, you can tell them yourself.'

I was so disappointed; I did not like to upset the girls. I could not think of a good excuse to explain why their dad would not go with them.

'Hey, we're going to Thailand, okay.' I told the girls.

'No, we want to go to Disneyland.' Teresa was not happy.

'Your Dad says he couldn't take two weeks off work.'

'I know, he said he's working to pay for our holidays.'

'Is that what he said to you?' I could not believe what I just heard.

'Yes, that's what he told us.'

'Why don't you ask him again? Tell him, I have offered to pay for everything from my wages. I did offer this before when I discussed it with him.'

The sad thing is I did not know if the children believed me or not. Looking back now, I think that he was quite critical of me towards the children, but I did not realise the extent of it, at the time.

I never did anything to the children that would jeopardise their relationship with their father. I have never indulged in that type of behaviour, whatever he did, he was still their father, and very important to them.

Eventually, he agreed to go with us. I booked our holiday with Thomas Cook in Newton Mearns shopping centre, on the last week of June 2006, when the children finished school. I booked a hotel in Disneyland, so we did not have to travel far every day. It was convenient, with a free bus shuttle to the park every fifteen minutes. I booked a family room, Nicola slept with me, Teresa shared with her dad.

I tried my best to have a happy family holiday. But, no matter how much I tried, we did not get along. We spent most of the time apart.

On the third day, it just got too much, I did not want the children to see us arguing, it was not good for them, and I did not want it to spoil their holiday.

'I'm sorry girls, I have done my best to do everything together, but it's really hard. Teresa, you come with me, Nicola, you go with your dad.'

'No, mum, I want to go with you and Theresa.' Nicola said.

Teresa said, 'I'll go with dad then, I don't want him to be by himself.'

He was lucky to have such a warm-hearted daughter. I remember, one night, we had a disagreement, he squeezed my jaw hard to force me to look at him. He broke my thumb when I tried to break his grip on my chin.

I had to see the hotel doctor because I was in so much pain. I told him that I fell. I never told the girls about their father's violence towards me. Look back now, I was stupid. He was clever enough not to abuse me in front of the girls.

He knew that I was a good mother, and I would not tell them, because that would upset them. He knew their well-being was paramount for me.

When we came back from holiday, we went to collect Avalanche from the girls' grandparents.

After a few days, it had become extremely hot, so, I left the windows slightly open. I cannot bear the thought of any animal being in a cage. I often left the cage open for Avalanche to run about downstairs.

'Mum, I can't find Avalanche.' Nicola shouted.

'Have you searched every room?'

'Yes, she's not in the house.'

'She must have got out somehow.' I helped the girls to look in very room but there was no sign of her anywhere

'Did you leave the windows open, Mum?'

'Yes, for fresh air. The opening is too small for Avalanche to get out.' I was sure Avalanche could never have squeezed through the small gap.

'Well, most rabbits are able to fit their bodies through three centimetres gaps.' Nicola said.

'How do you know?'

'I read a book about rabbits.'

'I'm really sorry honey; I didn't know that, otherwise I would have put her back in her cage before I opened the windows.' I felt bad, I should have realised she would be able to get out.

'Mum, we're going out to look for Avalanche in the garden, and around the neighbours' houses.'

They went out to look for Avalanche. I did not think, she would survive outside because she was a house rabbit. But, I did not want them to give up without looking for her first, so I let them go.

'Mum, we've looked everywhere and asked our neighbours, no one has seen her.' Nicola said.

'She'll be fine, she probably prefers freedom to being locked in her cage.'

'She's a house rabbit, Mum. She won't survive in the woods.'

'She'll learn to survive, there's nothing we can do about it now.'

'We want a new pet. We want a puppy this time. We'll take our responsibilities seriously. Granny has six dogs; you and my aunties had a puppy each when you were a kid. Why can't we just have one? It's not fair.' Nicola was annoyed, and desperate for a puppy.

'It's not much work to have dogs in Thailand. It's hot all year round. They live outside, you don't have to take them for a walk.'

'We'll take it out before and after school.'

'Okay, you need to ask your Dad first.'

I could not see that he would agree with the girls having a dog. In fact, he was never in the house to take any responsibility, so I suppose it made no difference to him if we had one or not.

TWENTY-EIGHT

I was still doing Bob's washing and ironing, even though we were not a couple anymore. After two years in our rented house, I could not help noticing that the amount of his washing became less and less. I decided to open his wardrobe, it was almost empty, there were only a couple of shirts.

I rang him. 'I want to talk to you about our rental home.'

'What about it?'

'Why has it taken you over three years to find a house to buy?'

'I'm still looking for one.'

'I know you're lying. You never take the girls and I to see any houses. I don't see why you want to waste money every month. I'm talking about £1,200 per month, £14,400 per year. Now you have already paid £43,200 for rent.'

'I try my best.'

'No, you don't try hard enough, you're up to something.'

'What do you mean?'

'You rent a house for us, but I don't know if you have bought another house to live in with somebody else. What's going on?'

'Don't be stupid!'

'I know you are up to something, but is whatever you are up to more important than buying a house for your children to secure their future in case something happens to you?'

'I'm looking!'

'Why don't we just get a divorce? It's not good for the girls seeing us argue all the time. Even though we don't see each other, we still argue on the phone.'

'I told you, I'll give you a divorce when I'm ready. I can't see the problem, I'm still paying all your bills.'

'Stop talking rubbish, you don't pay all my bills. Who do you think pays for the children's clothes, holidays, cinema, toys, games, presents for their friends' birthdays, petrol for driving them around? I buy them a Chinese take away every Friday night and I take them out for a meal every Saturday. You should be paying a proper amount to me based on your income.'

'I pay for the rent, council tax, electric and gas bill, and internet.'

'The rent, it's your choice to pay rent, because you forced me out of our family home, and sold it. I don't know what you've done with the money from that, where you live or what's going on? I'm not paying rent because you've forced me out of a house which I owned.'

'I do my best.'

'I've told you before, I have no problem to pay my share, if you show me your bank statement, how much your income is each month, and how much the bills are each month. We need to reach an agreement about the money from the sale of our house which you have kept for yourself. You're secretive, you've never treated me like a wife.'

He did not reply.

I wondered why he wanted to stay married. I was sure he had already bought a house with someone else. I thought it was impossible that there was someone else who was more important than his children, but he spent virtually no time with them.

The girls kept asking me. 'Mum, we want a puppy, please.'

'Have you asked your dad?' I do not know why I said that to the girls, he was never in the house, but I thought, he's their father, he should give his permission for a dog. I suppose I wanted the girls to be brought up properly, despite all these issues, and they should ask their father if it was okay to have a dog.

Teresa replied. 'He said, no. But Mum, we really want a puppy. Can you help us make him change his mind, please?'

I decided enough was enough. 'Your dad is hardly ever home, he has no responsibility around the house. If you two want a puppy, you can have it.' I wanted to say he took no responsibility for his children, never mind a dog.

'Really Mum, we can have a puppy?'

'Yes, you can have a puppy.'

'We love you.'

The girls were pleased and gave me cuddles. We looked through the pet newspapers for a puppy for sale.

'What breed of puppy do you have in mind? I asked the girls.

'I want a golden retriever just like Numwan.' Teresa said, she liked my mum's big dog.

'I want a Dalmatian just like the film 101 Dalmatians.' Nicola said.

'Well, I think, the golden retriever is quite sweet and calm. The Dalmatian is highly energetic, playful, and needs lots of exercise.'

'We don't mind either of them.' Nicola said.

I hoped that I had made the right decision to let the girls have a puppy. I would love to have a dog myself, but I was worried that one day it might become too much responsibility for me.

I worked full time, and I had my exercise routine, running or climbing every day, after work.

We saw one advertisement that caught our eye.

A beautiful litter of Dalmatian puppies have been born, black and white spotted, boys and girls available, mother is KC registered full BAER hearing and father is full BAER hearing.

Please enquire for more information, will only sell to wanted, loving homes, will be ready to leave 15th May 2009. These puppies have been raised with children.

'Mum, look at this picture. They're all so cute. Can you call to arrange to see the puppies?'

'Yes, they're all lovely, I'll give the owner a ring.' I called and arranged for the girls to see them.

'We can go to see the puppies this weekend.' I told the girls.

'We're so excited! Mum, we need to get stuff for it.' Teresa said.

'What do we need? We need to make a list before we go to the pet shop.' I was thinking aloud. 'We need a comfy bed, puppy food and treats, water and food bowls, leash, harness, collar, toys.' I did not realise that there were so many things to get.

The next day, after school, I took the girls to the pet shop and bought everything we needed.

At the weekend, I took them to see the puppies. We took one back home, it was a boy and we called it 'Domino'. He was four weeks old, he was big for his age, and we liked the pattern of his spots the best.

I spent over £1000 altogether, Domino was £600, but there was a lot more to pay for, such as food, insurance, and vet bills.

I ordered a personalised collar, a t-shirt, and a towel online. He was so adorable, we loved him to bits.

Bob was back home in the morning. 'Where did you get the puppy? He asked the girls.

'Mum bought it, she said, we can have a puppy.'

'I told you not to, why didn't you listen to me?'

'Mum said, we can have a puppy.'

'Why did you get them a puppy?' He turned to me.

'Because we want it, it's our responsibility, not yours. You're hardly in the house.'

'You can take it back tomorrow.'

'No! Why can't we just have a puppy, dad?' They both were crying.

'From the start, you didn't listen to me when I said no. This house isn't designed for having a dog. It'll destroy the furniture in the house.'

'We have the back garden for him to run about. We'll keep him in the kitchen, and in the washing room if we're not in.'

'There's a dining table in the kitchen. He'll chew the table and chairs.'

'We promise that we'll keep an eye on him.'

'Okay, if he starts to chew the furniture, he has to go.'

'Thank you, daddy.'

Nicola and Teresa were very happy. They took their responsibility well, they took Domino out for a walk before and after school. They spent most of their time playing with him after school.

'He's not a toy, you need to put him down sometimes.' I felt sorry for him, sometimes he wanted peace to sleep.

'We love him, Mum.' Theresa said.

'I know, but sometimes he just wants to be free. Look at your arms, Domino's scratch and tooth marks are everywhere.' He had strong jaws.

'I can't help it, he's so adorable.'

'Well, you wouldn't like it if I cuddled you all the time.'

'Okay, I get it, Mum.'

When Domino was ten weeks old, he was big and strong for his age. He was very energetic and playful. He did not like to be left alone. I worked full time; the girls were at school all day. He started chewing the dining table, chairs and kitchen units when he was bored. Bob was not very happy, he said to the girls. 'I'm sorry, he has to go.'

'No! dad, you can't do that. You can't take him away from us. He's our dog.' Nicola and Teresa were crying loudly.

'I can't have him destroy the furniture.'

'He's still a puppy, he won't do it when he gets older. Just like us when we were toddlers, we did things that we were not meant to do. Give him a chance please, dad.'

Bob was not very happy, he turned to me. 'This's all your fault! You should have listened to me!'

'I've listened to you all my life! This is not just about me, it's about the girls too.'

'You encouraged them to get the dog against my wishes! I'll get rid of him.'

'Don't you dare break their hearts.'

'It's all your fault, you shouldn't have gone against me in the first place!'.

I was worried, I knew that he could get rid of the dog. I could not imagine how the girls and I would feel.

A coupler of days later, I came back in from work, there was no sign of Domino. The girls were still in school, so it was not possible that they had taken him out for a walk. My heart sank, I had a feeling that Bob had got rid of him. I rang him to find out.

'What did you do with Domino?'

'I gave him to a new family.'

'How did you find a new family for him?'

'I put an advert in the local newspaper.'

'Have you told the girls?'

'No.'

'Did you think how they would feel when they came back from school and Domino's no longer here?'

'I thought, it would be better to give him away when they aren't there. They would be more upset if they saw him leaving.'

'Well, make sure you're home when they're back from school. You can tell them yourself.'

I was really upset; I could not imagine how the girls would feel. I knew Bob would not be home before the girls. It would be my job to break their hearts.

They came back from school. I had to tell them before they ran to the kitchen to see Domino.

'Listen, I need to tell you something before you go to the kitchen. I'm really sorry, Domino's no longer here.'

'I don't believe you, Mum.' They both ran to the kitchen.

'Where is Domino, Mum?' They both asked, I could see they were terribly upset.

'I'm sorry, he wasn't here when I came home from work. Your Dad's given him away to someone else.'

Nicola and Teresa could not stop crying. Bob came back home a couple of hours later. They went straight to him.

'What did you do with Domino?' They demanded.

'I gave him to a new family.'

'Why did you do that? He's our pet, we want him back.'

'I'm sorry, he destroyed the furniture. I want him to be with a family that can give him a lot of attention, that's what he needs. He's left alone all day in the house. It's not fair on him.'

'Whatever you did, it's not fair on us. We didn't even get a chance to say goodbye. Will you take us to see him?'

'No, I'm sorry. It would be better if you don't see him now. I'll take you to see him in a couple months, not now, okay.'

'You're cruel.' Nicola said.

'I did the best for him. His new family already have another dog. He has another dog to play with, and two children. The mother works part time, so there's someone in the house with him.'

'You've broken our heart. We don't want to speak to you.'

The girls were really upset, they spent most of their time in the bedroom. They did not have dinner that night, they did not come downstairs to watch television.

It turned out, I was more upset than the girls. I could not cope well with the guilt and grief. I could not eat, I could not sleep. I could not stop thinking about him.

I treated him like one of my children. I gave him the same food as us. If we had salmon, he had salmon. If we had steak, he had steak too. I remember, he loved meat balls and spaghetti.

I thought, his new family will feed him with dog food. He will not like it, he will be starving.

I could not cope with work. I cried time to time at work, my boss had to send me home. I lose weight. I was still upset two weeks later.

I spoke to Bob on the following Sunday. 'You need to take me to see Domino. I can't eat, or sleep. I have to see if he's okay.'

'I told you, he's fine with his new family.'

'I'm not fine, I need to see him, where he lives and how his new family are.'

'Okay, I'll call them first and ask if you can come over to see him.'

I went to see Domino; his new family was only a five-minute drive from us. I was so happy when he remembered me. He was barking with joy, wagging his tail, jumping all over me.

The mother spoke to me, she was very nice. She said to Domino, 'You're so happy to see you're old Mum!

'I'm really sorry if I bother you. I had to see if he's okay.'

'Not at all, you can visit him anytime you want. He's happy that he has another dog to play with. We also have two children, the four of them sleep in the same bedroom. We've a garden for them to run about. We take him for a walk every day.'

'Did you keep his name?'

'Yes, it's a lovely name.'

'That's great. I brought his personalised collar, t-shirt and towel. I wasn't sure if you would keep his name, but I brought them with me anyway. Thanks for keeping his name.' I was tearful.

'I know, it's hard. He's not just a dog, he's like your baby.'

'I'm feeling better now seeing him in such a good home, thank you. Is he eating okay?'

'Well, he didn't eat much the first a couple of days, maybe changing his food didn't suit him. I forgot to ask your husband what brand he likes. He's eating well now, he just took a couple of days to get used to the new food.'

'I'm glad everything is okay with him, thanks again.'

'You're welcome, you can visit him anytime.'

I was much happier now that I knew Domino was in a loving home. His love was sure to grow to include members of his new family.

I understood that he lived in the moment, he was not counting days. He was more settled where he was. I did not think, after seeing him, that it would make any difference to him if I was gone for two weeks or forever.

TWENTY-NINE

In 2009, I took Nicola and Teresa to Tenerife during the school summer holidays. They enjoyed going to the beach and sightseeing.

We ate out every night in different restaurants. When I walked down the seafront with them, on the way to the restaurant, sometimes I had an admiring look from guys.

'Mum, you always look nice, and guys are keen to chat you up. Why don't you go out with someone?' Nicola asked me.

'I don't know, is it okay with you?'

'Of course, it's okay with us. You and Dad will never get back together, we know that.'

'Your dad put me off men for the rest of my life. He broke my trust, I don't think that I could trust anyone again. Are you trying to get rid of me?' I laughed with the girls.

'No, we just don't want to see you grow old alone.' Natasha said. Theresa wasn't saying much.

'Thanks, that's very sweet of you.'

'You're forty-three now. You won't stay beautiful like this forever. You're getting older every day. I want you to give yourself a chance with someone else.'

I thought that was the sweetest thing I ever heard from my daughter. She was right, but I could not help thinking what if I met somebody and he did not get along with my daughters. I did not want anyone to come between me and the girls.

It was not easy for me to move on because of my culture, and the way I had been brought up. I could not live with any guys without being married. I knew most people in the UK would shop around first before they decided to try living together.

I was still enjoying my hobbies after work. I went climbing or running every day, during the week, after work. At the weekends, I was always climbing the Scottish mountains over 3000 feet, the Scottish Munros.

A couple of years later when I was up in the Cairngorm mountains in Aviemore. I met Chris, a mountain rescue dog handler. He and the team were on search dog avalanche training. He was in a Keswick mountain rescue team in Cumbria, but they were up training in Scotland.

We swapped telephone numbers and started to go hill walking together. It was nice to have someone with me in the mountains, especially in the winter.

Chris and I saw each other twice a month. He came up to see me in Glasgow once a month, and I would go down to see him once a month in the Lakes.

I love the Lake District; it is the place where I want to spend the rest of my life. It is surrounded with beautiful landscapes of lakes, mountains and waterfalls.

I told the girls about Chris, but I never took him to my place, because at the end of the day, I was still married, despite wanting to be divorced. It was a difficult situation for me.

At the end of 2010, after five years of living in the rental house, Bob spoke to me. 'I'm sorry, I can't afford to pay the rent for this house anymore. We need to move to a smaller place.'

These conversations used to annoy me a bit, because he did not live there, he was not part of the 'we.' I was only living there with the children because he refused to give me my freedom and divorce me or settle up regarding the sale of our family house.

Unfortunately, I did not realise that I could just divorce him or go to the police about the violence and mental anguish I was being put through.

'Are you telling me that you have run out of money?'

'Yes.'

'What did you do with the money from selling our family home? It was sold for £700,000, we owned that outright, there was no mortgage. Five years of renting is £72,000. It's not £700,000, where is the other £628,000?' I realised at that point, that I had never seen his bank account or business accounts since we married 20 years ago.

'Well, I paid for food and all the bills around the house!'

'We're talking about a missing £628,000. Also, you're working, what about your wages? Don't you use your wages to pay the bills?

'I used some of the money to start a new business. It didn't work out.'

'Well, I know nothing about that, in fact you have used our money to do that, it's not just your money. You should be discussing that with me too.'

'It's my money, my business, I made it, it's nothing to do with you. I'll do whatever I want with it.'

'Look, you're refusing to divorce me. I'm like a prisoner, I'm looking after the children for you, I don't even know where you live. I've made you an offer, I'll pay half of the bills around the house if you're honest and show me your bank statement. I need to know financially what is going on with you.'

'It's my money, I'm showing you nothing. Just stay out of my business.'

'I'm your wife, I'm the mother of your children. I don't know anything about you, your business, or your personal life.'

'You came here with nothing. You don't deserve anything; your job is to look after the children.'

'Actually, I had a good life at home with my family before I met you. I had a good job, I came here because I loved you, and you promised to look after me. You made vows when we got married. Beating me up and keeping me trapped in this relationship was not part of it.'

'I'm not answering any more of your questions. I don't have any money left.'

'That's good that you don't have money, you can't say anymore that I want a divorce because I'm after your money. Where are you moving us to?'

'I have found a three-bedroom semi-detached house in Giffnock, five minutes' drive from here. You can still shop and go running in the same area.'

'That's very thoughtful of you worrying about my shopping and my running route. After the girls settle in the new place, I'm getting a divorce. It's stressful packing and unpacking. I'm too old to keep moving around. I can't take it anymore.'

I was really upset worrying about the girls' future. I was so sick and tired of my life. Chris had asked me to move in with him and look for a new job in the Lake District.

But, I could not leave my daughters to go to another part of the UK before they finished school. I did everything for them, washing, ironing, cooking, helping them with homework and being their taxi driver.

'They're fifteen and eighteen, they're not kids anymore. They'll look after themselves if you're not there.' Chris told me.

'I'll worry about them and I'll miss them. I'm not leaving them.'

'It's only a two-hour drive from Keswick to Glasgow. You can see them anytime.'

'I need more time to think.' I said that so I did not hurt Chris's feelings, but I knew I could never move, until the girls were both finished schools, and managing independently.

'Okay, take as long as you like.'

There was no way that I could leave the girls before they both finished schools. I was not sure that I could start my life over again, with another man. I did not want to take any more chances.

Bob moved us to a three-bedroom rental house in Giffnock in November 2010. I hated him so much because of what he was putting me and the girls through. I kept telling myself, it had to end now.

On 21st August 2011, it was my father in law, Robert's 82nd birthday. I took him and the girls out on his birthday. I took him and the girls out on their birthday every year.

Sadly, my mother in law passed away in February 2007. Bob never made it to his parents or his daughters' birthday celebrations.

This year he came around on his Dad's birthday, it was odd because he was quite early. 'Do you mind if I join you all for dinner on Dad's birthday?' I was surprised that he asked, I was worried, I suspected he was up to something, whatever it was, it was not going to be good for me.

'Are you coming with us?' I asked.

'Yes. Is it okay to join you?'

'Of course, it's okay. I just want to make sure that I heard correctly, because you have never made it in the past.'

'He's getting old now, I thought I should make the effort.'

We went for a lovely meal in Glasgow city centre. Bob dropped his dad off after dinner then took us back to the house.

After the girls went upstairs to their bedroom, Bob asked me. 'Have you got a minute? I have something to talk to you about.'

'What is it?' I was worried because I now knew he was up to something.

'You always wanted a divorce. I kept telling you that I was not ready.'

'You were just not telling me, you threatened me that you would make sure my life is hell if we divorced!'

'I'm sorry, it was not nice of me. I'm ready for a divorce now.'

'That's good. I suppose, you have already hidden everything, if you're ready.'

'I don't have anything to hide.'

'The good thing about you having no house, no money is you can't say that I want a divorce because I'm after your money. I just want to remind you that when you were hiding your money from your creditors, you transferred it all to my name and the children's names.'

'I know that.'

'Once you did that, I could have kept it all and lived on the interest for the rest of my life. I would not have needed to put up with your domestic violence. I didn't need to transfer it all back to you, just remember that.'

'I know, you're not that type of person. That's why I could trust you and give you all I had. I thank you for that. Here's the divorce agreement, just sign at the bottom.' He handed me the papers and a pen.'

I looked through it quickly. 'Oh, you've already signed your part.'

'Yes, you just sign on your part.'

'Just give me a few minutes to read through this agreement.' I read through it quickly. 'It's says that, I'm not entitled to any of your properties, your business or any lump sum.'

'Correct.'

'Wait a minute. As far as I know, you don't have a house, you don't have a business and you don't have any money.'

'That's right. I'll keep giving you the money for the children's food every week if you sign it.' He looked happy I was finally agreeing with him.

'Why do I need to sign to say I have no claim to a house, business and money those you don't have, is it because you do have these things?'

'Don't worry, I'll still give you money every week.'

'But you don't give it to me every week, sometimes you give me nothing. I can't see how I can trust you because sometimes you don't give me any maintenance money. I get it when it suits you, if it doesn't suit you, I don't get it. How can I trust you after I sign this document?'

'If you don't sign it, you'll get nothing!'

'So, I'm still confused about why I need to sign for something you don't have?' He was getting angrier, I knew he would turn violent any minute. I was not going to back down though. I was used to the beatings, I would survive another one.

Bob was looking at me, but he did not know what to say now. I could tell he was getting angry but trying to hide it so I would sign his document.

I continued. 'I'm confused as to why you're asking me to sign an agreement for money or property you don't have! Do I look stupid to you?'

He said nothing, but I could see he was grinding his teeth.

'Don't you be smart, just fucking sign it!'

'I won't sign anything until I see a solicitor.'

Bob went crazy, he tried to throttle me, and slammed me back and forth against the wall. I was crying, I thought, I am going to die tonight.

'Nicola, Teresa please help me.' I broke free, shouting for the girls, but he grabbed me again. I was terrified. I thought the only way I would survive was if the girls came downstairs.

Normally, I just put up with the violence because I did not want the girls to see that side of their father.

I remembered how upset I was when I saw my father beat my mother, but I knew Bob would not hurt me in front of the girls.

'What is it, Mum?' The girls ran downstairs.

He let go of me, and stepped back, trying to make it look as if nothing violent had happened. 'Nothing, your Mum and I just had a disagreement. You two can go back upstairs now.'

'Nicola, can I sleep with you tonight?' I asked.

'It's fine, Mum.'

I walked upstairs with the girls and slept with Nicola. I no longer felt safe in my bedroom on my own.

An hour later, I walked downstairs for a glass of water. I thought he had gone. The kitchen door was slightly open. He was talking to someone on the phone.

'She's not signing the papers; she's going to see a lawyer tomorrow!' I could just make him out.

I walked back upstairs, wondering who he was talking to. I did not believe his friends would support whatever he was trying to do, because it wasn't right.

But what was he up to on the phone?

I discussed the divorce with the girls. 'Your Dad and I are getting divorced. I would like to know who you're going to live with? I need to know the situation before I see a lawyer.'

'Of course, we want to stay with you.' Nicola said, Theresa nodded.

I knew that was going to be their answer, because he was never around to do anything for them.

'That's good, tomorrow after school, we're going to put our names down for a council house.'

'Where will it be and how many bedrooms?' Nicola asked.

'I don't know, I don't think we'll have a choice. You'll probably have to share a bedroom with Teresa. I don't even know where we go to put our name down.'

'Don't worry, Mum. I'll ask Laura, my friend. She has a two-bedroom council flat in a high rise in Thornliebank.'

Nicola was on the phone to Laura for a while.

'Mum, Laura said, the office is on the second floor of her block. If you want to put your name down for one, bring your ID, your pay slips, and proof of your present address.'

'Will you go with me after school, tomorrow?'

'Yes, we'll go with you.' They both nodded.

The girls and I went to the office the next day. It was on the second floor as Laura said. It was a rough area, and the building smelled dirty.

It was the first time I saw the other side of life, in Glasgow, up to now we had become used to a comfortable life.

However, I was not scared or frightened for myself by having to move to a council flat. I was worried how the girls would cope.

But, I reasoned if I stayed with the girls, I knew we would all manage, somehow.

We picked up the application form, from the girl in the office, and went back home to fill it in. I took it back the next day.

I decided to talk to the girls about my financial circumstances, because I knew their father would not have been honest with them, or told them that his intention was to give me nothing, especially if they chose to stay with me.

'There are a few things that I would like to talk to you about. I can no longer afford to buy or do the things we're used to, because I'll have more bills to take care of. I don't think your father's going to give me any money to help look after you, buy food, clothes or anything at all. I can't afford to take you out after school or at the weekend, no more eating out, no holidays.'

'You mean we can't visit our cousins in Thailand, and we won't see granny and grandpa.'

'No, not at the moment.' I was upset.

I was so scared, I do not know where we would end up. I had to think how to start my life over again at forty-five. I had absolutely nothing to start off with. I had to pull myself together for the girls and pretend I thought everything would work out.

The day after, Nicola said. 'Mum, we think, we're going to stay with dad.'

'Who's going to feed you every day?'

'Dad said he'll come home early.'

'He only has meals with you once or twice per year, Christmas and New Year, not even your birthdays. What makes you think he'll change the way he is now?'

'We're grown up now, we can look after ourselves.'

'Okay, if that's your decision.' I was sad and disappointed, I would miss being with them terribly.

I was also quite scared to live on my own. I had never lived on my own before, that was a real fear for me. But I thought, his house was in a better area, and much safer for them than a council high rise. I would just have to be strong and get on with it.

I went to see a divorce lawyer in Glasgow city centre. It was embarrassing because I was unable to answer most of the questions about my husband during the first interview.

'What's your husband's occupation?

'I don't know where he's working now. He used to have seven Hi-Fi shops. His business went bankrupt about five years ago. I don't really know what he has been doing since. He keeps everything from me. He's extremely secretive.'

'Where does he live?'

'I don't know, he used to come home after midnight or in the morning to get the children ready for school, when they were younger. My eldest daughter is nineteen, the youngest one is sixteen, so he's hardly ever at home nowadays.

We sold our family home for £700,000 five years ago. I do not know what he did with the money. He could have bought a house somewhere, he could be living with someone else.'

'Where can I contact him?'

'I suppose you can post letters to my address. He'll see them at some point, I can give you his phone number and you can phone him. I'm sorry, my case is complicated.'

'Don't worry, we can sort it out. Any questions that you would like to ask me just now?'

'How does it work for you if I don't have money to pay you upfront?

'We'll apply for legal aid for you just now, and then we'll take something off your settlement after your divorce has been granted.'

'What is legal aid?' I did not even know what that was.

'It's the use of public funds to help to pay for legal advice and progress matters in court. You might have to pay small amount in contribution, it depends on your income.'

'Thank you, it sounds great.'

'We'll get in touch with your ex-husband. We'll let you know what's happening.'

I felt relieved about the cost, I did not know about legal aid, there is no such facility in Thailand. If your husband throws you out, if you have no family or friends you can stay with, you are on the street, and people often starve to death.

That's' why I was so frightened throughout all Bob's terrible behaviour towards me and was part of the reason I put up with it for so long.

I did not think I had any choice. I kept thinking back to how my Mum had to put up with violence from my father, in Thailand, for so long.

The girls arrived back from school, Nicola said to me. 'Mum, I talked to Laura about the council house. She said, you won't get it if you still have somewhere to stay.'

'But, I'm getting divorced from your Dad. I can't stay under the same roof. I know, he's hardly here, but he still has a house key, he can come in anytime.'

'I understand what you are saying. Laura said, at the end of the day you still have a roof over your head. If you're homeless and stay at the shelter, then they'll try to get a council flat for you. Laura had to stay in a shelter for a week before she had an offer of a council flat.'

'What's a shelter?'

'The place where homeless people sleep. There're about ten to twenty single beds in one room, of course, you'll share the kitchen if there is one, and the bathroom, with others.

'Where am I going to keep my stuff?

'I don't know, Mum. You'll have to hire a container for storage, or space in a warehouse, to keep your stuff.'

'I'm not sure if I could stay in a shelter.' I tried not to cry in front of the girls.

'That's the only way you can get a council flat any quicker.'

'Ok, I'll look for somewhere to hire a container for storage first.' I searched online for a self-storage business around Glasgow. They were quite expensive for such a small space. I had to be careful about money. I was stressed, there were too many things in my head to think about.

I had a two-week climbing trip in the USA coming up the next month. I had saved up for ages, and booked it about four months previously, before I was in this disastrous situation.

I did not know what was the right thing to do. Perhaps I should not go on the trip because my circumstances had changed. But, it could be my last trip, I would not be able to afford any trips again.

I had already paid for everything on this trip, including a group climbing instructor, air tickets, half-board accommodation. It was to be my trip of a lifetime.

I decided to carry on with it, it could be my last holiday for a while.

My flight was at six o'clock in the morning. Bob came home at 21:00 the night before I was due to go. 'I want you to sign this divorce agreement before you leave. If not, when you come back from your trip, there will be nothing left here. I'll throw out all your belongings. I'll get rid of your car and the girls won't be here! You won't see them!'

'Are you blackmailing me? I'm not signing anything. I'll let my solicitor know what you just said to me.'

I could see from the expression on his face how angry he was. He would have killed me if the girls were not in the house.

I sent an email to my solicitor because my flight was at 06:00, and I would not be able to ring him before I went.

Dear Mr Ross Robinson

I am off on my climbing trip in Arizona tomorrow morning. My flight is 06:00 therefore, I could not ring you before I leave.

My ex-husband came to the house tonight at 21:00. He tried to make me sign the divorce agreement.

I didn't sign the agreement, he then threatened me, and tried to blackmail me by saying that he would throw all my stuff out, get rid of my car and take the children away and that I won't see them again.

Could you please help me? Could you do something to stop him?

I am looking forward to hearing from you.

Your faithfully

Mrs N Smith

I went to bed after sending the email to my solicitor. I could not sleep, I still did not know what to do with my jewellery, which was quite valuable.

I packed it up securely to take with me. I was hoping that there was a security box that I could hire at the airport. I could not leave it with my daughters, their dad could forcibly take it from them.

Unfortunately, there was no security box that I could hire at the airport. I had no choice but to take all my jewellery with me.

I checked my emails every day during my trip. I never heard back from my solicitor; I was so disappointed. I feared what Bob might do with my property and what would happen with the girls. They were young adults; I was sure that he could not force them to do anything they didn't want to do.

When I arrived home after the trip, my car was gone. Some of my clothes, and boxes of belongings such as pictures and ornaments were in the back garden. I was upset by the sight of my clothes and other stuff in the garden, but I was more concerned about the girls, I ran upstairs to see them.

Teresa and Nicola were both asleep upstairs, I did not disturb them. I realised I had not seen my car when I rushed in. I knew that he must have got rid of it. I did not know what to do. At that time, because of the culture in Thailand, I did not realise, that in the UK, you could ring the police about behaviour like this from a partner.

I walked over to the council office to chase up my council flat.

'I'm sorry, you're still on the waiting list.' The woman in the office told me.

'How long will I have to wait?'

'I can't tell you, it depends on your circumstance and how many points you have.'

'What do you mean by circumstances and points?'

'For example, people who're disabled, pregnant, have small children, unemployed etc. They'll have more points than you.'

I was so disappointed, it sounded as if even a council flat was out of my reach. I needed to get out of this house. I could not sleep at night; I was scared that he would come in and kill me while I was asleep.

He had a house key, he could come in anytime. There was no lock on my bedroom door. I had to put a table against it when I was in bed, otherwise I could not sleep.

Before I left the house, I put my head out of the door first to check all around to make sure was no one waiting to attack me.

I did not think Bob would do anything himself outside of the house. He was too smart for that, but I thought he was capable of paying somebody to do me serious harm or worse. I lived in fear.

I had no car to go to work. I started too early for a public transport. I had to get a taxi for work every morning, it was twelve pounds. I took two trains back home after work.

I was really struggling with money. I could not afford to pay for storage to keep my stuff.

My phone rang, it was Nicola. 'Mum, I've got good news. Laura said, you can stay in her flat till you get somewhere else to go. She lives with her boyfriend in his flat at the moment. She has two bedrooms; you can sleep in one and you can keep your stuff in the other.

'That's great, that's awfully kind of Laura.' I was so pleased, at least I had a place to keep my stuff now. But, I did not have a car to move it.

'Can you come to Glasgow over the weekend? I rang Chris.

'I'm sorry, I can't go. Beck is on two weeks' assessment.' Chris explained that Beck, his mountain rescue dog, was having her assessment.

'Can't you just put it off?'

'I'm sorry I can't. If I put her off this time, then she'll have to wait another year.'

'It's okay, don't worry about it.'

I did not understand about Beck's assessment, she was already a qualified mountain rescue search dog. I was not sure why she had to do her assessment again.

Chris was so obsessed with mountain rescue, nothing else seemed to matter to him. Mountain rescue and his rescue dog came first. I suppose it had gone from a hobby to an obsession.

Because he was so busy with mountain rescue, and the fact he would never miss any call outs we started to see each other less, just once per month.

It was hard for me at weekends, I would drive the two-hundred-mile return trip to see him, and sometimes he would go straight out on a call out.

I knew others in the team did not go to every incident, there had to be a balance between your private life and mountain rescue.

It was a big team so there were plenty of people, sometimes only two or three people were needed on a call out.

It did not make me feel good, I felt guilty every time I argued with him about it, because he was trying to help people when he went out on a call. Unfortunately, it eventually led to arguments.

'Why do you always have problem with me when I go on a call out, I'm trying to save people's lives?'

'I know you don't have to go on every single call out. Don't make it sound like I'm a bad person.'

'You don't like it when I get a call out.'

'It's hard for me to drive two hours to see you, and you just shoot off every time there is a call. You don't need to go every time, the others in the team aren't doing that. It's not your job, it's a hobby. Your team is so busy, you're out nearly every day, nobody can sustain that, most team members go to about 50 percent, or less, of the calls. Otherwise, everybody in the team would be divorced. Many of the employers don't allow attendance at work, you're allowed to go then, so your attendance is very high in any case.'

'They need help, I'm trying to save people's lives.'

'It's truly kind of you but why do forty of you need to go to pick somebody up with a sprained ankle by the side of the road? That's not an emergency, and you don't need to go every time, you do need to spend some time with me when I visit.'

Chris did not say anything.

'We only see each other once or twice per month. You're need to prioritise our time. I have no problem if you're going out for a real emergency, or the team is short of people.'

He did not argue, he knew I was right, but I did not think he would change. He was obsessed.

I remember it came to a head when he was visiting me in Glasgow and his pager went off, he was 200 miles away, he just could not leave it for a second. He used to leave it switched on when we were on holiday.

I started to look around for a cheap second -hand car. I was worried about buying one on my own, I knew nothing about cars. I did not know if a car was in a good condition for the price, or not. Most of all, I did not have enough cash for a second-hand car.

I walked three miles down the road to the closest car hire company. I hired a car for £175 per week so I could get to work and keep my job. It was so expensive, it was almost as much as I got paid. But, I needed my job, and I was proud that I could support myself.

I tried to pack some of stuff away and take it to Laura's flat every day after work. Despite this, Bob wanted me out of the house. I found out later what he was up to.

On the 17th December 2011, I came back in from work. Nicola said, 'Mum, there was an old guy here, he knocked the door.'

'Who was it?'

'He said, Dad hasn't paid the rent. We must move out within five days, or else he'll change the locks! He left his name and phone number for you.'

I was in shock, I had no idea, at all, that he had stopped paying the rent. I was angry that this person spoke to the children and frightened them.

I gave him a ring. 'Hello, is that Mr. Macdonald?'

'Yes, I am.'

'It's Mrs Smith here. My children said, you came this evening, regarding the rent.'

'Yes, that's right. Your husband hasn't paid the rent for six months.'

'I'm sorry, I didn't know anything about it. He never told me. How much does he owe you?

'Four thousand, two hundred. If you can't find money within five days, I'll change the locks.'

'Don't you think, you should have given us more notice?'

'I told your husband three months ago. I have given him more than enough notice.'

'Okay, I won't be able to get four thousand and two hundred within five days. We'll move out. Next time will you wait to speak to me instead of my children.'

My heart sank, it was too much for me to cope with. I did not know any way to get out of this situation.

I did not realise that landlords could not force you out like this, or that threatening to change the locks is a criminal offence. I should have phoned the police, but I had no idea of my rights.

Looking back now, Bob knew that I had little knowledge of Scottish Law, he knew I was very vulnerable, and an easy target.

I was worried about the girls. I called Bob, 'Why didn't you tell me about the rent?'

'You didn't sign the divorce agreement, I warned you what would happen. You've brought this upon yourself.'

'It's not just about me, it's also about our children. I can't move out with five days' notice. I'm still waiting for a council flat. I'm working every day, I can't finish packing within five days.'

'You still have all the jewellery I bought for you. You can sell that to pay off the rent.'

'No, I won't sell my jewellery, that's the only thing I have left to pass onto the children. I don't want them to think that I have nothing left for them.'

'It's your choice, sell it or get thrown out of the house!'

'Yes, unfortunately, I can see that. I made a terrible choice when I married you. What are you planning for the girls?'

'They will stay with their grandad. But, because of our circumstances, my dad can't take you as well.'

'So, now I'm facing being homeless. I still can't believe what you have put me through. I'm the mother of your children. If I had known how nasty you are, and how you were going to treat me, I would have run off with everything when you put it in my name. You're lucky I'm not like you.'

I knew then that I should have listened to Bob's friend, Martin. I should have gone to Thailand when I had a chance. Looking back, with the benefit of hindsight, I was naive, too soft and so stupid.

THIRTY-ONE

I kept myself away from Chris, and most of my friends. I tried to sort out my life on my own, I could not bring myself to repeat what had happened to me. I think, maybe, I was depressed it was just too much for me to deal with.

First, I needed a car to keep my job and to move my stuff to Laura's flat. I could not afford to keep wasting so much money on car hire every week.

I went to the garage in Paisley and bought a new car. I could not really afford it, but I did not want to take any risks with a second hand one and end up paying more in repairs.

I chose the cheapest one in the garage; it was a Renault Twingo. I bought it on credit over 5 years.

It was hard to get credit because I had no credit history. At first, I was refused. The salesman told me he tried for ages to get a deal for me. I love that car, I still have it ten years later!

Alison, my close friend from the college, called me. 'Is everything okay with you?'

'I'm fine, thanks for calling.'

'I can sense that you aren't fine. I've not heard from you for ages, which is unlike you. You know, you can talk to me about anything. It's better than keeping it to yourself.'

'I'm going to be a homeless in three days.'

'What do you mean?'

'Bob didn't pay the rent on our house for six months, so we owed them four thousand, two hundred. The landlord came around and threatened to throw me out, he said he would change the locks in five days.'

'He can't do that with such short notice.'

'I had no idea that he hadn't paid the rent, maybe this is his way to get rid of me.'

'Listen Nuch, you need to phone the Women's Aid, organisation. Get the address and the phone number online. You need help, you need to talk to them.'

'I can't see how they're going to help me.'

'You're in the UK; you're not in Thailand. We have help organisations here.'

'Okay, I will, thank you.'

'Let me know how you get on.'

I searched for the closest Women's Aid organisation near me. I found one in East Kilbride, which was about thirty minutes' drive.

I sent them an email.

Dear Madam,

I do not know where to start, I just know, I need help. It is easier for me to talk to you in person than a phone call. I would be grateful if I could come to see you.

I am looking forward to hearing from you.

Kindest Regards,

Mrs N Smith

I had an email reply the same day, with an arrangement to come to see them two days later. I was pleased.

I went to the East Renfrewshire Council on Main St, Barrhead, Glasgow. I had heard nothing back from the council flat in Thornliebank. I thought my circumstances had changed now. I thought I would try a different council house organisation, this time.

I went with the girls, but I walked into the office by myself. I did not want the girls to see me upset and begging for a place to live.

'Hi, I'm looking for a council house to live in with my two daughters.'

'Do you have any ID with you?'

'Yes, I have my passport and driving licence.'

'Where are you living now?'

'A private rental house in Giffnock. I couldn't afford to pay the rent; the landlord is going to change the locks in three days.'

'Who is your landlord?

'I don't know, it was my estranged husband who found that place for us. It's too long a story to go through it all now.'

'I need the details of your landlord, otherwise I can't proceed your application.'

'I'll call my husband now for the landlord's address and phone number.'

I rang Bob straight away. 'Can you give me the landlord's address and phone number?'

'I don't know.' Bob struggled to answer.

'I know you like to keep everything secret from me, but I'm in the East Renfrewshire council office now. I need the details of the landlord so the lady can proceed with my application for a council house.

I'll pass the phone to her now, you can tell her yourself.'

I passed the phone to the lady but I could see it did not go well. 'It's really strange, I don't understand why he tried to avoid all the questions about the landlord.'

'I assume, you didn't get the address and phone number.'

'No, he said that he would call me back, but I have the feeling that he won't.'

'I know, he won't.'

'I'm sorry, I can't go forward with your application now.'

'I understand, you're just trying to do your job. Thank you for your time.'

I walked out of the office, I had no hope of getting a council house. I walked over to the girls who were waiting for me in the car.

'The lady in the office couldn't proceed my application.'

'Why, Mum?'

'Your Dad refused to give her our landlord details, without it, she couldn't go forward with my application.'

'I'll ask Dad for the landlord details tonight.'

'It's okay, don't waste your time.'

I remember, I took the girls to the supermarket. 'I'm sorry, I only have thirty pounds left for food now. Will you make sure we don't spend more than that?'

I felt so sad to tell them this but, I thought, it was better to tell them the truth.

'Okay Mum, we don't need much.'

After shopping, I returned to my packing. I packed my stuff to go to Laura's flat. I packed the girls' stuff so they could go to their Grandads.

I did the best I could with such a short notice period. I was still working; I did not have much spare time to pack.

While I was packing, I saw Nicola's purse on the floor. I lifted it up to put it on her desk. I could not help noticing that she had plenty of cash in her purse, there was nearly three hundred pounds.

'Where did you get this money from?' I asked her.

'Dad gave it to me.'

'Why didn't you say something in the supermarket when I said to you that I only had thirty pounds for food?'

'Dad said not to tell you, or give money to you.'

'It's okay, just so you know, I didn't buy any food for myself. I just wanted to make sure that you two had enough food.'

I was hurt and disappointed. To me, if I had money, it would not matter what my Dad said, I would give money to my Mum to buy food for us, if she did not have any.

That was the first time I saw how Bob had brainwashed the girls. I thought back to when they had said they would stay with me, then after they went home, they changed their minds. It was frightening for me; I did not know what was going to happen next.

The next day, after work, I went to the Women's Aid office. I met Kirsty in the office reception. She was friendly, I felt I could share anything with her.

It was hard to tell someone, who I had just met, what I had been through. I did not know where to start.

'I'm here to listen to you and help you. You can talk to me about anything.'

I felt more comfortable telling her about my life.

'Have you told the police?'

'No, never, I was afraid he would kill me after the police left.'

'Do your daughters know about the domestic violence?'

'He never did it in front of the girls. I never told them because I won't do anything to upset them. Until the day he tried to force me sign the divorce agreement.'

'No, don't you sign anything. We have women's aid solicitors who can help and give you good legal advice.'

'Thank you, I'm relieved.'

'Just now, I need to sort out a place for you to live. It's coming up to the Christmas holiday season, so it'll take longer, but I'll do my best.'

Kirsty went back to her office and started the search on her computer. I sat down in the waiting room. She came back to me a few minute later. 'I have a refuge place available for you next week. I'll get back to you.'

'Thank you for helping me to get through this. I was at my wit's end until I came here and saw you.'

I was so grateful to Kirsty, I had never met her before, but she worked hard to help me.

I still could not believe how my husband could possibly do this to me. I was not just the woman he married, I was the mother of his two daughters.

Four days before Christmas, on the 21st December 2011 at 10:00, the landlord came to the house and changed the locks.

With such short notice, Nicola and I could not pack everything on time. Teresa was with her Dad. I left some of my stuff and some of the girls' stuff in the back garden because I could not shift it all, in time.

I told the landlord; I would come back for it and remove it all later that night. He just nodded and carried on changing the locks.

Looking back now, I do not know why I never asked to see paperwork, I think I was so stressed that I just could not think clearly. I did not really know what paperwork to ask for. I thought it was all legitimate, and because of that I never explained the details to my solicitors or contacted the police. I suppose, I was quite vulnerable.

It was my first night in Laura's flat. Fortunately, Nicola was with me, helping me move my all belongings. My stuff covered the floor, I had no sheets. I was crying.

'Mum, I'll stay with you tonight.' Nicola said to me.

'Thank you, I will drop you off tomorrow. I need to go to work, I can't afford to stay off work. I need money.'

We cried and cuddled each other in bed and fell asleep with exhaustion. I took Nicola back to her grandads the next morning.

Teresa was already with there, she was upset and crying.

'Look at them, they're upset and crying!' Bob shouted at me, he was putting on a show for his parents and the girls. Goodness knows what he had told them.

'Is it my fault?' I still could not believe that he tried to make out it was my fault.

'If you had just signed the divorce agreement then it wouldn't have ended like this! The money that I have had to waste on a lawyer, we could have kept it for their education.'

I realised the scope of the lies and brainwashing that was going on between him, the girls and his parents. It was nothing to what I found out later.

It was hard for me to argue in English, I could not reply quickly, especially, when I was so upset.

'Is that what you are telling the girls? That I made you waste money on a lawyer instead of keeping it for their education?'

'That's a fact, I'm wasting money defending myself too, that's also your fault.'

'I don't have money for a lawyer, I had to apply for legal aid, you've left me on the street with nothing.'

He was just looking at me, saying nothing. Then his brain started working again. 'I didn't leave you on the street, you went to Laura's flat.'

'That was nothing to do with you, as far as you knew, I was out on the street.'

I could see he was getting angry. I did not care; I was not going to let him away with all these lies. 'You should apply for a legal aid too if you don't have money. But, you can't, can you? You can't be honest with Legal Aid, so you can't ask for it.'

He changed the subject. 'Listen, I only have two thousand cash. You can have it now, if you don't drop the case, you'll end up with nothing.'

'Keep it, I won't drop the case. I won't let you get away with what you have put me through. Is that what you value me at, two thousand pounds? If I could turn back time, I would do what Martin advised, run away from you, and keep the money you hid in my bank account, instead of being honest and giving it back to you.'

He said nothing, he knew it was all true.

I drove back to Laura's flat. It was my first day on my own, my second day in this place, I just could not stop crying, I missed the girls, I could not live like this.

In the past, I would go climbing, running or walking, but I knew they would be there when I came back.

But, from now on, it would be different. I had no one to come home to. I came back to an empty house.

I was in so much pain and lonely. There was no reason for me to live any more, I had nothing left.

THIRTY-TWO

Kirsty took me to the third-floor refuge flat in Cambuslang. There was no lift, but I was relieved, I did not need to worry about who I was going to meet in it.

'We've installed a security alarm that goes straight to the police station when you press the buttons. One at the front door, one in the kitchen and one in your bedroom. I'll show you.'

'Thank you.'

'There are three bedrooms in this flat, later, you may have to share the flat if we need another room for somebody, is that okay?'

'Yes, it's fine.'

'Here's a food box for you, there are some tins of food, soup, puddings, fruit, tea bags and jam. We have two hundred pounds cash here for you, from our organisation, just to help you out a bit, until you get back on your feet.'

'That's very generous of your organisation.' I could not believe it; I had no idea this sort of help existed. It was a lifesaver.

'Do you mind if I ask, how does your organisation afford the food and money you give to people like me?'

'From government funding and donations.'

'I wish I had known about you earlier. I put up with my abusive ex-husband for so long because I didn't know there is help out there in the UK.' I think one reason I did not look around for help was, that in my country and culture, I was brought up not to wait around for help from others, the only person who can help you in Thailand, is yourself.

'You know it's different now. I'm going to leave you to get settled in. Here's my card, if you need anything, just call me. Tomorrow, I'll take you to put your name down for a council house.'

'I did try before, I went with my daughters to East Renfrewshire Council Housing. They said they couldn't progress my application until they receive details of the landlord from our rental house. My husband refused to give them the details.'

'Don't worry, I'll help you go through it with them.'

'Thank you very much for helping me.'

After Kirsty left, I started to cry. I was scared and worried about my finances. I was 46, I had nothing to start my life over again with.

I felt so lonely, I missed my daughters. I was not used to living by myself. I lived with my family, in Thailand, before I was married. I had never had a serious relationship before my husband.

I left my family, friends and everything I had, when I came to Scotland to start my life with him.

At work, the next day, Lisa, from HR called me into her office. 'I would like to talk to you about your absence record. It's been very high lately.'

'I know, I'm sorry.'

'Is everything ok with you?'

'No.' I started to cry.

'I can't help you if you don't tell me.'

'I'm getting through a tough divorce. I was kicked out of the house with nothing. I just moved into a refuge flat yesterday, that's why I couldn't make it to work.'

'You need time off work to sort out your life.'

'No, I can't afford to stay off work. I need money.'

'Don't worry. You wait here, I'm going to see Brian.'

Lisa left to see Brian, my manager. I knew I needed some time to sort out my life. But, I just could not afford to be off work. I had so many bills to take care of, I had nothing to kick start my life over again.

Ten minutes later, Lisa walked back into the room. 'I spoke to Brian, he's given you two weeks off work. If you need more time, just phone in.'

'It's ok, I need money, I can't take time off work.'

'Don't worry, you'll get full pay.'

'Thank you so much, it's very generous of you and Brian.' I was amazed that Lisa and Brian were doing so much to help me. I suppose, it is a reflection on how good a company M&S were to work for. I could hardly accept that it had happened.

This would have been impossible back at home in Thailand. If you do not work, nobody pays you, you starve to death if your family cannot afford to help you.

But, it does mean, that nobody takes a day off work when they are not genuinely sick! You get 2 weeks annual leave, and that includes your sick days.

I was relieved to have some time off work, I only had a few clothes with me in the flat, most of my clothes were still in Laura's flat.

Later, Kristy took me to the Lanarkshire Council Housing office.

'Are you on any benefits?' The lady in the office asked me.

'No, I don't know anything about benefits. I've worked all my life.'

'Okay, I'm just trying to find out about your income. How many bedrooms do you need?'

'Two, if possible.'

'It's quicker if it's one bedroom.'

'She has two daughters, she needs a spare bedroom for them.' Kirsty said to the lady in the office.

'Nuch, go outside a minute.'

The door was slightly open and I could hear some of the conversation. 'I need you to find a good home for her, and definitely not in a high-rise block.'

'Okay, I understand, we will do our best.'

Kirsty came out of the office. 'Nuch, they will be back in touch as soon as they find something.'

'Thanks Kirsty, I don't what I would do without you.'

I was truly grateful, it was so kind of her to take such good care of me. I would not be here today without her, or Women's Aid. They saved my life.

THIRTY-THREE

Chris rang me two days before Christmas. 'Are you having Nicola and Teresa for Christmas?'

'I don't know. They've not replied to my messages, yet.'

'Do you want to come to mine?'

'I want to wait and see if they're coming, or not.'

'Okay, I'll come to yours then.'

'No, if you come to Glasgow, then your mum will be by herself.'

'She doesn't mind.'

'No, I don't want her to be on her own at Christmas.'

'What about you? If you don't have Nicola and Teresa, you'll be by yourself.'

'I'm okay, it's just another day to me, nothing special, and I'm not in the mood for celebrations.'

'Okay, if you change your mind, you know where I am.'

I was sad, if the girls did not come, then it would be my first Christmas without them. I received a text from Nicola later that day. 'Mum, Dad is taking us and grandad out for Christmas dinner.'

I texted her back. 'Okay, that's fine. Will, I see you both on New Year's Day?

'No, Uncle Steven has invited us to his house.'

'Okay, have a good one. When will I see you?'

'I'll let you know later.'

I was so disappointed, I did not know what their Dad had arranged or why, but they were adults, they had their own minds. Why did they not realise how awful I felt?

I decided not to go to the Lake District to see Chris. I was not in a mood for celebration, and I did not want to fall out with him which was happening regularly. I was upset enough.

I had a few invitations from friends for Christmas. I thought, if I cannot be with my children, then I don't want to be with anybody. I should have gone to a friend's house, but I was too upset.

I was up early on Christmas day, I made a tuna sandwich and decided to go hillwalking to Ben Lomond. It was dry but dull, there was no one else there, just how I liked it. I had the whole mountain to myself.

After two weeks in the refuge, I tried to return to normality. I bought a Chinese take away every second night to save money. I ate half and kept the other half for the next day.

I thought it was time to start cooking and eating healthily again. I walked up to the local Co-op supermarket for some groceries.

I picked up a basket and walked down the aisle, I started to cry, I missed the girls. I used to choose whatever they ate first, and then some things for myself, afterwards.

A lady noticed I was crying. 'Are you okay?'

'No, I'm not. I miss my daughters.'

'Where are they?'

'They're with their Dad.'

'Don't worry, they'll come around. Can I help you with your shopping? Or would you like me to get one of the staff to help you?'

'No, it's okay. Thanks, that's very kind of you. I'm going home now.'

I walked back home in tears, with nothing. I had lost too much weight, I was not eating or sleeping well.

I was running and climbing much more than usual. I tried to exhaust myself so I could sleep.

I know some people turn to alcohol or drugs to help them through tough times, but I used exercise.

On 26th January 2012, Kirsty took me to see a Women's Aid solicitor in Motherwell. Brenda was twenty-three, I think she may have just qualified.

'Have you seen a solicitor before?'

'Yes, I've seen Mr Ross Robinson, a solicitor, in Glasgow city centre.'

'When was that?'

'Late last August, we had our first meeting, but I've not heard back from him since then.'

'I can't act for you until you withdraw formally from him.'

'How do I do that?'

'I'll write a later to him and you just sign it.'

'Thanks, that would be great.'

'What about legal aid?'

'Mr Robinson did mention that, but as I said, he never got back to me.'

'No worries, I'll sort that out too. Okay, now you can tell me about your marriage situation. I'll ask questions as we go along.'

I gave her as much detail as I could. I felt that I was repeating myself, over and over, to everybody, but nothing moved forward.

'We'll send your ex-husband a letter, and let you know if we receive a response from him, or his solicitor. We'll also check with the Land Registry regarding the ownership of the property at Church Road, Giffnock, and let you know the outcome of that.' Brenda summarised the meeting before I left.

I did not understand, at the time, why they had to search the Land Registry about the ownership of our rental house. The only reason I could think of was because he refused to give the details of our landlord to the council when I tried to rent a council house.

I called the girls every day, but they never answered my calls. I could only assume he told them not to answer.

I sent Nicola a text message. 'When are you two coming to see me? I've not seen you for a month now.'

For once she replied. 'Okay mum, we'll see you over the weekend.'

I was so pleased and looked forward to seeing them. Bob dropped them off on Main Street, I walked down to meet them.

I gave them a cuddle. 'I miss you, how are you doing?'

'We're fine.'

'Why didn't you answer my calls?'

'Dad said, it's better not to talk to you just now.'

'Okay, that's hurtful. I thought you were adults and have your own mind. It's okay, let's forget about it. Shall we go to do food shopping? I'll cook your favourite dish tonight.'

Neither of the girls replied. I did not know what to make of it. I changed the subject in case they broke off communications again.

I cooked spicy mince with noodles for them. It was the only Thai dish that Teresa liked. She was not keen on Thai food, at that time. Nicola loved Thai food; I knew she missed my cooking.

They stayed overnight with me. There were only the basic channels on the television and there was no internet.

The girls slept on two single beds, I slept on the floor. I was so happy to have them, I knew I would be sad to see them go tomorrow.

Kirsty came round to check how I was. 'Did you see your daughters?'

'Yes, their dad dropped them off on Main Street. It was lovely to see them. They said, their dad told them not to answer my calls. I don't understand, they're adults.' I started to cry.

'Are you scared of your ex-husband?'

'Of course, I am.'

'If you're scared of him, what makes you think they're not. They just do whatever they've been told, not because they don't love you. You don't know what he told them about you. He won't say anything good about you, that's for sure.'

I was really upset, I tried not to be, but it was hard.

Kirsty was right, he was not going to say anything good about me, and I was not there to defend myself.

I could not help thinking that I was the one who had been there with them twenty-four hours, every day, throughout their childhood. I still could not understand what he had said to make them behave that way, it made no sense to me. It occupied my mind.

On the 1ˢᵗ February 2012, I received a letter from the Women's Aid solicitor.

Dear Mrs. Smith

We refer to our letter of 26ᵗʰ January 2012 and enclose copy search results from our searches in the Land Register. You will see that in respect of the property on Church Road, Giffnock this is, in fact, owned by your husband and was purchased in 2007. The records show that there are no charges i.e. mortgages or securities affecting the property.

If you wish to discuss this, then please do not hesitate to contact our legal representative Brenda McTavish.

Yours faithfully,

I almost collapsed reading the letter. I read it repeatedly just to make sure there was no mistake. That was the house that we had just been evicted from!

I rang Ann, my close friend from work, she who lived five minutes' walk from my flat. 'Ann, are you free just now?'

'Yes Nuch, I'm doing nothing at the moment.'

'Can you come over to mine?'

'Yes, no problem. I'll walk down now.'

'Thanks, Ann.'

Ten minutes later, Ann knocked on my front door. 'Is everything ok?'

'I got a letter from my solicitor through my door after work today. I've already read it five times, but because English is not my first language, I just want you to read through it again to make sure there's no mistake.' I handed the letter to her.

Ann read it through. 'The letter says, your ex-husband owned that rental house where the locks were changed and you were forced out. It was his house. He bought it outright, with no mortgage.'

'That's what I thought, Ann. I just didn't want to believe someone could be that evil. I'm talking about the father of my two children. He must have sent somebody round to pretend they were the landlord and threaten to change the locks.'

'I'm terribly sorry. What are you going to do?'

'I don't know, I'm still in shock.'

'Well, for a start, you should tell your daughters.'

'I don't want to hurt their feelings. How can I possibly tell them that? Their own father sent someone round to kick us out the house.'

'I know, Nuch. It's incredibly sad.'

'I know what he's capable of, but I never thought, for one second, that he could be this evil and dishonest. It was quite deceitful, cunning in an evil way, to send someone pretending to be the landlord, so he could force us out of our house.'

'You should tell the children.'

'I'll think about it.'

'Don't you be stupid. They have to know how nasty he is.'

I could not stop crying after Ann left. I was sad, I was angry. I asked myself how he could sleep every night. I could not kick a dog out of my house, never mind my own children. He was an evil person, much worse than I thought.

It made sense now why he could not give the landlord's details to the council lady, because there was no landlord.

I sent text messages to the girls every day. There was no point calling them because they did not answer my calls.

However, after I had not heard from them for a week I decided to call. There was no ring tone and no answer machine from either of their phones.

I could not sleep, I could not eat, I couldn't cope with work. I cried every day. I called Brenda. 'Can you do something to make sure that he can't stop the girls from contacting me?'

'I'm sorry, I can't. Your daughters are twenty and seventeen. They're adults, it's up to them.'

I just could not stop crying. I was in so much pain, I did not know how to get in touch with them. It left me with no choice but to phone their grandad. 'Hi, it's me. Can I speak to Nicola and Teresa?'

'Bob's here, I'll pass on the phone to him.'

Bob replied. 'They're not back from school.'

'I could hear their voice on the background, you let me speak to them now!'

'Hi, Mum.' Nicola answered the phone.

'Why didn't you reply to my text messages?'

'I didn't get your messages. Dad bought us new phones.'

'Why didn't you give me your new numbers, how am I supposed to contact you?'

'I couldn't remember your number.'

'Your Dad knows it, can you pass the phone to him?'

I was so frustrated with his behaviour, he was stopping the girls from contacting me. I said to him. 'I want you drop the girls off on Main Street this Saturday at midday.'

'I can't this weekend, I'm busy.'

'Okay, fine. I'll pick them up at granddads, midday on Saturday.'

There was no reply from him, but I did not care.

I kept the letter regarding the house ownership for a month, I did not want them to think their father was that bad, I knew it would really upset the girls.

But, I decided to tell them, because he was a liar and he was good at it. He would say anything to harm me and make me look like a bad mother. He was turning the girls against me, without feeling any guilt whatsoever.

I did not know what he had been saying to them, but whatever it was it had he to stop, because it was upsetting the girls equally as much.

My main concern was not revenge, it was the girls' welfare, he was behaving in such a way that he left me with no choice.

I had to make sure they knew there was a high level of deceit going on, some of it very calculated to damage me and my relationship with the girls. I remember he threatened I would never see them again. Was he putting his threat into action now?

I spoke to the girls when I had them over the weekend. 'I have a letter from my lawyer, I've kept it for four weeks because I wasn't sure that I wanted to show it to you. I didn't want to upset you.'

I gave the letter to Nicola. 'Just read loudly so Teresa can hear as well.'

Nicola read the letter, she was in tears. 'I don't think this is true, Mum.'

'Are you telling me that my lawyer made this up? I know it's hard to believe that your own father sent someone to kick you and your mother out of their house. The worst part is that you two were threatened when I was out, you were told we had five days to pack.'

'I'll ask dad if it's true.'

243

Nicola was upset. Teresa had a strong personality, she could hide her true feelings, she did not show any emotion, or make any comment.

I was amazed that even when I showed them absolute proof of what their father had been up to, they still did not accept it. I know now that this is not uncommon in these cases. It demonstrates the power he had over both girls.

I saw the girls a couple of weekends later, they seemed okay, they never mentioned the house issue. I wondered what he had told them about it.

I did not ask the girls again about the house. I just left it there, I did not want to spoil my quality time with them or make them feel as if they were stuck in the middle of a matrimonial dispute.

THIRTY-FIVE

On the 9th March 2012, after twelve weeks in the flat, Kirsty called me. 'There's a housing association flat available, it's in a block of four in Newton Avenue, five minutes' drive away. Would you like to go to see it?'

'That would be great, I'm so excited!'

'Okay, I'll get you after work tomorrow. We'll go together.'

I kept thinking about moving, it would be great to get my own place. I was grateful for the refuge, but it did not feel like home. It looked so empty.

I had not been able to decorate or move in my own pictures or ornaments. It had been a safe place for me, but I wanted somewhere I could make my own. I could not wait until tomorrow.

Kirsty picked me up in her car after work. We parked outside the flat, I could see it was a nice situation, in a quiet area with private houses opposite.

The flat was on the ground floor with gardens front and back. It looked great, exactly right for me.

'I don't have a key to show you inside. If you really like it, I'll call the housing association to give you one to look inside.'

'So, it's not a council house?'

'No, it's a housing association.'

'What's the difference?'

'With rented council housing, the council owns the houses and is responsible for the upkeep.

With housing association properties, a private company owns the house and is responsible for the upkeep but rents them out to tenants.'

'How much is the rent per month?'

'I'm not sure, ask someone in the office tomorrow, when you go for the key.'

The next day I to get the key went with Ann. There were two bedrooms, a bathroom with toilet, but no shower, a kitchen and living room.

The main bedroom in the front was decorated with strong colours, black and bright pink!

The second bedroom was half painted, there was black mould covering parts of the walls. There were lots of holes in the toilet walls, and black burn marks on the ceiling. A painter told me later that the black marks came from burning heroin.

There were big holes everywhere in the hallway. The kitchen was completely undecorated, just bare plaster. It was more or less empty apart from some units on the floor, there was not any wall cupboards. There was no cooker, fridge or washing machine.

The living room was the only room that looked okay to move in to. It had white wallpaper and laminate wood flooring. There was no flooring in the rest of the house. There were filthy window blinds, no rooms had curtains.

'It looks good, you've got your own doorstep, your own garden, you can put your washing up. Will you call them tomorrow and say you'll take it? Ann asked me.

'Yes, I will.' I agreed with Ann, at the time, because I did not want to seem ungrateful, but I was wondering how I could sort out such a mess.

My main concern was, I knew nothing about DIY, and I had no money to decorate it. The way the house was just now, I knew I could not live in it, or have the girls around.

I was disappointed, I had been so excited after seeing the outside and the nice quiet area but now it horrified me.

I had never seen anything like it before. I could not imagine living there, how I could possibly sort it out myself?

Ann called me the next day to check that I had called the housing association.

'Have you called the office?' She asked.

'Yes, but I didn't take it.'

'Why?'

'It looks terrible inside, I don't think I could live in it.'

'Listen; you've not been in many council houses. I've been in loads, that's the best council house I've ever seen!'

'It's horrible inside.'

'You can decorate it. We can go to B&Q and paint it ourselves; I'll help you.'

'We can't just paint over the old decoration, there are holes everywhere on the walls.'

'We'll just fill the holes in with filler before we paint.'

'I don't have any furniture.'

'You can get lots of good second-hand stuff in the charity shops, these days. I'll give you a microwave, I'm sure the housing association will give you a cooker. You can do your washing in my house. You can get a small fridge to start with.'

'I don't have any money.'

'It's not easy to get a two-bedroom house, when you live by yourself, especially on the ground floor, and with your own front door. No sharing with others, a front and back garden. You don't know how lucky you are. If you don't take it, you might end up in a tall block, and that house will have gone to somebody else.'

'You're right, I agree with you, but I've already turned it down.'

'Call them now, and say you've changed your mind. I'm sure that house will go quickly.'

I agreed with Ann, I could end up in one-bedroom flat in a high rise, having to share the lift with unpleasant people. No garden to sit in, or dry washing.

I called the office and explained that I had changed my mind and would like to take the house.

I picked the key up the following day. I was overwhelmed by friends at work who gave me a dinner set, coffee table and chairs. Ann gave me a microwave, a kettle, mugs and glasses. I did my washing at her house. I was lucky I had such good friends. In difficult times, you I realise how good some people are.

The housing association gave me a cooker and carpeted two rooms. I still needed money to pay for a painter and joiner.

I called Alison. 'Do you know any place that I could give them my jewellery for cash? I don't want to sell it, though.'

'No problem, I know a few places in the city centre, they're called pawnbrokers.'

'Are they safe?'

'Yes, I do it all the time, I've never had any problems.'

'That's great, can you come with me tomorrow?'

'Yes, meet me in Glasgow city centre and I'll take you. Bring your ID and proof of your address.'

'Thanks, see you tomorrow.'

I met Alison in town.

'I've brought all my jewellery.'

'Don't worry, it will be safe enough.' She took me to the pawn shop in the city centre.

I walked up to the counter and said to the lady. 'Hi, I have some jewellery with me, I need some cash.'

She had a good look through it. 'How much do you need?'

'One thousand pounds.'

'I'll give you back this Rolex, we can't take it. It's too high a value for us. It's too risky to keep it here.'

'Okay, what about the rest?'

'I'll give you back this wedding ring, it's also too high a value. I'll have a look at the rest.'

'Okay, thanks.'

'I'll take this necklace for three hundred and fifty. This bracelet for three hundred and fifty, and this ring for three hundred.'

'That's great, how long do I have to pay you back?'

'As long as you like, but you have to pay the interest every month.'

'How much is it?'

'About thirty pounds each item, per month.'

'So, about one hundred-pounds interest, each month, for a loan of one thousand pound.'

'That's it.'

It was a rip off, but I had no choice. The lady did not ask me for ID or proof of my address. She handed me one thousand ponds in cash and asked me to sign their contract.

Linda, my close friend from work, took me to B&Q so I could use her pensioner discount card.

She was good at DIY, she helped me to put up the curtains. She built the wardrobes, drawers, changed my light bulbs, took out all the window blinds and washed them for me. She also showed me how to cut the grass.

I will never forget, Ann and Linda, they helped me through that tough time. I could not have got through it without them.

I was on and off with Chris most of time. I asked him one evening, 'Can you come and help me, most of my stuff is still in Laura's flat. I need your car to help move stuff, my car is too small.'

'I'm sorry, I've dog training this weekend, can I come next week instead?'

'It's fine if you're too busy.' I knew, we would end up arguing again, I could not cope any more stress, I had too many issues to think about.

'I can't see why you make your life so difficult. Why don't you just give up your job and move in with me in Keswick. You can find a job here.'

'Because I can't see myself living with you and arguing every day.'

'We won't argue if we live together.'

'I can't see that, you're obsessed with your dog training. You don't know how or when to limit it. You don't have time for a relationship!'

'That's not fair.'

'You're so busy with dog training and attending every mountain rescue call you're your house is a mess. Your clothes are in piles on the floor because you don't have time to buy wardrobes or any storage. I can't live like that!'

'I'm not that bad!'

'I just couldn't live there, you don't tidy up, there's stuff everywhere! You know I love Beck, but there's dog hair everywhere, I can't stand it.'

Chris was silent, he knew I was right about his house. I had told him often enough.

'Listen, it's okay if you're busy. My stuff has been in Laura's flat for over three months. I suppose, I can wait for another week.'

I could do without any more arguments. I was happy with my new home, all my neighbours around me were pensioners. They were all nice and kind to me.

This was my home now.

I went to the library to use the computer. I wanted to update my details on my car insurance. It was still in my old address. I did not change it to the refuge, because I knew it was temporary.

I could not log on to my car insurance policy for some reason. I called them and explained this to customer service.

The guy told me to hang on while he looked into it. 'I'm sorry, your policy has been cancelled.'

'I don't understand, I never cancelled it.'

'No, you didn't cancel it. We cancelled it.'

'Why did you do that?'

'Because we sent you some papers which needed your signature. You didn't sign and return them to us within the time limit.'

'When did you cancel it?'

'In January.'

'Are you telling me I've been driving around without insurance for four months?'

'I guess so.'

'I didn't receive the documents because I was moving. I've just settled into my new address now and tried to update my details.'

'I'm sorry, there's nothing we can do about it now.'

'What did you do with the money, I paid in full when I took out the policy?'

'We refunded it back to the card you paid with.'

'I paid with my credit card, I've not used that card since, that's why I didn't know. How much will it cost to renew?

'It's about two thousand pounds.'

I could hardly believe it. 'That's much more expensive than when I first took out the policy. I remember it was just over three hundred and I paid in full. It can't be two thousand.'

'It is because your policy has been cancelled, so it's much more expensive to take out a policy again.'

'Please, I'm getting through a difficult divorce. My ex-husband didn't pass on my mail.'

'I'm sorry, you should have phoned in and let us know about your situation.'

'I moved into a women's aid refuge. I didn't know how long I would be there. I don't have that kind of money. Can't you understand my circumstances?'

'I can't just remove the cancellation, I'm sorry.'

'Okay.' I gave up arguing, he was not going to help me. I found out later that the insurance company should have also tried phoning or emailing before they cancelled my policy. Unfortunately, I did not know that at the time, or I would have written a letter to them.

I was so upset and mad at Bob, he could have easily passed on my mail, or given it to the children for me!

I rang him. 'Why didn't you pass my mail on to me?'

'What mail? I don't know what you're talking about.'

'The mail that came through the door with my name on it! I just found out that my car insurance policy has been cancelled because you didn't pass it on to me.'

'I didn't see any mail.'

'Are you telling me that since you kicked me out of the house, there was no mail for me?'

'No, otherwise I would have passed it on to you.'

'I don't believe you, I've been driving about for four months with the girls in the car without insurance.'

He did not reply.

I just could not stop crying. I searched online, the cheapest policy I could find was fifteen hundred. I did not have that kind of money.

I called Chris to let him know that I could not drive without insurance. He searched online for me and managed to find one for four hundred and fifty pounds. I took it, I was really grateful.

THIRTY-SIX

In April 2012, I called my solicitor. 'I want to collect some of my belongings, and the children's, from his address, can I do that?'

'Of course, you can. He can't stop you uplifting your stuff.'

'That's good. Can you let him or his lawyer know that I'm going this Saturday at midday?'

'Don't worry, I will. If there's any problems, let me know.'

I went to his place on Saturday to get some of the girls' stuff, such as their bedsheets. I wanted their pictures and their handicraft projects that they made for me when they were in school.

Bob was waiting for me at the front door.

I asked him. 'You were meant to deliver the girls' beds yesterday, why didn't you do it? There's no beds for them to stay overnight.'

He did not answer my question. 'Why did you apply for a legal aid?'

'Because I don't have money for a lawyer. You didn't give me anything from our house to start my life over again, not even a dinner set.'

'You're not allowed in here. I won't deliver the girls' beds until you drop your case.'

I was angry and confused. At first, I was not sure if his lawyer had told him or not, or if it was just him being nasty to me. But then I realised, he had been waiting for me at the front door, obviously, he knew I was coming.

I called my lawyer to let her know what had happened. It was not so much about my stuff. I wanted the girls' beds so they could stay overnight with me some weekends.

'Don't worry, I'll send his solicitor a letter.' Brenda told me.

'Can you send me a copy of the letter as well?'

'Yes, I will.'

We refer to the above and our telephone call to your office on 24 April 2012 when you advised that you had met with Mr. Smith and obtained his instructions but were awaiting approval of a draft letter to our firm. We note that we have heard nothing from you to date and our client is anxious for the matter to be progressed.

We understand that our client attempted to attend at your clients address at the weekend to uplift items which belong to herself and the children however your client refused to allow her access to the property. We understand it had been agreed that the children's beds would be delivered to our client on Friday, however your client advised that as our client had applied for legal aid to raise a court action he was unwilling to deliver the children's beds.

The fact that our client has required to apply for civil legal aid is as a direct result of your client's failure to correspond in respect of this matter. We have attempted on several occasions to contact Mr. Smith direct but have heard nothing further from him in response. Please let us hear from you as soon as possible with confirmation of your client's position so the matters can be progressed on an amicable basis.

I was happy with the letter. I need to do something; two months had passed and the girls could not stay over.

A week later, I had a phone call from Brenda. 'I've the good news for you. You'll get the girls beds delivered this weekend and you can go and get your belongings at his address.'

'How do I know it'll be okay?'

'I had confirmation from his solicitor.'

'I don't want him to be there when I arrive. I'm frightened he does something or hits me.'

'Okay, I'll let his solicitor know that you don't' want him to be there, someone could let you in, his dad or the girls.'

'Thank you.'

I know now that the Women's Aid solicitor was very inexperienced, she should have advised me to report the abuse and assaults to the police. A lot of the behaviour I was on the receiving end of was mental torture, which is a form of domestic abuse.

I was perfectly entitled to go and collect my possessions from our old matrimonial home or from their grandad's house, and if there were any objections then I should have been advised to phone the police.

The circumstances regarding our eviction from what transpired to be my own house should also have been reported to the police.

Unfortunately, I was vulnerable and an easy target, for a man with no conscience. I had little or no knowledge of the law surrounding these matters,

Despite these issues with the Women's Aid lawyer, I still hold them in the highest regard, and consider they saved my life.

I was worried as I drove to Bob's house, but I wanted the girls' nursery and school things. I saved everything they brought home, pictures and the projects they had made in class. I have kept it all since they were born.

I even have Nicola and Teresa's hospital bracelets. They are all important to me. I knew if I left them with him, they would be thrown out or lost, he had no idea what was there. He saved nothing from those days.

He did not even know what I wanted because he had never taken the slightest bit of interest, at the time. As, I have pointed out before, he may even have been living a double life with somebody else. I do not have any idea where he was every night, until midnight. He certainly was not working!

The girls opened the door for me when I arrived. I noticed Nicola was sending a text message to someone. I hoped that she was not texting her dad to tell him that I was there.

He turned up five minutes later.

'Don't you take anything out of this house.' He was extremely aggressive, I knew his moods, I had been hit enough by him, in the past, to know what was coming.

'I've had a confirmation letter that it okay to collect my stuff, from your solicitor. So, your solicitor and my solicitor know that I'm here today, at this time. Don't you do anything stupid.'

'I want you sign this divorce agreement if not, you won't get anything out of this house.'

I was shaking when he said that. I knew he was close to violence. It looked like he would hit me wither the girls were there or not.

'I'm not signing anything, I'm leaving now. Bear in mind, I'm not living with you anymore, we might still be married on paper for now, but you can't treat me this way anymore. I don't live with you.'

I walked towards the door, I thought I had better leave for my own safety.

He grabbed my wrist hard and pulled me back into the house. The girls were watching, they said nothing. I could not believe it.

He blocked the doorway to prevent me from leaving. 'You're going nowhere until you sign this divorce agreement.' He shouted and handed the paper to me. He continued to say I could not leave until I signed the agreement. He was extremely abusive.

I could see the girls still watching.

I took my phone out of my pocket. 'I'll call the police if you don't get out of my way. Also, Kirsty will call me if she doesn't hear from me.' I was quite terrified now; I really did not know what he was going to do next.

I could see he was thinking about what I said, weighing up what he should do. Eventually, he unblocked the doorway. I was shaking with fear. The situation had changed, he knew he could abuse me in front of the girls, and they would do nothing. I did not want them to see that side of their dad or think that it was normal to behave that way.

I was still shaking when I arrived home. Kirsty called me, 'How did you get on? Did you get what you want?

'No, I didn't get anything.'

'What happened?'

'He wasn't there when I arrived, he turned up five minutes later.'

'I thought you agreed with his solicitor that you didn't want him to be there.'

'I did, but he turned up.'

I told Kirsty what had happened. She was not happy and did not understand why he was there when we agreed with both solicitors that I would go on my own.

'Did you call the police?' Kirsty asked me.

'No, I didn't.'

'You need to call the police, if you don't call the police there will be nothing recorded about this, and he'll do it again. You need to call the police now.'

'Yes, I'll do it.'

I was stupid, I just could not do it. I could not call the police when I was his wife. Now I was separated, I still could not do it.

Ten minutes later, Kirsty called to check if I had called them. 'Have you called the police?'

'No, I couldn't do it, at the end of the day he's still the father of my kids.' I started to cry.

'You've let him get away with this for long enough, it's got to stop now. You can't let him get away with it anymore, otherwise it'll never end. Clearly, it's not going to end just because you're no longer his wife, you're not living under the same roof with him and he's still doing it.'

'I know, you're right.'

'I'm going to call the police now, they'll come and take your statement, shortly.'

Ten minutes after the phone call, the police came to my house to take my statement.

I told them what had happened when I went to collect the children's stuff. I also went through how he tricked me in to leaving the house by pretending it was rented. I explained to them that I had been assaulted then and kept in the house against my will.

'Where were your children when this happened?' One of the police officers asked. They seemed to be only interested in what had just occurred, and not any past issues. His questions only related to the recent incident.

'They were in the house.'

'So, they saw what happened.'

'Yes, it was right in front of them.'

'I'll go and take your estranged husband's statement and your children's statements.'

'You can take my husband's statement, but he won't tell you the truth. Please leave my daughters out of this. I don't want to put them in the situation where they have to choose between their Mum and Dad.'

'How old are your daughters?'

'Twenty and seventeen.'

'I'm sorry, they're adults. I have to take their statements. I'll let you know what is going to happen next, after we've taken their statements.'

If I had known that the girls had to give statements, then I would not have reported it. At the time, I felt stupid, I felt bad about involving them.

The policeman called me a couple of hours later. 'I'm sorry, I couldn't arrest your ex-husband. Your daughters did not corroborate what happened. They weren't telling us the truth, they said that they were not there at the time. They said, they saw nothing.'

I did not know what to say, I just agreed with the police, and they left. They advised me to call if anything else happened.

Unfortunately, I didn't know enough to question this, and ask them why they were doing nothing about the fact I had forced out of my house, assaulted, and threatened with assault, and worse, if I didn't sign a divorce agreement to give up my entitlements as a wife.

I know that police procedures are much stricter now, so that this sort of poor response to domestic violence does not happen as often.

Nowadays, the police must arrest the suspects, to prevent this sort of poor treatment of domestic violence victims.

Sadly, it has taken the murders of many women for the police to improve their handling of this type of crime.

I broke down. It was so hurtful knowing that my children, who I carried in my tummy for nine months, and then put food in their mouths every day for twenty years, did not tell the truth.

I knew, I did not want them involved in this, but knowing they lied was very hurtful.

A mother's love is unconditional love, I tried to forget about it.

Kirsty phoned me later to find out what had happened. I told her.

'Don't be upset, they just said whatever their Dad told them to say, it's not because they don't love you.' Kirsty tried to make me felt better.

'The police must think I'm a liar.'

'I don't think so, the police said your daughters didn't tell the truth. From their experience, they would know what happened.'

A few days later I got a phone call from the police officer. 'We hold a class every Tuesday night at the police station in Cambuslang or Rutherglen for those who have been victims of domestic violence. If you want to listen to others or share your experience, you are welcome. They try to help each other to cope and help you to get out of this situation.'

'Thank you, I would love to.'

I thought it was ironic that they were asking me to attend a domestic violence class but declined to deal with the violence when they were called! I suppose somebody could tick the tick the box to show I had attended.

When I went along to the class I realised, I was not the only one in the world. Sadly, my case was the toughest and the longest.

'Can I write your story?' The policewoman taking the class asked.

'The people at Women's Aid asked me the same, they said my story would help others, especially those who are not born here, and know little about British Law.'

'That's what I thought too, that's why I asked you.'

'I'll think about it when this is over. But, I can see it's not going to end easily.'

'Yes, no problem.'

I could not cope with think telling my story over again or writing a book. I tried to deal with all the emotions going on inside my head. I did wonder why they wanted to write a story they would not take any action over!

I decided the girls were being brainwashed by their father. God knows what he was telling them to justify his behaviour towards me. I was really hurt; I felt the girls did not love me.

I know Kirsty said that they were frightened of him, but I thought there was more to it than that. I did not understand why they accepted his behaviour.

The only thing I can think of is that he told them to say nothing or else he would go to prison, and then they would have no financial support from him.

I do not know what was said, but the fact they said and did nothing about it really hurt me, and still does to this day.

I was struggling to cope with my finances. I was in debt with the car and my jewellery was in the pawn shop.

I tried to keep up with the payments, but it was too much for me. I lived very frugally, I drink rarely, and do not smoke.

I decided to give up my car, I just I could not afford to keep it anymore.

I called Chris 'Just to let you know, I'm giving up my car. I can't afford to keep it anymore.'

'You can't get rid of your car.'

'I've already called the credit company. The saddest thing is, I don't even have enough money to get rid of my car. They asked for fifty pounds for an admin fee, and one hundred seventy pounds to pick my car up.

If I drop it off, I won't have to pay the fee. It's a forty-minute drive, I was ringing to see if you can give me a lift back home.'

'If you get rid of your car, how will you come to see me?'

'You'll have to come here whenever you're free from your dog training.'

'What about indoor climbing during the week, and hill walking at weekends, how are you going to get there?'

'My climbing wall annual membership is three hundred sixty pounds and expires in August, I don't have money to renew it, anyway. I'll just go hillwalking whenever you're here.'

'Climbing and mountains are your life, I can't see how you can manage without a car.'

'I don't have a choice, for now, hopefully things will be better next year.'

'I'll come this weekend; we'll talk it through.'

'Okay.'

I knew, I could not manage without the car. Climbing and hillwalking keeps me alive, it makes me feel good about myself. It was the hardest decision that I had to make.

Chris came over for the weekend. 'I'll help you out with a hundred pounds each month for your car, until your finances improve.'

'It's okay, I know that you don't have much money yourself.'

'I can help you out with the climbing wall membership, we can talk about it when it's due. I'm sure you can pay monthly.'

'Thanks for helping me out, I'll pay you back when I've got more money.'

'Don't be silly. You should have another think about moving to Keswick.'

'No, I can't, I'm sorry.'

'If you move in with me, you won't have to pay rent, you'll save a lot on your bills.'

'It's not about saving money. You're helping me a lot, I'm very grateful, but I don't want to spoil our weekend with an argument about why I can't move in with you. In any case, the most important fact is, I couldn't leave the girls.'

'They're twenty and seventeen, they're adults.'

'They're still, and always will be my babies; it doesn't matter how old they are.'

'It's their choice to live with their Dad, it's only two hours' drive between Glasgow and Keswick.'

'I know, but I'm staying here for now, thanks for all your help.'

It was very nice of Chris to help me out, but I knew he would only come to Glasgow once a month to see me. He was too busy at weekends with his mountain rescue hobby. This was the only time we could see each other.

He had made very clear which was the most important to him.

I needed to sort out my life first before I started to think about moving in with someone else.

In fact, I did not think that I could live with anyone again, after what I had been through, and what I was still going through.

Also, it was complicated for me to move in with somebody. I had been brought up to get married before I lived with a man. I had moved in with Bob, before we were married, I was not going to make that mistake again.

Unfortunately, this horrible experience was by no means over, I was still married to him, and it seemed impossible to reach any type of divorce settlement, unless I complied with his demands to sign away any rights I had.

I was not after his money, but I was not going to be beaten and bullied as if I was a worthless and disposable product for him to throw out when he was finished with it.

I had put up with his violence and abuse for too long.

Nicola asked me. 'Dad doesn't have money, why are you taking him to court?'

'Is that what he told you? Did he explain that if he doesn't have any money then the court can't force him to give me money that he doesn't have? What is he worried about if he doesn't have any money?'

'Dad has to pay for a lawyer if you're taking him to court. He wants to keep his money for our education, not waste it on a lawyer.'

'What makes you think that I have money for a lawyer, I was put on the street by your father with nothing. He made me homeless.'

Nicola said nothing.

'I applied for a legal aid. Your dad can do the same, but he must be honest about his income and assets. He won't do that. I was his wife for twenty-two years and knew nothing about his finances.'

'Maybe he wants to keep it private.'

'I'm his wife, he even bought the house in Giffnock behind our back. He isn't honest with any of us.' I found out later, he bought two houses secretly.

Nicola did not reply. She did not look upset by what she heard.

'Anyway, what reason has he given you for making me homeless?' I could not help but bring the house issue up because I was so annoyed with her for supporting for her father.

'You're a mother, it's your job to bring your children up with nothing in return.'

I could not believe what she said. 'You sound like your Dad, but it's much more painful hearing you say it.

'Dad said you had an affair with a Korean man.'

I was quite shocked by this, but I started to realise the sort of things that were being said about me to the children.

I tried to think about who he could have meant. I did know one Korean guy when I worked in a restaurant, part time about 10 years ago, but that was the only one I could think of.

'That's complete nonsense. If I was seeing somebody, I would tell you. The only person I am seeing is Chris.'

Nicola said nothing.

'Did he tell you that he hired a private investigator to follow me, he didn't find anything out about me, apart from the fact, I was a good mother.'

She looked shocked but did not say anything.

I tried to explain further to her. 'Did he tell you how many times I had to quit my job because he refused to come home after work to take care of you? Was that fair?'

'Dad said you never worked.'

'You're twenty years old, I can't believe I'm listening to this. You know I worked really hard. How can you believe that nonsense? You used to see me in his shop every day, and you know I work in M&S now!'

'Dad said you never saved up.'

'Who do you think paid for your holidays every year, your clothes, laptops, games, cinemas, restaurants and the car to drive you around?'

'It's doesn't matter what you say, Dad doesn't have any money now.'

'I've saved up all my life, I was brought up to do that. I saved all the child allowance for you and Theresa, plus a hundred pounds of my own money, every month since you were born. That money was eventually transferred to your father, I've still got the receipts for it.'

Nicola did not reply to that either. I suppose she was trying to work out who was telling her the truth.

'Do you mean he doesn't have any money to give to me as part of the divorce? I want you to know, it's not about money, it's my dignity. I'm not a disposable asset, I don't deserve this awful treatment from him. Never mind the criminal aspect of it!!'

She did not reply.

I had to drop it, it was causing me more pain hearing his words from my daughters, than when I heard it from him. I wondered how they could go to bed and sleep every night.

I still wonder how he explained his behaviour to the girls. I wonder what he said that made the girls believe him. Kirsty was probably right, it was brainwashing.

On the 11th June 2012, I received a letter from the legal aid informing me that they had decided to grant my application for the following proceedings, capital sum, orders under matrimonial homes (Scotland) Act, and divorce on the grounds of two years' separation.

My legal aid was granted with a contribution of seven hundred and ninety-eight pounds. It was payable in thirty instalments of twenty-six pounds and sixty pence.

On the 9th July 2012, I received a letter from the Women's Aid solicitor.

We now attach a draft initial writ which we have prepared on your behalf and would intend to lodge at Hamilton Sheriff Court to raise an action for divorce against your husband, including additional financial orders.

Mr. Smith has failed to produce any financial information despite repeated requests, we have applied to extend your legal aid so that we may ask the court to grant an order to force him to disclose any other assets for investments which he has. The relevant date being the date of separation over and above the matrimonial home. We shall notify you immediately once you have considered the terms of the attached draft writ. Please check the draft writ carefully for factual accuracy and confirm to us if any changes require to be made or whether you have any additional information you would wish to be included in the Writ. We look forward to hearing from you.

I did not know much about British law, but it sounded good to me, I was happy with it. I called in to confirm and told them to go ahead.

A month later, on the 9th August 2012. I received another letter from Brenda.

We understand from Mr. Smith's new agents Mr. Smith does not agree with your date of separation being March 2009, and that, in fact, he considers the date of separation to be sometime in 2001. We understand that on or around 2001 you left the family home to go to America and that at that stage you both considered the relationship to be terminated.

Obviously before any initial writ is lodged with the Court we will require to clarify with you the position in regards to the date of separation and your comments in relation to the allegations by Mr. Smith that in fact the date of separation was 2001.

In addition, you will note that the former matrimonial home on Church Road has already been transferred into the names of your daughters, that this was carried out in around March or April this year.

We further understand that Mr. Smith has produced to them emails from yourself stating that you wished the matrimonial home to be transferred into your daughter's names and that you would not be seeking any other financial provisions.

I saw that he had changed lawyers. Every time I tried to get him in court, he changed lawyers and delayed proceedings.

I was so shocked by the allegations in this letter. He was such a liar.

He knew what he was saying was not true, and that I would easily be able to prove that. For example, I had been working in Marks and Spencers for the last 14 years and had my pay slips to prove it. Also, there was no USA immigration stamp on my passport in 2001.

The reason he did this was because it delayed the proceedings whenever he alleged something like this. He just wanted to drag things on as long as possible.

The legal issues involved in the divorce were incredibly stressful for me, just reading and understanding the letters in English was hard work.

The behaviour of my daughters was very hurtful, I could not describe in words how hurtful it was.

I remember calling Nicola after I had not heard from either of them for a week. A week might have made little difference to them, but for me it felt like a month.

Nicola answered, she obviously held the phone away from her mouth, but I could still hear. 'Dad, am I allowed to speak to her?'

I was so upset. 'Listen, you're twenty, you're an adult. You don't have to ask your dad for permission to talk to your mother. And I'm not a her! I'm your mother.'

'Sorry, we're not in Glasgow.'

'It doesn't matter where you are, you can answer my calls without asking your dad's permission. Anyway, where are you?'

'We're in Ireland?'

'How long are you there for? Is Teresa with you?'

'Two weeks, yes, she's here with us.'

'Okay, I'll see you when you get back. Have a nice holiday.'

'We aren't on holiday; we're just visiting Auntie Sadie.'

'It's okay, whatever the reason, will you visit me when you get back?'

'Yes, we will.'

'You should have let me know you were going away.'

'Dad said, we don't have to tell you where we're going.'

'Okay Nicola, I shall let you go now.'

I could not stop crying, I was so upset.

I saw the girls when they came back from Ireland. 'This is the letter from my lawyer.' I handed it to Nicola.

'It's okay, Mum. I don't want to read it.'

'It's okay if you don't want to read it. I understand why you don't want to read it. But, I'll keep all these letters until the day I die, you can ask to see them anytime. There are a few things in the letter about our house being transferred into your names. Why did you do this behind my back?'

'I don't know what you're talking about?'

'About the house. Your Dad transferred the house to you two, and you accepted it.'

'Dad has already transferred the house to us. Aren't you happy that your daughters have a house?'

'Of course, I'm happy that you two have a house, but it's my house. Are you happy that I have no house, and that I was homeless?'

Neither of them replied.

'Do you really think that there is a good and honest reason that your father wants you two to have our house? Or do you think it is because he thinks it will protect the house from the divorce proceedings?'

'I don't know, maybe he has his own reasons.' Teresa said. Unfortunately, she always believed whatever he told her.

'Whatever the reason, it's not acceptable for him to do that, it's dishonest. When I'm talking to you, I feel like I'm talking to him. You believe everything he tells you.'

'Dad says, sometimes it's too complicated for him to explain.' Nicola said.

I showed the girls the letter from my solicitor. 'Look at this, he says I left the family home to go to America in 2001. You know that's totally ridiculous! If he is saying things like that, do you not think he will be lying about other things too?'

'He could be mistaken about the year.' Teresa still took his side.

'I never left home to live in America, ever! You know that!'

Neither replied.

'Teresa, do you believe I left the family home when you were six! Did I not take you to school every day, make all your meals, and entertain you at weekends!?'

Teresa just looked annoyed that I had disproved what her father had told her.

'I've had enough of this. I don't need help from either of you. I can prove it with my national insurance number, my pay slips, my bank statement, my bills.'

'Maybe Dad meant that you went on your climbing trips.'

'I never went on holiday to America until 2008. It says clearly that I left the family home, in 2001, to go to America, that is a complete lie. I saw you every day during that period of your life!'

Neither replied, they just looked sullen. I realised I was not getting anywhere. I was worried about what he had told them to brainwash them to this extent.

'Okay, let's drop it. I wish that he would stop trying to drag things out. What type of father is he? This transfer of the house is a fraudulent transaction, he knows he can't transfer the house without my written agreement.'

'I don't understand.' Nicola looked worried.

'I know you didn't understand what you were signing for, you signed whatever your father asked you to sign. I know he didn't care enough to explain to you that what you were doing was fraud. You have dishonestly answered questions on the property transfer forms which relate to me, so the house could be transferred without my knowledge or consent. You have been party to a fraud.'

The girls were silent, I continued, 'Did he tell you about council tax, gas, electric, home insurance? Did he explain that he was stealing the house from me? Did he explain that it is illegal to treat your wife like this?

'No.' Theresa said.

'Do you realise how painful it was when my solicitor said we have advised the Registers of Scotland of the fraud which has been carried out by Nicola Smith and Teresa Smith?'

They both looked worried.

'I wouldn't have been upset if the solicitor had said, the fraud which has been carried out by your father. He is so selfish, he only thinks about how much he can get away with. He has dragged you two into this fraud, he didn't care about the consequences.'

'You put us in the position that we had to choose between you and Dad.' Nicola said.

'I didn't put you in that position, I didn't ask you to do anything wrong. But, I agree that you have chosen to believe him and not me.'

There was no answer from either of them. I did not understand why I deserved this. I was struggling to cope and control my emotions toward my daughters.

I was starting to doubt if they loved me until I realised, I was the victim of a sophisticated campaign of parental alienation.

THIRTY-EIGHT

Bob appeared to be getting worried about the impending divorce hearing. He was making some quite wild accusations about me to his solicitor, and these were going to my solicitor. Unfortunately, Brenda appeared to be taking these at face value, and started to write to me to explain accusations which were quite obviously false.

I felt that when she received these accusations, she should have asked Bob's solicitor for proof before she accepted them. I knew she was inexperienced and possibly working for nothing, as an intern, to gain experience, but she was causing huge delays in progressing these matters to court. I felt I could do better myself.

'Please let us hear from you with your instructions particularly in relation to Mr. Smith's comments with regards to your extra marital affair and your intention to relocate to the United States of America.'

There were no details about who I was supposed to have had an affair with, when it happened, and what the evidence was that I had any intention to go to America.

I had no intention of emigrating to America. Even if I had, there was no way I would have passed the immigration requirements, because I had no money, no visa and no job in America. In any case, I would never leave the girls!

A previous letter from her queried if I was living in America, despite the fact she was aware that I had been working in Marks and Spencers for the past ten years!

I instructed her to start asking for proof of such statements, instead of appearing to accept them, and asking me to disprove them.

On the 14th November 2012, I received a letter from Brenda, regarding the date of separation. My ex-husband considered the date of separation to be 2002, therefore the property did not constitute a matrimonial home.

We refer to the above and your meeting with our colleague on the 9th November 2012. At the time we discussed in detail the history of your marriage with your husband and also why you consider the date of separation to be March 2009. At the time you accepted that you and your husband didn't sleep in separate bedrooms from March 2009 and that you both continued to reside within the matrimonial home with you continuing to carry out cooking, cleaning and washing for your husband. This information which you provided to our office at your meeting with our Brenda is at odds with the statement you had initially given to support your legal aid application in March 2012.

On that basis we have no option other than to withdraw from acting on your behalf. The information which has been produced to the legal aid board and which is the basis on which you were granted legal aid is untrue and incorrect. We have now required to notify Mr. Smith's solicitors and also the legal aid board that we no longer act on your behalf. Should you wish to continue pursuing your husband for a financial claim in terms of the divorce you will now require to instruct new solicitors or to continue matters on your own behalf.

I did not understand the letter, it was very confusing. It appeared to be saying that we had not been in a separate bedroom since 2009, and that I accepted that. This was not true.

I was so upset with the letter. I just could not stop crying. I called Kirsty, she said she would come to see me after work.

'Is everything okay?' She could see I was upset.

'No, I got this yesterday.' I handed the letter to her.

Kirsty read it through 'I don't understand what's gone wrong. We filled in the application form for legal aid together. It was truly clear what you meant.'

'I know, and Brenda sent it on my behalf. If something wasn't right, she should have spotted it then. The only thing I can think of is, my last meeting with Brenda.'

'What about it?'

'It was to discuss the date of separation. My ex-husband said it was 2002, of course he wanted to make sure there was ten years of separation, because that affects the status of the matrimonial home. Brenda asked me when we started to have separate bedrooms.'

'What did you say?'

'I said it was a long while ago, 2002.'

'What did Brenda say?'

'She said, so your ex-husband was correct, it was 2002.'

'I said, it depends on what you mean by separation? I explained to her that I still did his washing, cooking and looked after the children, we were still a couple but we didn't sleep, every night, in the same bedroom because he came home so late and woke me up.'

'Yes, I remember that.'

'That was since Nicola was born in 1992.'

'Yes.'

'Then later, since about 2002, he was still living in the house with me, but he came home very late. We weren't getting on, and I no longer wanted to have sex with him, but he forcibly had sex with me, whenever he felt like it.'

'Yes, I remember you told me about that.'

'So, when Brenda asked me when about the separation date, I explained all of this, and asked her if that meant we were separated?'

'What did she say?'

'She said no, in that case, you were not separated.'

'I'll call and make an appointment to see her, we'll go together.'

'It's okay. She has made a decision to drop my case. Maybe, in my case, the word 'separation' was too complicated for her.'

'Well, she's a Women's Aid solicitor. It's not going to be a straightforward case.'

'It's okay Kirsty, she's let me down badly. She hasn't even called to discuss it; she's just dumped me.'

'What are you going to do?'

'There's plenty of other solicitors in Glasgow, I'll find one.'

'Okay, you let me know how you're getting on. If you change your mind about Brenda, give me a call.'

'I won't change my mind about her, she's let me down.'

I started to cry after Kirsty left. I could not eat, I could not sleep. I could not understand why Brenda had let me down.

I knew, my case was complicated, and my husband and his various solicitors were very difficult to deal with. I thought Brenda did not have the experience or the knowledge to deal with them.

Maybe it was also more complicated for her because English is not my first language, and it was hard for me to explain some of the issues.

It appeared to me that she believed some of the wild accusations that were in my husband's lawyers' letters.

It did not help matters when I received another letter from the legal aid board:

'We cannot continue to provide legal aid to a person who is not represented by a solicitor, we have now suspended your grant to legal aid. If you want to continue with your action, please tell us who your new solicitor is within ninety days from the date of this letter. If we don't hear from you within ninety days, we will terminate your grant of legal aid.'

I had three months to find another solicitor. I would have to tell my story over again to another stranger. I hated telling my story, I hated going through it repeatedly. I had lost my confidence, I could not face being let down again.

I cried all the time, I could not eat or sleep for three nights, I was not sure where to start looking for a new solicitor.

I could not face watching TV. Eventually, when I started again, I saw a news story about, Bob's friend, Martin talking about his shop.

I remember he used to disagree strongly with the way Bob treated me. He used to say to me, if I needed help, to call him anytime.

I rang his shop. He was not in, I left a message for him. An hour later, he phoned back.

'Hi Nuch, it's Martin. How are you?'

'I forgot to leave my number; how did you get my number?'

'I kept it on my phone.'

'Thanks.'

'How are you?'

'Not so good. I need somebody to talk to, and maybe you can help too.'

'Why don't you come to my office tomorrow, after your work?'

'Okay, see you tomorrow.'

I went to see Martin, he was always glad to see me. 'It's nice to see you, tell me what's happening?'

'Here, these are the letters from my solicitor from day one until today.' I handed him the folder.

'Oh my gosh! I had less than ten letters when I had my divorce!' Martin read through them quickly.

'I can leave them with you if you need more time.'

'I'm not surprised you're so upset. He was one of my good friends, I've known him for years, and most of these allegations about you, are complete rubbish. I really don't agree with the way he is behaving. It's quite wrong.'

I nodded.

'I had no idea he was as ruthless as this. I did warn you that he was dangerous, and to be careful.'

'Yes, I'm really sorry now that I didn't listen to you.' I started to cry.

'Right, don't worry. First, we need to sort out a lawyer.'

'I'm not sure where to look, maybe online. But, because the Women's Aid solicitor let me down. I feel embarrassed and self-conscious telling my story.'

'Forget about her, she didn't do a good job. I'll take you to see Kevin, my lawyer.'

'I hate telling my story.' I started to cry.

'You need to make an appointment to see your doctor first.'

'Why?'

'You're depressed, you need antidepressants.'

'What makes you think I'm suffering from depression.'

'Because you're crying.'

'I'm crying because I'm upset telling you what he put me through, not because I'm depressed.'

'You can be suffering from depression and not realise'

'I don't believe in taking tablets. People in my work often sent in sick lines with depression. I grew up in a country where if you don't work, you starve to death, depression doesn't exist.'

'Okay, when was the last time you saw the girls?'

'A month ago, they seem to have made a decision that I'm the one at fault.'

'He brainwashed them, don't you worry, one day they'll see it all clearly.'

'When was the last time you spoke to your mum?'

'A year ago.'

'That's not good.'

'I don't have enough money to call.'

'You can get cheap calls through call centres online. I'll ring for you; can you give me your Mum's number.'

I was so grateful to Martin. I spoke to my Mum for thirty minutes. I did not tell her everything that was happening to me.

I did not want her to worry about me. I could imagine how she would feel, being on the other side of the world, not able to help

Martin took me to Boots. He bought me vitamins, supplements & herbs for depression. 'You take them every day, I'll call you when I have an appointment with Mr. Murray, my solicitor.'

Before we parted, I promised that I would take the tablets, but I never took any. I do not believe in tablets, I do exercise. I thought it was okay to be upset and cried again.

THIRTY-NINE

On 29th November 2012, Martin made an appointment for me to see his solicitor, Mr. Kevin Murray. He took me to his office in Shawlands.

'Hi Kevin, this is Nuch Smith, the friend I told you about.'

'Can you tell me about your marriage history.' Mr Murray looked at me.

Martin replied. 'Is it okay if I tell you. Nuch has been through enough. If you have any questions just ask her to clarify. If I say something incorrect, not right, she'll clarify it anyway.'

'Yes, I'm happy with that if that's okay with Mrs Smith.'

I nodded in agreement.

Martin started to explain my marriage history to Mr Murray.

Mr Murray turned to me. 'I'll do my best to help you. I know Mr Smith, I've met him before.'

'Are you friendly with my ex-husband?'

'Oh no, I only know him through his business. I also deal with business and employment law.'

'Okay, so you have an idea about his business.'

'Yes, and it doesn't matter to me if he says he has no money now. He has to prove to me where it's disappeared to. For example, if his assets were five hundred thousand, he has to show me the paperwork detailing exactly where his five hundred thousand has gone to.'

'What about if he refuses to do that? That's what happened with my previous solicitor. He refused to explain anything, and the solicitor kept sending him letters to chase up replies, but she never got anything back.'

'I'll send him a reminder letter with a time limit on it. If I haven't heard from him by then, I'll get a court order.'

'That sounds much more positive.' I was pleased with the new solicitor, he sounded really positive.

'Any more questions that you would like to ask before you go?'

'What's going to happen with my legal aid?'

'Just leave it to me, I'll sort that out for you.'

'What happens when my legal aid contribution of £795 is used up?'

'I'll take something off your share of the joint assets at the end.'

'Thank you.'

'I'll sort out the legal aid first, and I'll get back to you.'

I felt much better after the meeting Mr Murray. I felt he knew what he was doing. I didn't feel the same way about Brenda.

Martin took me to a cafe before sending me home. We had a little chat during coffee. 'I can't believe that you went to stay in that terrible high rise, and then moved to a refuge flat.'

'I had no choice, it was there or on the street.'

I've got a four-bedroom house just ten minutes' drive from yours. Why didn't you call me?'

'I didn't want to trouble you. I felt that I had to sort it out on my own. Also, I'm seeing someone, I didn't think it would be a good idea.'

'So, where is he? I didn't know that, it looks like you're going through this on your own.'

'Chris is in the Lake District, we see each other once or twice per month. Our relationship is on and off, most of the time.'

'That's not good, after all you have been through already. Anyway, I'm going to check out your previous marital house tonight. We'll talk later.'

Martin went to check out the house. I thought, it will not make any difference, but I wondered what Bob was up to and if Martin knew or suspected something.

Two days later, I met up with Martin. 'I went to check out your old house, there was a sign at the window 'for rent' with his phone number.'

I was aghast. 'He kicked his family out of the house, so he can rent it out!'

'I know, what's a nasty person. I also went to B&Q.'

'Why?'

'To get the lock. We need to move fast, I'll change the lock, you can move back in before he gets a tenant.

'Are you kidding, right?'

'No, it's your house, why waste money on renting somewhere else. And he is making money on the rent.'

'I don't know if it's a good idea. What if he calls the police?'

'It's good if he calls the police, but he won't dare. He would get locked up, not you. He is nothing less than a criminal.'

'I can't stay in the house anyway; I wouldn't feel safe. I would worry that he would send someone to attack me. I was in fear of that when I lived there before.'

'If you change your mind let me know. I've already bought the new locks. I'll help you as much as I can. I don't care if he doesn't speak to me again.'

'Thanks, you've already helped me a great deal. Without you, I wouldn't have found Mr Murray. I didn't know I could move back into the house, nobody explained my rights to me before, not even Brenda.'

'She was useless.'

'I think people assume I know basic law, like other British people, but I don't know anything. And thanks again for telling Mr Murray about my marriage history. It's unhealthy for me to keep going through this with strangers, over and over again.'

'It's my pleasure, you're my friend. I'm happy to listen any time, don't worry about that. I fully understand the emotions, having gone through a terrible domestic time myself.'

'He was very good at destroying my life, he put me through so much pain and anguish.'

'You need to write and complain to East Renfrewshire Housing about the house transaction and the landlord registration.'

'I still couldn't believe that he would put his children at risk of prosecution for fraud.'

'That's right, for example, if a fire was to occur and a fault was found for which the landlord was liable, your children could be placed in the appalling position of facing a criminal prosecution. being a landlord is a serious responsibility.'

'I've no doubt that he never explained that to the girls.'

I wrote a letter to East Renfrewshire Housing complaining about Bob failing to disclose the fact he was landlord. Also, the property was our matrimonial home and I had not given my permission to rent it out.

I could not have done nearly as much without Martin's help. Sadly, in January 2018, he died suddenly after a heart attack.

On the 13th December 2012, I have received my first letter from Mr Murray.

The Scottish Legal Aid Board have confirmed we can act on your behalf in term of an award to you of Legal Advice & Assistance pending the transfer of your file from your former agents.

Please, however, note the Scottish Legal Aid Board have indicated the based upon comments by your former agents, relaying to the date of your separation as had been referred to in their correspondence to you, they now require to consider whether your Legal Aid Certificate should be transferred.

It would therefore be of assistance if you could contact ourselves in writing confirming the date you consider you did indeed separate from your husband, albeit you may still have been residing together at the same address.

Please also confirm the date when you both began to reside at separate address.

I made an appointment to see Mr Murray as soon as he was available.

'Hi, I received a letter regarding the dates of separation. This was the issue with my previous solicitor, Brenda, from Women's Aid.'

'When do you consider that you separated from your husband?'

'That's tricky for me to answer, it's not straightforward, but I'll explain to you exactly what I explained to Brenda.

We had separate bedrooms not long after we were married, it was not because we didn't love each other. When it comes to sleeping, I like my own space, we were still in love, at that time, despite the separate bedrooms.

He started being violent and very controlling after our first child. After that, I no longer loved him. Our marriage was on the rocks. I told him that I did not want him to come to my bedroom for sex anymore.

But he still did, he said he could come and have sex with me when he wanted, and that was Scottish law, because I was his wife. I did his washing, ironing, cleaning and cooking until 2009.

The reason I stopped doing it, was because he moved his clothes somewhere else, and came home very little. I still lived at the same address with him, until the day he had me evicted in December 2011.

It's easy to prove that I lived at the same address with him. If you need evidence regarding the matrimonial home or my occupancy rights, I can provide you with letters, bills and my pay slips.

I couldn't give you a one-word answer because of these reasons. I'm not sure exactly what separation means in cases like mine. I explained all of this to Brenda.'

'If he still came into your bedroom and you still did his washing, and cooking then, you were not separated in law, as far as divorce goes. In fact, you have grounds for divorce with unreasonable behaviour, such as domestic violence, controlling behaviour, threats, insults and manipulation.

At this time, we'll concentrate on separation, that's what your legal aid was granted for.'

I felt much better after talking it through with Mr Murray.

Brenda never explained to me that I could have other grounds for divorce. I still do not understand why this was. I can only assume that she was very inexperienced.

Martin called me. 'How did you get on with Kevin Murray?'

'Legal Aid confirmed that Mr Murray can act on my behalf.'

'That's good news. What are you planning for Christmas?'

'No plans, I don't like Christmas, I was evicted four days before last Christmas.'

'Are you having the girls?'

'Yes, I didn't see them last Christmas or New Year. I'll have them this year, I'll cook them something.'

'Why don't you and the girls join me and Andrew. I'll book a table in a Thai restaurant. Andrew will be pleased to see Nicola and Teresa again. He last saw them on his thirteen birthday.'

'I don't think it's a good idea. The girls will tell their Dad, he might send someone to kill you!' I did not really want to go, I did not want to get too close to Martin, I knew he liked me, but I was only interested in friendship with him. I did not want to say no, because he had been helping me so much.

'I'm not worried, I'll kill him first! I'm kidding. I'm not scared of him; I don't care if he doesn't speak to me again.'

'I'm not sure how to tell the girls about New Year.'

'Why don't we just accidentally meet each other in the Thai restaurant?'

'How?'

'I'll book a table for Andrew and me, and a table for you and the girls. We can just pretend that we met there by accident. Then I can ask to join the tables together.'

'Sounds good.' I decided it would not do any harm, the children would have a nice time.

'Don't forget to act surprised!'

On Christmas day, we went to the Thai restaurant. Martin and Andrew were already there, as planned. Andrew was the same age as Nicola. I thought it was great for the girls to have company their own age.

After we had finished our meal, the Thai chef came to say hello to us, she knew Martin.

'This is Nuch, Bob's ex-wife.'

She was silent for a few seconds. 'Nice to meet you, I didn't know Bob had a wife, he never told me. I've known him for a few years now.'

'Yes, I'm not surprised he never told you. This is Nicola and Teresa, my daughters.' I replied.

I was hurt when the chef told me she did not know Bob had a wife or two grown up daughters. It was still hard to hear about my husband's double life from other people.

On the 3rd January 2013, I received a letter from Mr Murray's secretary.

We refer to our previous correspondence. We have now received notification that your Civil Legal Aid Certificate has been transferred to ourselves subject to our confirming, following a study of your former solicitors file, as to whether we consider it reasonable that an award of Civil Legal Aid remains in place.

Unfortunately, today we have not received your file papers as your former solicitors state their file had been forwarded to their Law Accountants. We have also been advised that they require an undertaking from you to the effect that should we receive any money following the division of the matrimonial assets, that we would settle their Legal Advice & Assistance account. They are making such a request as they considerate unlikely the Scottish Legal Aid Board would make settlement of their legal fees incurred under the award to you of Legal Advice & Assistance in such circumstances, this being the usual

position adopted by the Board in relation to the division of matrimonial assets.

    Please therefore contact our Mr Murray initially by telephone to confirm you would

agree to providing such an undertaking.

I read the letter over a few times, trying to understand what they were saying. I could

not understand why Brenda; my former solicitor just could not make it simple by

transferring my file to Mr Murray.

I could not understand why she could not just be happy that I had a new solicitor. I

could not understand why she was so negative about my Legal Aid grant.

However, I was sure that Mr Murray knew what he was dealing with. I could feel that

I was in a good hand.

On 24ᵗʰ January 2013, I received another letter from Mr Murray.

We have now received in your file from your former solicitors. We have also had your

Legal Aid Certificate transferred to us. The Scottish Legal Aid Board have now processed

what is called a Stage Report confirming that we can continue to act on your behalf at

this time in terms the Legal Aid Certificate granted to your former solicitors.

    As your legal Aid Certificate has now been transferred to our Mr Murray, we have

now also written to your husband's solicitor advising that we are acting and requesting

they provide us with copies of any recent correspondence which may not be in your

former agents file.

    We will therefore contact you again once we have heard from them and have been

able to confirm their exact position at this time.

I was pleased and hoped I was getting somewhere. I knew it would take time because of Bob's lying and underhand behaviour, but I did feel, at last, I was moving forward.

I still could not understand why my former solicitor dropped my case or her comments to Mr Murray about my Legal Aid.

On the 15th April 2013, I received a letter from my solicitor.

We have written to your husband's solicitor; we have not as yet received his response. We have therefore issued a reminder letter to them, our initial detailed letter concentrating upon the transfer of title of your former home on Church Road, Giffnock and the date of separation.

We will contract you again as soon as we receive a response.

I was not surprised that my solicitor had not received any response from him. If he was honest and had nothing to hide, he could have replied quickly.

The next weekend my daughters stayed overnight with me. They brought some homework from school with them.

I tidied up their notebooks after they went to bed. I found some invoices among their notebooks, one of them must have accidentally taken it from their Dad's car.

The invoice was signed by Bob as a director in a Limited Company, Total Heat Recovery Limited, registered office, St Vincent Street, Glasgow with a business address at Newton Terrace, Glasgow.

I forwarded the invoice to my solicitor.

I received a letter randomly, in the post, asking me if I knew the contact details of my ex-husband's private pension contributions. I also passed it on to my solicitor.

On the 31 May 2013, I received a letter from my solicitor.

We have now had the Initial Writ requesting the Court grant decree of divorce and a financial payment against your husband warranted by Glasgow Sheriff Court.

We are therefore now arranging to service this documentation on your husband and will contact you as soon as we receive a response from his solicitors.

Initial Writ

1) *To divorce the Defender from the pursuer on the grounds that the parties' marriage has broken down irretrievable as established by the parties non cohabitation for a continues period of two years or more;*

2) *To grant Decree against the Defender for payment to the pursuer of a capital sum of one hundred thousand pounds sterling (£100,000) payable on such date and by such method as the Court thinks fit, with interest thereon at the rate of eight per centum per annum from such date as the court deems appropriate until payment;*

3) *To find the declaration that the property on Church Road, Giffnock, Glasgow is a matrimonial home within the meaning of the Matrimonial Home (Family Protection Scotland) Act 1981.*

4) *To grant and order the Defender to lodge details of his resources, assets and investments within 14 days of service of this Writ and to grant such an Order ad interim.*

5) To find the Defender liable in the expenses of the action.

I started to see light at the end of the tunnel. The divorce had been ongoing for eighteen months, I hoped it would be over by the end of the year. Surely, it would not take more than two years.

FORTY

In June 2013, I found out. Tann, my niece, was diagnosed with colon cancer, she was in the final stage. It was incredibly sad, there was nothing the doctor could do for her.

Her mum, Sang, passed away with colon cancer, aged thirty-five. Tann was only twenty-eight, I thought she was too young for this to happen to her.

I found it really hard to cope with. I loved Tann like my own daughter. I had sent money to Thailand, to my Mum, to look after Tann, since my sister died. Tann was thirteen at the time.

I was not coping well with work, there were too many things in my head. It was hard to find a way through the difficulties Bob was causing during the divorce proceedings.

The problems in the relationship with both my girls was very upsetting, and now my niece's illness made it hard to concentrate on work.

On the worst days, I could not help crying at work, because of this, I was sent home. This was always done very sympathetically, and I am grateful for the compassionate way I was treated.

One day, during our lunch break, Ann said to me 'Nuch, you need to go to see your niece.'

'I know, Ann. I would love too; she is not just my niece. I've taken care of her since my sister died, I love her like my own.'

'Then you should go while there is still time.'

'I can't afford six hundred pounds for the flights.'

I was desperate to go. I would never forgive myself if I did not see her for the last time. People at work collected money for my flights. It was really generous of them. I was overwhelmed by their generosity. I never asked anybody for money, it was a spontaneous gesture from my friends when they found out what I was going through.

Ann handed me her debit card. 'Here is my cash card and my pin. Please go and take out some money. I know you need money to spend, on top of the cost of your flights.'

'I can't do that, Ann. You can't just give your cash card and pin code to anybody.'

'I don't just give my card to anybody. I only give it to you, I trust you.'

'Thanks, but I still can't do it.'

'Okay, I'll go and take it out myself to give to you. Don't worry, you just pay me back whenever you can.'

That was what she did. It was truly kind of Ann, she always helped me out. She often took me out for lunch and never let me pay. 'You can pay when your divorce is over.'

Sadly, Ann passed away with cancer in 2018. She will always have a place in my heart.

I booked the flights to see Tann as soon as I could. I called my Mum every day before I left, to check how Tann was. I did not want to speak to Tann myself, because I did not know what to say, and I thought I might burst into tears when I heard her voice.

I thought this might upset Tann, and I wanted her to remain strong.

Just before I left, I noticed that my monthly wage was much more than usual.

I showed it to Ann. 'Look at my pay slip, they've given me too much, that's a manager's rate.'

'That's great. Someone up there is looking after you.'

'Shall I tell HR?'

'No, you can do with the extra money. You need to go to see Tann.'

'What if HR find out? I won't be able to pay them back if I use it all up in Thailand.'

'Don't be silly, don't tell them, they've plenty money. If HR find out later, just say you never noticed because you were in Thailand. Don't worry if you don't have money left, they won't take it all out at once from your wages. They'll take a small amount off each month.'

So, I never told HR, and they never noticed. Maybe Ann was right, someone up there was looking after me.

When I arrived in Thailand, I went straight to the hospital.

Tann was so skinny, only skin covered her skeleton, no fat or muscle. I could see a big solid lump inside her tummy, it was the tumour.

She looked exactly like her Mum, before she died.

I was so upset, I tried my best not to cry in front of her. 'You have to fight, you're still young.' I told her.

'Don't worry auntie, I'm a fighter, I'll fight until my last breath.'

She acted as if it was a normal illness, and she would get better the next week. She still enjoyed having her meals, watching telly, and having face call with her friends.

She always had friends coming around to visit, and they enjoyed taking pictures together, and uploading them to Facebook.

She uploaded her routine in hospital to Facebook every day. That was how I first found out about her illness.

At first, I thought, it was a joke. I wondered why she had never called to tell me. She told me later, she did not want to upset me, she did not know what to say.

I understood what she was saying but, the truth was, it still upset me to find out from Facebook.

Since my sister died, I had taken care of her and her brother's financial needs until they both graduated. I worked hard to be able to do this and went without much myself.

I understand that it is hard for people, in this situation, to tell people about their illness, however, finding out from Facebook was awful.

Her hospital was in Chiang Mai, roughly two hours' drive, so my Mum and I stayed over with Tann, in hospital, every day during my three weeks in Thailand.

She was in a private room covered by her health insurance, but I had to pay extra for the beds for Mum and me.

During the second week in hospital Tann said. 'Dad is coming to see me this afternoon.'

'When did he last get in touch with you?' I asked. I was surprised he had been in touch, he abandoned them as soon as he knew Sang was pregnant.

'Last year.'

'How did he find you?'

'On Facebook.'

I was angry, I just could not accept it. 'I'm sorry, you have to make a choice between him and me.'

Mum said to me. 'She's dying, just let her see him, if she wants to.'

'Okay, Mum.' I nodded.

An hour later, there was a knock at the door. I did not look at him, I walked out of the room, banging the door behind me.

I was angry because he walked out on Sang as soon as he knew she was pregnant. He saw Tann once, after she was born.

He never paid a penny to Sang to help with Tann, despite coming from a wealthy background and having a good job.

In Thailand, there is nothing like the Child Support Agency, to help women in this situation.

I felt he did not deserve to be a part of her life now, to ease his conscience.

I was the one who had to take on his financial responsibilities. That was part of the reason that I had to put up with my husband's behaviour. If it had not been for this, then I would have been able to leave Bob much earlier.

I went down to the hospital canteen, I was upset and cried at the table. I am not sure if I did the right thing, sometimes I think I was wrong to walk out like that. It was not my decision, it was Tann's decision to meet her estranged father.

Ten minutes later, Mum called me. 'Just come back, he's gone.'

I walked back up to the room

A couple of days later Tann was strong enough to leave hospital to recover at home. I was due back in Scotland. Leaving was the hardest thing I have ever done. I knew it would be the last time that I saw her.

I could not say, I hoped she would get better. I could not say, I will see you next time. I gave her a cuddle and walked away without saying anything. We both cried.

On the 5th July 2013, I received a letter from my solicitor.

We can confirm that the Sheriff Clerk has now processed your application for divorce on the basis that your current address not be disclosed to your husband. We are therefore arranging to serve Court papers on your husband.

Please note, initially service will be made by recorded delivery letter. We will therefore contact you again in some seven to ten days to confirm that service has been affected.

Your husband will then have a period of twenty-one days to consider whether he wishes to defend these proceedings. As we are seeking financial payment from him, we assume this will be the case and we therefore also contact you again once we hear further from his solicitors.

Every time I received a letter, I read it over a few times. Sometimes, it was hard to understand the legal terms, they were completely unfamiliar to me.

My husband had a period of twenty-one days, I wondered what he would come up with this time. Whatever it was, I knew it would upset me.

I collected and dropped the girls off at their grandfather's house every second weekend. For six months, I noticed a new Ford Mondeo parked there, I asked the girls about it. 'Is that your Dad's new car?'

'No, Mum it's his friend's car.' Teresa said.

'Where's his friend, why does he park his car there?'

'He parks here when he and Dad go off to work together in Dad's car.' Nicola said.

'Every time I have collected or dropped you off in the past six months, it's been here. Are you sure it's not your Dad's car?

'Yes, it's the truth, that's what Dad told us.'

I was angry, I knew they were lying. 'I'm not stupid. It's hurtful knowing that you are lying. I'm struggling to keep my car, I almost gave it up. Now, I see your father has two cars, and you know he took mine from me.'

They both were silent.

The day before my forty-seven birthday I bought a mountain bike for myself as a birthday present. I bought it second hand on E-bay for thirty-five pounds. It was pink and looked in good condition, I thought it was a good bargain!

The seller said. 'There's nothing wrong with it, it's still in a good condition. I'm selling it because my daughter grew out of it, she needs a bigger one.'

'My daughter will like it, she loves pink.' I was too embarrassed to say it was for me!

The seller helped me to lift the bike into my car. I did not know if it was in really in good condition or not, I did not know anything about bikes.

I thought it was the time for me to deal with my cycling phobia

I reasoned it was not too late to learn to ride a bike at forty-seven, but it was now or never.

There were cycling paths just five minutes' walk from my flat. It would be good to go cycling with the girls when they came over at weekends.

I called Nicola. 'Will you and Teresa come over tomorrow to teach me how to ride a bike?

'Have you got a bike, Mum?'

'Yes, I bought it from E-bay. Can you ask your dad to drop off your bikes here later?'

Chris had attempted to teach me a couple months before, but unfortunately it had ended in failure, and damaged my confidence further.

His bike was too big and heavy, it did not fit me at all. I could not put my feet down when I was sitting on the seat. I feel off a couple of times, and it damaged my confidence further.

Now I had a smaller bike, I was more confident starting and getting on and off, because my feet could touch the ground.

The girls and I went to the cycling path early one morning. We only had my bike, their father refused to drop their bikes off.

'Mum, don't worry I'll hold the back of the saddle to help you learn how to balance yourself.' Nicola said.

'Okay, if you promise that you won't let it go.'

'Okay Mum, I promise.'

Nicola started pushing my bike, it was wobbling, I fell over every time she let her hands go.

'I don't think I can do this.'

'Mum, you're a climber, that's much harder than cycling.' Teresa raised her voice.

'But, I fall off every time you let go.'

'Come on, you've no problem hanging onto crags with your fingertips, it can't be harder than that.'

'I agree with you. I can do this!' I decided to try again.

'Don't look down at your feet! It makes it harder to balance. Look ahead in front of you.' Nicola gave me some tips.

'It's easier to balance once you get going. I think you're wobbling because you go too slow.' Teresa said.

'Come on, you can do this, Mum. Look at the five-year-old kid in front of you!'

'Thanks for trying to embarrass me!' I was not amused.

I went off slowly, forgetting Teresa's advice. I fell off into some bushes and landed on dog poo!

The girls killed themselves laughing, instead of helping me to get up. I was mad, 'Are you two going to help me get up, or just stand there laughing!?'

'Sorry Mum.' They both helped me to get up.

I grabbed the bike off Nicola and scooted off fast downhill. I was so excited, I managed to stay on the bike, without help, at last.

Teresa was right, it was easier to balance if you go faster.

'Woohoo, I can ride a bike now.' I shouted to them.

'Well done, Mum. We knew you could do it!'

'Okay, you know how to balance yourself, now you need to pick up speed by pedalling faster on the level and uphill.' Nicola said.

'Remember Mum, if you don't pick up speed, the bike will wobble. Keep your head up and sit straight, don't lean forward.' Teresa reminded me.

I was so proud of myself, I had managed to overcome my phobia. I thought I had done well to learn within an hour.

I had a sore bottom, my arms were sore from over gripping.

'You need to relax and keep your arms loose, don't over grip the handlebars, it won't help. Your bottom will get used to the saddle.' Nicola told me.

It was harder learning to ride a bike as an adult than as a kid. I am still nervous on narrow paths or passing someone. I looked forward to cycling more with the girls. They were not keen on running, hillwalking or climbing.

Nicola did some climbing with me, but I was not sure if she did it because she enjoyed it, or if she just wanted to make me happy.

Teresa tried indoor climbing, but she was not very keen.

I was pleased to find something that we all could do outside together.

We were resting and watching television back at my house. Teresa heard the ice cream van chimes in the distance. 'Mum can we get ice cream?'

'Of course, you can.' I gave her a five-pound note.

'Is this enough for two ice cream cones?'

'Of course, you're not in a posh area, five is more than enough here. Nicola, you go with Teresa.' I opened the front door for them.

The ice cream van was about a hundred yards away. The girls were wary because they saw a few teenage boys hanging around the ice cream van. They looked rough, and the girls were not used to this side of Glasgow.

'It's okay, I'm standing here.' I said to them.

I kept my eye on them from my front door. I could see the girls looking back to me. I gave them a wave to make sure the boys knew that I was Nicola and Teresa's mother.

'Mum, we were so scared.' Nicola said when they were back in the house.

'What were you scared of?'

'Those boys were talking about a fight two nights ago, someone was stabbed to death, one of them was in the fight.'

'Oh yes, I remember the police cars going up and down my street, and the police helicopter was flying above.'

'That's scary.'

'Yes, that's normal here. You can tell your Dad about it, he's responsible for me living here.'

There was no reply from either of them.

It was another side of life for me. I checked my back door at least ten times per day. I knew it was locked, but I could not help it. Every time I walked past, I had to check it was locked.

My entrance hall had an inner and outer door. Half of the outer door was clear glass; the inner door was frosted glass with a pattern that I could still see through.

'Mum, you need curtains at your front doors.' Nicola said.

'Why?'

'People can see inside your house from the road. Maybe not at the clear outer door, but you definitely need one at the inner door. I know you haven't bothered to get them because you prefer to see who is at the door.'

'Yes, that's the reason, I want to see who is at front my door before I open it just in case it's your Dad, or he's sent someone.'

'Okay, if you're going to be horrible about Dad, I'm not talking anymore.' Theresa said.

I felt safe with my double front door, it meant I could ring the police before anyone could break through the second door.

I always kept them both locked, I could see immediately who was at my front door. Sometimes, I woke up for the toilet in the middle of the night. Even then, I was so nervous I could not help but check the back door to make sure it was still locked.

I was so frightened of my husband in any case, the fact I was in a bad area, just increased my fears to the extent it made me ill.

Most nights, there was a lot of disorder from drunken teenagers. It kept me awake or woke me up.

On the 29th July 2013, my forty-seventh birthday, I received a letter from my solicitor. It was a good one for a change.

We write to advise you that no Notice of Intention to Defend the action we had raised on your behalf has been intimated to us.

We will now Minute for Decree. Please, however, note in order to Minute for Decree for Divorce you will require to attend at our office to complete an Affidavit. We will also require to obtain an Affidavit from a friend or relative to support your Minute for Decree.

Please arrange for yourself and a friend or relative to contact our office as soon as possible to have this documentation completed.

I was pleased I was one step closer, but it was still hard to believe my husband had not come up with any more delaying tactics or accusations, it was out of character.

I took Ann with me. I thought about Martin, but I decided to go with Ann.

'Ann, will you go with me to see my lawyer, and come with me to court later?'

'I'm not sure, Nuch. You know I always help you if I can, but I'm not sure about anything involving a lawyer or court. I'm too nervous.'

'You'll be fine, please.'

'I'm too nervous, I might forget and say something not right. I don't want to cause you any problems later.'

'You just have to be honest and tell the truth. There's nothing to remember because it's not a made-up story. But, if you don't want to, then it's okay. I won't force you to do anything you don't want to do.'

'It's okay, I'll go because it's not a made-up story, there's no script for me to read and memorise.'

'Thanks, Ann.'

I took Ann to the solicitor's office after work.

'Can you give me your full name, your address, contact telephone number and your work number? Mr Murray asked.

Ann looked nervous, but she managed to remember it all.

'How long have you known Mrs Smith? Mr Murray continued.

'Since she started work, I was there before her.'

'When was that?'

'About eight or nine years ago?'

'So, that would be 2004 or 2005.'

'That's correct.'

'Did Mrs Smith have a long career break to the USA after she started working?'

'No, she's never had any career breaks. She went climbing to the States twice for two weeks, each trip. She always showed us her climbing pictures when she came back from her holidays.'

'Have you met Mr Smith before?'

'A couple of times, in person.'

'Do you remember the last time you met Mr Smith?'

'About three or four years ago. He picked her up from work when her car was in for service, and then he gave me a lift. That was because Nuch always gave me a lift after work.'

'Okay, that covers everything I need.'

Ann did well, she need not have worried. But, I did understand, I would worry too, with any legal process.

On the 13rd August 2013, I received a letter from my solicitor.

Following the further change of solicitors by your husband, they have now effectively indicated that no matter what procedure may or may not have been undertaken before, it is their intention to place your court action on hold in order that your husband can apply for Civil Legal Aid.

My heart sank, despite the solicitor's letters, I knew it had been too good to be true.

This is what he had been up to. He changed solicitors three times now I knew he would take as long as he could to apply for Legal Aid.

I did not see this one coming; how could he possibly apply for the Legal Aid. How could he send them a bank statement?

I had never seen his bank statements since we were married, but I knew there had been very large sums of money in his accounts. I did not think it would be possible to hide that from Legal Aid, but I was still worried about what he was up to.

I kept telling myself, it cannot take much longer. It only took me a month to have Legal Aid granted, surely, he will not take a year.

On 24th August 2013, I called Mum.

'Mum, what's the plan for Tann's birthday tomorrow?'

'Her friends are having a surprise birthday party for her.'

'It sounds lovely, I wish I was there. Will you give her the parcel I posted tomorrow?

'Yes, I will, I hope she makes it, she looks really tired.'

'I'll call you tomorrow to see how she gets on with her party.'

'Why don't you call her yourself?'

'I can't, Mum. I'll be too upset to speak to her, especially on what will be her last birthday.'

I went climbing in Glencoe the next day. It clears my mind because I only concentrate on my next move when I am rock climbing.

When I was in the middle of the cliff, the phone rang in my pocket. I did not want to answer, I had a bad feeling, I could not answer anyway, whilst climbing.

I finished the route, I was at the top of the mountain. I hesitated to check my phone just in case it was a missed call from Thailand, because I still had over three thousand feet to descend, and a two-hour drive back to Glasgow.

I checked my phone as soon as I arrived home. It was a missed call from Thailand, my heart sank with the message, Tann had passed away.

I called Mum. 'Are you okay?'

'She died in the morning; she did not make it to her surprise birthday party. She put her arms around my neck, she said, I love you, Granny, those were her last words.' Mum was upset and crying.

Mum was the one who brought her up, my part was only giving Mum the money so she could afford to look after Tann.

It was so sad, she died on her twenty-nine birthday. She was too young to die. I still look at her Facebook when I miss her.

FORTY-TWO

On the 5th September 2103, a month after the last letter from my solicitor, I received another.

We refer to previous correspondence and write to confirm the Court action we had raised on your behalf has now been put on hold pending a decision on your husband's application for Civil Legal Aid.

Given we have still to receive intimation of any such application, we will press this solicitor for an update and contact you as soon as we hear further from them. We will also indicate that if no application is submitted within the next 4 weeks we shall seek to have the sits in the action, this is the Order placing the Court procedure on hold, recalled and further Court procedure set.

A month passed; his application wasn't even finalised for Legal Aid. I thought, this is madness.

I knew what he was up to, he would drag things on as long as he could.

I had the girls over the weekend. Teresa said. 'Mum, Dad is not keeping well.'

'Really?'

'Do you have to take him to court?'

'No, I don't, he can agree to a reasonable divorce settlement. He's going to court because he refuses to disclose his finances. However, he has also made me homeless, amongst other things, so that's why the court is dealing with it.'

'Dad doesn't have any money. Don't you understand?'

'If he doesn't have any money, the court can't force him to give me something that he doesn't have. Didn't he explain that to you? I guess not.'

'He said, it's too complicated.'

'It's complicated because he doesn't have any answers to all the lies, he's told. He has never been honest to me, you or the courts.''

I did not want to argue with the girls every time I had them. I was afraid that they would not come to see me again. I knew he had the power and influence over them to make this happen. I feared I might lose contact with them at any time. I lived in fear of it.

Sometimes, I just kept my mouth shut because I knew they had been brainwashed into believing I was the bad mother. Trying to defend myself provoked arguments, it was a no-win situation.

On the 6th November 2013, a month later, I received a letter from my solicitor.

We have been advised that your husband's application for Civil Legal Aid was submitted at the end of October 2013.

We are pressing his solicitors for an update regarding same and will contact you as soon as we hear further from them.

On the 5th December 2013, a month later, I received a further update.

We still have to receive confirmation from the Scottish Legal Aid Board that they are in a position to process your husband's application for Civil Legal Aid.

Given, however, the Board have confirmed they have received in documentation from him, we will request and update in 14 days' time with a view to contacting you then to discuss your options and the possibility of asking for the Court to set a date for an Options Hearing.

On the 21st January 2014, a month later, a letter from my solicitor.

We still to receive a decision from Scottish Legal Aid Board on your husband's application for Civil Legal Aid.

We will therefore contact the Board have if we do not receive an update from them within the next 14 days.

On the 10th February 2014, a month later:

Please note your husband's solicitors have indicated they still await a decision on his application for Civil Legal Aid.

Hopefully, a decision will be made in the near future and will contact you at that time.

On the 24th March 2014, another letter arrived.

Please note your husband's solicitors have indicated they intend to oppose our Motion seeking that further court procedure be assigned in connection with your action for divorce. This is due to the fact they still await a decision on his application for Civil Legal Aid.

We will therefore contact you again once a court hearing date has been assigned and a decision intimated by the Sheriff following his having heard ourselves and your husband's solicitors as to further court procedure.

The whole thing was a joke, another year had passed going around in circles chasing his application for Civil Legal Aid.

I did not understand how it was possible that he could get away with this. Did nobody look into this properly, did nobody care about the damage to my health.

I knew he would continue to do this as long as he could, unless the court took a grip of it, and stopped it becoming an even bigger farce than it was already.

I remembered when the girls were at college, I tried to apply for a bursary for them and helped them with the application form.

I filled in my part on the form and told them to give it to their dad to fill in his part.

I kept asking them if they had submitted the bursary application. 'We've not submitted it yet, Mum.' Said Nicola.

'I gave it back to you two and half months ago, I'm giving you a week to submit it.'

'Dad is too busy to fill in the form.'

'He can't be that busy to fill in a one-page form. It's because he won't, or can't answer those questions honestly.'

In the end, because of his long delays, the girls' application was never submitted, they never got their bursary. I was disgusted.

On the 10th June 2014, the next letter arrived:

As your husband has been granted Legal Aid, the court has now set a timetable for further procedure. As part of this timetable, a period of time has been allowed for both parties to adjust their pleadings, that is the written outline of the basis for the proceedings, and, the defence of the proceedings.

We therefore enclose a copy of the First Note of Adjustments from your husband's solicitors. Please now contact our Mr Murray to discuss the content thereof.

I knew he would be granted Legal Aid, eventually, because he was highly skilled in covering his financial dealings.

I read through a copy of the First Note of Adjustment from his solicitors. It was full of untrue statements about me, which were easy enough to disprove, but it meant more wasted time.

It made me mad, it seemed he could say anything which came into his head, there was no sanction if turned out to be complete rubbish.

I made a list of the many points in the First Note of Adjustment which were untrue and then set out where I could get documentary evidence to disprove them.

It was maddening, and was obviously going to be very time consuming, but I was determined to do it.

The first allegation was that he had to move the family out of Church Road because he could not afford the rent there. This was the house that he owned outright! He later paid somebody to evict me from it, because, even I, as his wife, did not know he owned it at the time. His dishonesty was blatant!

I went to the East Renfrewshire Council Office on Main St, Barrhead, Glasgow.

'Good morning, how can I help?' The girl in the office asked me.

'Hi, I was here in December 2011 to apply for a council house. To cut a long story short, at the time, I believed I had three days to move out of a private rental house. One of the ladies filled in my application form.

She said, she could not go ahead with my application because my husband refused to give her the landlord's details when they spoke on the phone. I would like a copy of that application for my solicitor.'

'I need to check first to see if we still have that form, I'm sure we do. Can I have your details?'

'Certainly.' I went through my details and the girl went off to look for me. She was really helpful.

'Yes, I found it.'

'Does it say why my application was put on hold?'

'Yes, waiting for the previous landlord's details.'

'That's great, can I have a copy of it?'

'Have you got a house now?'

'Yes, I have got a council house through the Women's Aid organisation.'

'That's good, if you already have a house, we'll bin the application form, so you can have the original one if you want.'

'Ok, thank you, that's great.'

I was relieved she had found it so easily.

The next lie to deal with was the fact that he was stating that our house on Treemain Road was bought in his sole name. I knew it was in joint names because he had throttled me to try to force me to sign a legal document allowing him to sell it. He would not have needed to do that if it was in his sole name.

I went to Allen & Harris Estate Agents on Ayr Road, Newton Mears.

'Hi, I need your help, but I'm not sure if you can help me.' I said to the gentleman in the office.

'Sure, what can I do for you?'

'You sold a house for me in 2005, it was on Treemain Road, Lower Whitecraigs. I need the copy of the agreement to sell. I'm getting through a difficult divorce, I need it for court.'

'We normally keep files for ten years, so we should still have it.'

313

'That's great.'

'Can I make a call first, I need to check with the manager.'

'Please, I can wait.'

After a couple of minutes, he came back to me. 'There's no problem, I'll look for the file for you. Can you remember what month?

'In April.'

He found it quite quickly and handed it over to me. My name was on the agreement.

'Thank you so much for helping me.' I was elated, I had proof my name was on the house documents. I could prove he was lying again.

The next lie to deal with was the allegation that we had separated in 2002. I remembered that we had all gone to Disneyland, Florida in 2006. I headed to the travel agent, Thomson or Tui, in Newton Mearns.

'Good afternoon, how can I help you?' The young girl in the office greeted me.

'I'm not here to book a holiday today, but I need help with a previous booking. Could I speak to your manager?'

'Hi, what can I do for you?' The manager came to talk to me.

'I'm going through a difficult divorce. My husband claims that we have not been together for over ten years so that I won't be entitled to anything. I need a copy of my booking details for my solicitor, to show that we were still together at that time.'

'Do you remember when the booking was?'

'June 2006, I was the one who made the booking, Mrs Smith. I can give you my address.'

'Can you give me a few minutes?' She started typing on the computer.

'Sure.'

'Yes, I've found it. I'll print it out for you.' She gave me a smile.

'Thank you so much.'

She handed the copy of the booking details to me. 'Good luck with your divorce!'

'Thanks so much.' I was happy with my progress. But, I wished it was all over, I was sick and tired of it all.

But, I had a feeling, it was not going to end so easily. It had carried on for four years so far, but I was not giving up.

I made an appointment to see Mr Murray to discuss the First Note of Adjustments.

'Your husband has indicated he found it increasingly difficult to meet the financial costs of your maintenance, so he decided to remove himself and the two children to his father's house.'

'I have proof now that he owned that house outright, at that time. He sent someone claiming to be a landlord who told us that my husband had not paid rent for six months. He gave us three days to move out unless I paid three thousand pounds immediately.

I have my application form for a council house, which was put on hold waiting for the details of the landlord. I discovered later that there was no landlord because the house belonged to my husband.'

'That's great, the application form will be very helpful at court, it shows he is a liar.'

'Yes, he's really dishonest.'

'Next, your husband says, you intended to leave Scotland to start a new life in America. You left around September 2011. You returned two weeks later.'

'No, I didn't intend to leave Scotland. I went on a two-week climbing trip in October. I have proofed my return ticket was for two weeks, and also my climbing insurance was only for two weeks.'

'That's good evidence, thanks. Now, if you leave work for good, you will need to give your work written notice in advance?'

'That's correct, otherwise I wouldn't get paid. I will ask HR to write and confirm that I never handed in my notice.'

'It's okay, you don't have to. There is enough proof with your booking details and your climbing insurance.'

'Your husband said he never threatened or used violence towards you. He states that you never went to Women's Aid or any other organisation, for help?'

'Obviously, he's not going to admit it. I regret now that I never reported that to the police. I was worried about the affect it could have on the girls, so I decided not to report it.'

'Have you told anyone about it or has anyone seen your bruises?'

'Yes, a few of my friends, and his parents, but I'm not sure if they would give evidence in court. More recently, my children saw him try to strangle me. I did report that to the police, but they said there was nothing they could do because my children would not corroborate what had happened.'

'Okay, I'll contact Woman's Aid to provide a letter to confirm how you appeared, physically and mentally, when you contacted them.'

'Kirsty said she would be happy to do that for me.'

'Your husband says you invited him to your flat on many occasions. The averment made by you that you do not wish to disclose your current address to protect yourself from a perceived risk of harm at his hands is both disingenuous and dishonest?'

'Seriously? I'm not going to invite someone to my place who put me out on the street with nothing. I don't have proof of that I never invited him. But, you could ask his solicitor for his evidence that I invited him.'

'Yes, ok.'

'Can you ask him for text messages or whatever proof he has, then it will be clear he has no proof of these lies.'

'I'll ask his solicitor for details of any such evidence.'

'Your husband states your first home together was bought in his sole name, because he had only known you for a short period, six months. The property was not subject to a mortgage.'

'I agree that the property was not subject to a mortgage, but it was in joint names. I have a copy of the sale agreement, in joint names, from the estate agent. By the way, I was in the UK six months before I was married to him, but I knew him a year before I came here, so it wasn't six months, it was eighteen months.'

'Your husband said, you were rude and aggressive. You were demanding. You would make frequent and extensive requests to him for money.'

'I have a Thai bank book and a supporting letter from my bank manager. He hid twenty million baht in my account in Thailand. I know now that he was money laundering.'

'Excellent, more good evidence.'

'Regarding the fact, I was rude and aggressive, that doesn't make sense. He hid money in my account when his business went bust. I returned it right away when he needed it back. In fact, I'm very honest, and this shows that, it also shows he trusted me, or he wouldn't have hid money in my bank account.'

'Yes, I see that now.'

'I didn't have to make frequent and extensive requests for money. It was already in my account, which was in my sole name. I could have disappeared with the lot if I had been dishonest.

'Yes, quite.'

'I almost forgot, I also have the girls' bank books, they were joint accounts with me. He hid substantial quantities of money in those accounts.'

'Can I have those bankbooks and the supporting letter from the bank manager?'

'Of course, you can send a copy to his solicitor too.'

'Your husband said, he began to suspect you were involved in relationships with various other men. He states that around 2002, you accepted that you were involved in a relationship with another man, a Korean national.'

'This is getting better. Yes, he suspected me having an affair, Martin told me that he hired a private investigator to follow me and record calls on our house phone. Nothing incriminating was found. I was not involved in a relationship with another man.'

'I see.'

'In fact, for some time, he's been in other relationships. I, and others have seen him with a Chinese woman. He has also been living with her or another woman for years.'

'I see.'

'Do you think he would hide his money in my account if I was involved with various men, as he says?'

'No, of course not. He says, he paid you a weekly income, originally set at approximately one hundred and fifty pounds per week, but soon increasing to a higher sum.'

'Yes, he paid me one hundred and fifty pounds per week for the children's expenses prior to 2010, but not after that. I can give you a copy of my bank statement showing how much I paid out for the children per month.'

'Yes, that will be very useful'

'I took them out on activities, and we ate out every weekend. This does not include their shopping, petrol and holidays every year.'

'Yes, teenagers are awfully expensive!'

'I would like you to ask, can you ask his solicitor to provide proof of these wild allegations. It is really time consuming for me to have to disprove whatever he comes up with.'

'I'll make that point. Your husband said, you would also frequently make payments to your parents who continued to reside in Thailand.'

'That's correct, and that was nothing to do with him, because it came out of my account. That account only had my money in it which I earned at work.

I sent money to my parents every month to take care of my niece and my nephew after my sister died with cancer. There is no benefit system whatsoever, in Thailand, no free schools, no NHS.'

'Okay, it is your business what you do with your own money.'

'I'm not a heartless person like him. His parents were over sixty when we met. They lived in a third-floor flat, with no lift. I made him buy a house for them before we got our own.'

'I see.'

'I caught him sending money to a girl in Thailand behind my back, she was fifteen years old at the time. Disgusting! I can prove that, I kept her letter to him.'

'That will be useful.'

'I will make sure I still have it.'

'Your husband said he purchased the property in Thailand in which your parents lived.'

'My parents had two houses and land before I met him, they owned them since I was a young girl. I will call my Mum to send me a copy of their land registration showing when it was purchased. I have plenty of pictures of my parents two houses, before I met him. He did pay something toward the new house, when it was rebuilt, to suit our daughters.'

'That document will be good evidence.'

I made a note to follow that up.

'Your husband said you made no contribution to the running costs of the household.'

'He asked me to pay for our council tax, landline, phone, gas and electric. I said, I would pay if he was honest and showed me his bank statement every month so I could work out how much maintenance and child support he should pay. He refused.'

'I understand he was very secretive in all his dealings with you.'

'He has also said that he paid for my personal things such as my mobile phone. That's nonsense, you can see from my bank statement there is an O2 direct debit every month.'

'Your husband said you wanted the property to be transferred into the names of your children.'

'It doesn't make sense, I didn't know he had bought two houses secretly. After we sold our first home, we moved into the three-bedroom house in Lochinch Place, Newton Mearns. I never mentioned this place to you because we were only there for a year. I didn't know he also bought that place secretly. He told us it was a rental house. If you hadn't checked, I would never have known he actually owned that one too.'

'Your husband admits that he is a director of a Limited Company, Total Heat Recovery Limited.'

'Yes, he had no choice but to admit it. He didn't volunteer this, my daughter accidentally brought a receipt to my house which showed him as a director. Otherwise, he would have kept that secret too.'

'Your husband determined that the separation date was around 2002.'

'I have with me our family holiday pictures in Disneyland, Florida. The date on the pictures is June 2006, the booking details show I paid for the holiday. Will you send these copied documents to his solicitors?'

'Yes, we will also use them in court.'

'Thank you.'

I left the office, and on my way home I remembered that when we moved into the first rental house in Lichinch Place, Newton Mearns, I found lots of Chines stuff, such as sauces, bowls, and chopsticks.

I know now that he had bought this house and was no doubt living with the Chinese girl, I saw him with. In a way, it was sad, I found out much more about my husband through the divorce proceedings than when I lived with him.

FORTY-FOUR

A week later, I had a phone call from Nicola. 'Mum, we're having lunch in the Premier Inn, Cambuslang. Would you please come and join us?'

'Who do you mean by we?'

'Teresa and Dad are here too.'

'What make you think, I want to have lunch with your Dad?'

'Please, Dad just wants to talk.'

'You tell him to speak to my lawyer.'

'Please Mum, Dad just wants to end this.'

I decided to go, for the sake of the girls. But, looking back, he was manipulating them. I should not have gone. I went, I thought he would not be violent in a public place.

'Please sit.' He invited me to have the seat next to Teresa.

They had already ordered their meal before I arrived, I ordered mine.

'You always have steak.' He started the conversation.

'What you are saying is you still remember that my favourite dish is steak.'

'I don't want any more arguments. I just want to end this nicely so we can still be friends.'

'I'm losing my mind trying to deal with you. Now you make out, I'm the one who doesn't want a happy ending. Do you realise what you have put me through for the past four years? And for sixteen years I had to deal with your violence, controlling behaviour and affairs?'

'I just want to end it now, I'm depressed.'

'I'm not surprised you're depressed with all the bullshit you made up about me. Now you're facing a court order regarding your assets, you've no way out. Please let my solicitor know whichever way you want to sort this out.'

'No, I don't want to sort it out through lawyers.'

'Sorry, I don't trust you and I never will. I'm leaving now, you're still abusive and controlling.'

'Mum, please.' Nicola was begging me.

I turned to him. 'You know what, this is the most painful thing you have done, alienating the girls from me. I'm their mother and you know I will always be there for them. I don't deserve the lies you've told them to excuse your own evil behaviour. I don't deserve what you have put me through as a wife, and a mother.'

I was crying, people in the restaurant started to look at me, so I left. He followed me to the car park and grabbed my wrist, trying to stop me get into my car.

'Please drop the case, I've three thousand pounds with me, I can give it to you now.' He grabbed my wrist harder.

'Don't you get it, if it's about money, I would have run away when I had everything in my name. I wish I could turn back time now that I know this is the way you would pay me back for my honesty. I'm done with you, let me go!'

I tried to break free from his grip. He would not let me go.

'You let her go.' A passing motorist shouted to him.

'This is between husband and wife.' He replied.

'If you want to hit someone, be a man, hit another man.'

'It's not your business.' He still did not let go of his grip.

The stranger stepped out of his car, he opened his car boot. He lifted a hammer out. 'If you don't let her go, I'll hit you with this.' The guy looked like he meant it.

He let me go. I said thanks to the stranger and drove away.

I could not believe, that even although I was separated, and living in my own house, he was continuing his controlling and violent behaviour.

I had a phone call from Nicola later. 'Dad said he was almost killed by a stranger because of you!'

'Was that what he told you? Well, he deserved it.'

'You are so clueless! Who is going to look after us if something happens to Dad? You don't love us, you don't care about us.'

'Just in case you've forgotten, before this disaster, I was the one who put food in your mouth every day since you were born.'

I was really upset, I felt it did not matter what I said. I would always be the bad one. It was really hard for me to accept the way my daughters talked to me. I had never spoken to my mother like that.

On the 28th July 2014, I received another letter from my solicitor.

The court has now assigned the 30th October 2014, as a date for a proof to determine the date of your separation.

You will require to attend at court on the date along with a witness to support your position that the date of separation is not as stated by your husband.

Please, therefore, contact our Mr. Murray, initially by telephone to discuss who would be able to attend as witness on your behalf.

I gave Mr Murray a call, 'Hi I received you letter today regarding the court assignment.'

'Have you made a decision as to who will you bring to court with you?'

'I'll have Ann and Donna, my friends from work with me. I did ask my neighbours but because they know both of us, they don't want to get involved.'

'I think, I've got enough proof with your papers, bills, bank statements, agreement of selling the house and your family holiday booking details. I'll get in touch with you when I find out what's happening next.'

I still believed that it was not going to end easily, I feared he would come up with something else.

Later on, I got a phone call from somebody called Mike. He said, he was a close friend of my husband and would like to talk to me in person. I agreed to meet him to see what was going on.

'Hi, I'm Mike, we met before when you first came to Scotland, you might not remember.'

'No, I'm sorry, I don't remember. Why do you want to see me?'

'Bob asked me to come and talk to you.'

'Are you his fourth lawyer?'

'No, I'm not a lawyer, but I do work in law. Bob ask me to help you and him come to an agreement without fighting.'

'You mean without processing through the court? You're his friend, how are you going to help me?'

'I'm not going to be on his side or your side.'

'I don't trust him, I only negotiate through my lawyer.'

'It's too complicated for Bob with solicitors and court.'

'You mean he can't provide honest information?'

'Yes, it's not easy for him.'

'I'm not surprised, he has never been honest or faithful. You'll have heard only one side of this story. Did he tell you about his money laundering using my Thai bank account?'

'No.'

'Did he tell you that he is violent towards me?'

'No.'

'Did he tell you that he bought two houses behind my back, then he sent someone pretending to be the landlord to throw me and the children out?'

Mike was silent for a few seconds. 'No, I didn't know.'

'What makes you think you can help with an agreement between us when you've only heard one side of the story. You think you know him, obviously you don't. You can leave now, thanks for your time.'

'I'll talk to him.'

I shut the door. I wondered what was coming next.

Whatever he did, I decided I would not give up.

FORTY-FIVE

Three months later, the 30ᵗʰ October 2014, I received another solicitor's letter. I wondered if anyone else's divorce took as long as mine.

The writer appeared for you at today's calling of the case. The proof was discharged and the Court was advised that it was now agreed that the date of separation was 5ᵗʰ April 2002.

Both sides now have to produce schedules of the matrimonial property held at the date of separation. This exercise will obviously take time and effort. The case has been continued to 13ᵗʰ January 2015 for both side to produce this information and to amend the pleadings accordingly.

Can you arrange a meeting to go through the information you have. Please bring with you any documents you mays still have going back to that date? We would like to be able to lodge this information within six weeks in order to allow us to carry out the amendments and other consequent work.

I made an appointment to see my solicitor after reading the letter. 'I don't understand why the court was advised that the date of separation was the 5ᵗʰ April 2002?'

'Maybe from the statement where you agreed that you were in separate bedrooms by that time.'

'Yes, but he still came to my bedroom whenever he wanted. I still did the cooking, cleaning, washing for him after that.'

'It's hard to prove that. Also, his solicitor advised that he said he never came into your bedroom.'

'So, what proof did he have that the separation was the 5th April 2002? I had proof it was definitely not 5th April 2002, such as the 2006 family holiday pictures.'

'Sometimes the date on pictures can be Photo shopped.'

'I also gave you the copy of the holiday booking details. I have my web albums that I could print out pictures of any month in any year.'

'I know you have a lot of documents showing that you were still living together under the same roof after 2002.'

'What's going to happen if we don't come to agree with the date of separation?'

'It could be complicated. You will have to go back to court and prove it was a later date.'

Suddenly, I realised why the date of separation was such a big deal. 'I get why he wanted to be in 2002, it means I won't be entitled to anything after 2002?'

'Yes, that what he hoped for, but don't worry, it's not that simple. From my search his business assets were five hundred thousand, the house he sold was seven hundred thousand, and there is the money that you transferred back to him. He has to prove to the court where the money has gone to.'

'So, it is not worth arguing about the date.'

'Yes, correct, it'll just cause further delays.'

I realised that my husband thought he would continue to make my life hell as long as he could. However, I could see that he was in hell too!

It was not going to be easy for him to provide any financial paperwork because he had never been honest in the first place. He could not fill in the bursary application for his daughters, so what chance had he to comply a court order regarding his finances.

I remember not long after that, he called me. 'I have prostate cancer and it spreads fast when I'm stressed.'

'I'm sorry to hear that, but you're causing all the stress in this divorce.'

'Please, I might not live till next Christmas.'

'I hate Christmas, it always makes me cry every time I hear Christmas songs. Do you know why? Because it reminds me that you sent someone to kick me out of the house four days before Christmas. And that was the end of me living under the same roof with my daughters. The fact I'm asking for a reasonable divorce settlement should not cause you any stress, you should be happy to give it to me, and be thankful I haven't reported all your domestic violence to the police.'

I put the phone down. I did not know if he had prostate cancer or not, I knew he had it about 10 years previously, but as far as I knew he had recovered from it.

I was so stressed, I knew what was going to happen when the girls came over next weekend.

'You're such a heartless person, Dad is dying with cancer, and you're still taking him to court. He has already transferred the house to us. Are you not happy that your daughters have a house? Dad brought you here from Thailand, you came here with nothing!' Nicola raised her voice to me.

'Will you call your dad to pick you up, I'm not feeling well.' I could no longer cope with the way they talked to me. It was so hurtful.

'Fine!'

He came round to get the girls. 'You two wait in the car, I need to speak to your Dad a for a few minutes.' The girls walked to the car.

'Have you told them that you're dying from cancer?'

'Yes, they have right to know that I'm dying.'

'They said horrible things to me. I just want to tell you that you're doing a pretty good job for someone who's dying. If I was dying, I would make sure that my daughters were happy and in good hands. If you're die tomorrow, who do you think will take good care of your children? Me or your new woman?'

He did not reply, he got back in the car and they left.

It was real heart ache for me. I felt devastated, hurt, confused, angry, misunderstood, shocked, invalidated, and empty. I just could not stop crying about the horrible things the girls said to me. I could not understand why I deserved all of this.

Was I a bad mother, was that why God was punishing me? This was the worst heartache I had ever experienced. It was much worse than the treatment and stress he caused me. This pain was killing me slowly, day by day.

On the 15th January 2015, another letter arrived from my solicitor.

We attended at the court on your behalf yesterday for the hearing to determine further procedure.

Mr Smith's solicitor advised the court that they were able to confirm approximate value for the matrimonial home as at the date of separation. This information has been lodged at court.

Your husband's solicitor then indicted due to Mr Smith's ongoing health problems; they had not been able to obtain further information.

We indicated to the court that Mr Smith should have been attempting to gather information for some time now and that a further court date should be set. Your husband's solicitor stated that the case should be placed on hold to enable them to obtain information. Despite our abjections, due to your husband's health situation. Sheriff Liddell decided to place the case on held until further information is available. Pleas therefore contact our Mr Murray by telephone to discuss the effect of this decision.

I was not sure if he was dying with cancer, as far as I knew, he had recovered and was clear.

I did not trust him, and I never will, for what he put me through.

I felt guilty about doubting he had cancer, but I knew he was evil enough to hit me, terrorise me, and lie to the children about me. He was quite capable of lying about having cancer, and the fact he might dead by Christmas.

I decided to call my solicitor to ask for evidence to be produced regarding his alleged cancer.

I went hillwalking up Ben Nevis at the weekend. I knew it was dangerous to go up there in winter on my own, but I was past caring.

The girls would probably be happy if I did not come back. It was horrible to think about your children that way, but I could not help it. I did not feel love from them towards me anymore.

Looking back now, I suppose the words they were using were not their words, but the hurt remains, they said some awful things.

A month later he phoned me late at night. 'I just called to let you know that Nicola is in hospital.'

'Is she okay? What's happening? My heart sank.

'She's crying and screaming, she also has fever and high temperature.'

'Which hospital?'

'Southern general hospital.'

'I'm going to see her now.'

'No, it's too late, the doctor is keeping her in tonight.'

'What did the doctor say? Will she be okay?'

'The doctor said that she has a mental health problem, and she will end up in the psychiatric hospital if she doesn't get better.'

'I'll go to see her tomorrow, what ward is she in?'

'No, you better not come, I'll tell you when she is out of hospital.'

'She's my daughter, she's twenty years old. I can go to see her when I want it's nothing to do with you.'

'She might not want to see you. I don't think it's a good idea to see her just now.'

'What makes you think it's not a good idea for me to see her?'

'She can't cope with the way things are between you and me at the moment. That's why she has a mental health problem now.'

'Are you telling me, it's all my fault, that it's nothing to do with you?'

'There's no point talking about whose fault it is.'

'It was you that involved our children in this. I did my very best to keep them out of it, I even hid your domestic violence from them. I know you have alienated me from them. I could see it from the way they talked to me. You pushed them to join you in your battle, you used them as weapons to destroy me. What kind of father are you, lying to turn your children about their mother.?' I put the phone down.

I was frightened by what he told me about Natasha. With hindsight, I doubt very much if any of it was true.

I had always done my best to manage my own emotions when I was around the girls. I thought that if their father told them that I was a bad mother, and then I acted as a bad mother, I would just confirm their father's twisted version of the truth.

It was normal to feel angry, scared and defensive when the children were being used as pawns in a divorce battle. In the end of the day, it was about money and control.

The children were now being brainwashed into coercing me to accept a divorce with no financial settlement at all. I could see he was obsessed by money and control. The children were his main weapon against me, he knew my vulnerability.

I did not know how to deal with this, I spent little time with the children, I could only see them every second weekend, I had no idea what was said about me in the meantime. It did not matter what I said or did, I was always in the wrong in their eyes.

Looking back now, I was suffering with mental health issues because of the extreme stress he was causing me.

However, I ignored it, because in Thailand, at that time, depression was not really accepted. People just had to get on with their life. Taking time off work or relying on the state for help was not an option. If you could not work, the reality was, you starved to death. That was my culture.

Nicola left hospital late the next day after her temperature dropped. I was relieved that she was better.

But, I felt guilty, the result of his behaviour and manipulation was to make me feel that I was the one who was putting my interests before those of my daughters.

At the time, it made me feel that I should drop any entitlement for financial settlement in my divorce. I felt that if I continued to pursue a normal financial settlement then it could result in harm to my children.

On the 15th March 2015, I received another letter from my solicitor.

We have received in various papers from your husband's solicitors. Please contact our Mr Murray's secretary to arrange an appointment to discuss the content of these papers.

I made an appointment to see my solicitor a week later.

'I have not received a letter yet from your husband's doctor confirming his alleged medical condition. Otherwise the case is looking good with these latest papers.'

'It's okay, I'm giving up my right to a financial settlement. I would like to drop it.'

'Are you sure? If you drop it now, you can't change your mind in the future. Would you like a couple of weeks to think about it?'

'It's okay. I have made my decision. My daughter has mental health problems now because of the stress of the case. I can't risk anything happening to her.'

'Okay, if you have made that decision, you'll get a letter from us in a couple of weeks. You still have time to think this over until you receive our letter.'

'Thanks for your time helping me.'

I did not really want to let him get away with what he did to me and the children. Especially all the lies he had told the girls, and to the courts.

I went to see Ann, I told her what had happened.

'Don't be stupid, don't you let him get away with it. You can't give up now, you've already been through four years of this.' Ann was not happy.

'I didn't plan to give up, Ann. But, I don't want to take any risks with Nicola.'

'You know what he's like. How do you know he told you the truth? Nicola might just have had a fever, and he may well have made up the rest to make you feel bad and give up. You should know him by now, he's evil!'

'I just don't want to end up with the girls not speaking to me or refusing to see me.'

'One day their eyes will open, they'll see the truth in time.'

I thought about it repeatedly what if Ann was right. But, if anything happened to Nicola, I could not live with the guilt. I would never forgive myself.

On the 30ᵗʰ April 2015, the last letter arrived from my solicitor.

We refer to your meeting with our Mr Murray earlier this week. We note you have decided not to pursue a financial claim against your husband.

As discussed with you at your meeting, if you decide not to pursue a financial claim against your husband, and decree of divorce is then granted, you would not then be able to make any financial claim against him at a later date.

Please therefore confirm that you do not wish to pursue a financial claim against Mr Smith.

Please also confirm that you do not wish to pursue a financial claim, whether you now wish us to proceed to obtain decree of divorce.

Maybe the girls were right, as a mother, it was my job to bring them up without expecting anything in return. I had never expected anything in return, but I deserved better than this, at least some respect from them.

He asked me to come to Scotland with him and marry him. He said he would protect me and make me felt safe in a foreign country. Instead he kept pushing me to the edge until I almost committed suicide.

On the 5th May 2015, I decided to write a letter to my solicitor.

Dear Mr Murray,

Divorce Proceedings

I am writing to confirm that I do not wish to pursue a financial claim against my husband Mr Bob Smith and please proceed to obtain decree of divorce.

Your faithfully,

Mrs N Smith

I abandoned the financial settlement side of my divorce because I thought it was the only way to repair the girls' health. I was left with nothing.

One thing that is certain about life is that it is about all about letting go.

I wanted to rebuild my relationship with the girls after their father had damaged their natural affection for the mother.

I tried to focus on reconnecting with them, and not worrying about the outcome. I would do the best I could for them.

Now, I live one day at a time, I only focus on one day.

I feel less hopeless and desperate.

I do not feel personally defeated, because I had terrible difficulties in this area of my life. I do whatever I feel is best for me and my children.

I am still climbing, hillwalking, cycling, and running, it makes me feel good about myself.

Printed in Poland
by Amazon Fulfillment
Poland Sp. z o.o., Wrocław